# PRAISE FOR
## *THE McAVOY SISTERS BOOK OF SECRETS*

"The perfect read for a summer day."
—**Jill Shalvis,** *New York Times* **bestselling author**

"Mothers and daughters, sisters and secrets… Molly Fader delivers
a delicious summer read populated with spirited characters, a
charming lakeside setting, and just enough mystery to keep the
pages turning. A warm-hearted delight of a book!"
—**Jamie Brenner, bestselling author of**
***The Forever Summer* and *Drawing Home***

"Mesmerizing and soul-searching. A story that makes you believe
in the power of family."
—**Carolyn Brown,** *New York Times* **bestselling author**

"The talented Molly Fader will keep you turning the pages right
down to the oh-so-satisfying final twist."
—**Susan Wiggs,** *New York Times* **bestselling author**

"An emotional, tender, simply wonderful book. I loved everything
about it, from the beautiful prose to the perfectly layered plot to
the strong, compelling McAvoy women. Once you start this book,
you won't be able to put it down until you discover all the secrets
within."
—**RaeAnne Thayne,** *New York Times* **bestselling author**

"A riveting, emotional blend of family drama, mystery, and
romance that you will not want to put down—but neither will you
want it to end."
—**Jamie Beck, national bestselling author of** *Before I Knew*

MOLLY FADER

*The*

# McAVOY
# SISTERS
# BOOK
*of*
# SECRETS

A NOVEL

GRAYDON
HOUSE

**GRAYDON
HOUSE**

ISBN-13: 978-1-525-83424-0

The McAvoy Sisters Book of Secrets

Copyright © 2019 by Molly Fader

GraydonHouseBooks.com
BookClubbish.com

**Printed in U.S.A.**

For Mom and Dad...and yes, Dad, you can read this one.

# The McAVOY SISTERS BOOK *of* SECRETS

# ONE

## *May 2018*

## *Delia*

Delia Collins was not proud of her glee. It was unbecoming, she got that. And truthfully, she couldn't even say where it came from. What awful spring of motherhood created this kind of joy in catching her teenage daughter sneaking back into the house past curfew?

If she was a different kind of mother she'd be worried. Or angry. Even guilty.

And she was angry, worried and guilty (this had to be partly her fault—hers and Dan's—they were too lenient, too forgiving, let her sleep too long in their bed when she was a baby—something). But somewhere between her gut and her head the anger, worry and guilt morphed into this…giddiness. Delia and Dan had told her they were trusting her. That this was—for real this time—her last chance. Brin had promised she wouldn't be late.

And Brin had blown it.

Dan shuffled into the room, bleary-eyed, up way past his

bedtime, and she felt a sudden rush of affection for him in his worn-thin Cleveland Browns pajama pants.

"Go on to bed," she told him as she dragged her old blue rocking chair across the carpet.

"What are you doing?"

"Nothing. Actually, can you…?" The chair got stuck on the edge of the coffee table and she couldn't twist it away.

Dan reached down and pulled it loose, the momentum nearly knocking her sideways. "Careful," he said and reached out to steady her.

"I'm going to be the first thing Brin sees when she walks in the door." She glanced down at her watch. "A half hour late."

"Did you call her cell?" he asked.

"Yep. She didn't answer. But she texted to say she'd be home soon."

She texted because she'd been drinking and she knew Delia would be able to tell.

Delia ran into Jenny's mom the other day outside Giant Eagle and she'd clearly thrown up her hands trying to control Jenny.

*She's mad at me all the time anyway*, she'd said. *Why make it worse?*

*Pick your battles*, she'd said.

But what if Delia picked the wrong one?

"When was that?"

"Ten minutes ago."

"Are you…supposed to be enjoying this so much?" Dan asked.

Probably not. But Delia was the breastfeeding perimenopausal mother of a teenager and an infant. *Enjoyment* was wired wrong these days.

"What's your plan?"

"Plan?"

"She walks in the door and what?"

"Dan, I'll handle it. Just go to bed."

"You're gonna scream?"

"No." *Probably.*

"I'm worried about you," he said.

"Me?" Dan was stressed. Clearly. His appearance after 10:00 p.m. in the living room on a weekday was proof that something was cooking in that head of his.

"Between the baby, Brin, the store and your mom—"

She sat down in her rocking chair, now conveniently positioned in front of the door. "I'm fine."

His silence seemed to imply that he thought otherwise.

The front door swung open and Brin walked in, curtailing the conversation. Brin, her beautiful daughter, looked from Delia to Dan and then back again.

And then her lip curled in a totally new and devastating way.

"What? You're like waiting up to yell at me?"

Delia's bright-eyed baby who had once slept curled like a question mark in the curve of Delia's body had turned into this teenager. Surly and sleepy-eyed, wearing cutoffs that were way too short.

Time folded like a fan and Delia was struck—anew—by how much Brin now looked like Lindy. It was shocking. They were carbon copies in different clothing. It was like having a ghost in the house.

Lindy. Delia still hadn't called to tell her sister about their mom. She just didn't know how to tell her.

The number of times over the last few months she'd sat at the kitchen table, her cell phone in front of her, was too many to count.

One touch of her finger and Lindy would come back. She knew that.

But then what?

Lindy had been the wild McAvoy sister, playing chicken with her reputation and her future, and in the end she left and broke Delia's heart.

All Delia wanted in this world was to stop Brin from doing the same thing.

# *Meredith*

*T*he lake got inside Meredith McAvoy's head on a Sunday.

She knew it had been a Sunday because she'd been sitting on her back deck, working the crossword, the yellow tabby stretched out beside her, when she heard the screen door slam. Her first thought was that it was William. Which wasn't right. He got swallowed up by the lake years ago.

But still, she turned, her heart pounding hard. Hope like that never really went away. It was a loyal dog, sitting at her feet every day, waiting for a chance to break its chain.

Next thing she knew she was waking up in the hospital, her daughter Delia looking over her like Meredith had survived a shipwreck.

"You're okay," her youngest daughter said as if it were an order. And it was an order Meredith was trying her best to obey. Because Meredith McAvoy was no burden. Not on Delia. Not on anyone.

And some days she was okay; the lake in her head was still and flat. Calm. The world recognizable. The old blue house, gone gray in the sun, was her home. There was Gwen on the corner, who overwatered her yard, and Mike Porter next door, who shoveled Meredith's walk all winter long. Her life. Her grief. The imaginary dog of hope at her side. All of it her own, just as it was supposed to be.

But some days the Lake Erie storms roared up and the sandbars shifted and she didn't know what was real. She didn't know where her William was. Or why her Lindy had left. All she had were the secrets she had swallowed, and Meredith was afraid she'd open her mouth and they'd all fly out like bats at dusk.

"Mrs. McAvoy?"

She had given the babysitter Delia'd hired, that Tiffany woman, the slip after lunch. Meredith was supposed to take a nap like some kinda toddler, but when Tiffany went to sit on the back porch, Meredith had skedaddled out the front door.

In her quick escape she'd left without her hat and the sun was hot on the top of her head. It was William's hat, actually. The brim white with salt and sweat and sometimes she put her tongue against it just so she could taste him again.

"Mrs. McAvoy?"

*Hold on, now, I am Mrs. McAvoy.*

Meredith stopped and there was Garrett Singh walking along beside her.

*How long has he been there?*

His boot kicked a piece of gravel and it flew off the narrow spit to land with a thunk in the lake. Erie was still shallow at this part. The sand like clay. The water, when calm, a bright blue-green.

"Garrett," she said and got back to walking. *No time for chit-chat.* Her palm was sweating so she switched the flare gun to her other hand. "If you're looking for Lindy, she's not here."

"I'm not looking for Lindy, Mrs. McAvoy." He kept along beside her.

"Probably for the best," she told him. "I love that girl but she's tough on the nice boys."

If William was still around maybe that wouldn't be true. Maybe Lindy would be less wild, but it was just Meredith and she was doing the best she could.

"Can I ask where you're headed?"

"It's obvious, ain't it?" The spit only went out to the Ful-bright House.

He smiled. "I suppose that's true."

"Oh no, boy." She wagged the flare gun at him. "You save that smile for someone your own age."

He vanished that grin real fast. "Can I ask what you're doing with that gun?"

*I've got to do something, don't I? You can't expect me to sit at home and do nothing. Not while he's out there.*

She was about to tell him all about it, glad actually that he was there in case she needed his help, but then they rounded that last curve and Fulbright House came into view.

And it didn't look at all like it should. It wasn't the grand mansion with bright white gingerbread and ruby-red door. The gardens—a Fulbright point of pride—were overgrown and full of them pesky reeds that crept in when you weren't looking.

And Garrett, he was wearing a uniform. Not the high school lacrosse jersey Meredith remembered, but something new. Something…

*He's Police Chief Garrett Singh. Not that high school puppy following Lindy around.*

Just like that the waves receded and the waters were still.

"Do you need help, Mrs. McAvoy?" Garrett asked.

Meredith McAvoy never needed help before, and there was already that Tiffany woman in her house these days, a baby-sitter in nurse's scrubs.

"Do you want me to call your daughter?"

Meredith wanted Garrett to call her husband. More than she could say, she wanted her William. He would know what to do.

She closed her eyes. This was a new kind of tired. Used to be, she could work for hours out on the boat and then come back and close up the shop and still go home and make dinner for the girls, play a couple hands of gin rummy on the porch. Every day she did that, for years, without even thinking about it much. The days were just days. The work just work.

But now her bones wanted a rest. *How long have I been walking?*

"Lindy will know what to do," she finally said.

"Mrs. McAvoy, Lindy doesn't live here anymore," Garrett said. "I can call Delia."

Delia's head would pop right off her shoulders and no one needed that. Meredith had caused that girl enough grief.

She remembered she had a cell phone in the pocket of her soft shorts. Delia'd insisted she have one, which seemed ridiculous.

Meredith and Lindy sometimes talked every week, but it had been a while. Time was a slippery fish these days, but Lindy had promised she'd come home if Meredith needed her. No matter what Delia had to say about it. And she'd wanted her daughter home plenty. Longed for her and missed so much it sat like a stone in her stomach.

But Meredith never *needed* Lindy before.

Meredith pulled out the phone. "Call Lindy."

# TWO
## *Lindy*

*Welp.*

This was it. Another highlight in the Lindy McAvoy story. Though, this one felt different. Special. In a lifetime filled with near misses, this might *actually* be rock bottom.

Sitting on the curb outside her apartment, her clothes raining down on her, thrown by her—now ex—boyfriend from her—now former—second-floor apartment, Lindy decided with the thunk of a Michael Kors knockoff hitting pavement that yep, this was rock bottom.

It had to be, because she sure as hell couldn't get any lower.

"Screw you, Lindy," Ben shouted. The window slammed shut and she flinched.

What could she say? Lindy made really bad decisions about men. She liked them talented, jealous and borderline unstable.

It was a flaw. One of many.

And in the case of Ben Ming, she liked them to be the genius chef at TAO where she worked. So now she had no boyfriend, no apartment and no job.

While this might be the lowest she'd ever been, she'd been

in training for just this kind of emergency for seventeen years and she gave herself to the count of five to get her act together. That was the rule for a woman with too much experience putting her chin up and getting on with things. Five seconds to wallow and curse and wail and then she had to get back up on her feet.

She put shaking fingers to her lips and refused to cry. Refused. She didn't love Ben, and knew he didn't love her. But she'd naively believed he respected her more than...this.

*Two...three...four...*

"You all right?" a girl asked as she picked up a pair of Lindy's underwear and handed it to her.

The kind pedestrian looked like she was on her way to some internship at a tech start-up or her brand-new job as a bank teller. Her glasses were ironic. Her hair, a day-old blowout, frizzing up in the Ohio humidity. This girl was putting her best foot forward.

In equal parts, Lindy wanted to push her away and invite her to sit down. So Aunt Lindy could tell her a few horror stories about how the world really worked.

"Do I look all right?" Lindy asked her. Wondering really.

"Nope."

"Yeah. I didn't think so." She sighed. "Word of advice," Lindy said as the young girl slowly backed away. "Don't go for the jealous types."

"I never do," the girl said before melting into the trickle of pedestrian traffic.

*Well, bully for you, kid.*

Lindy stood up—literally from the gutter—and picked up her black bra and her e-reader—now probably broken; *thank you, Ben.* The kimono from San Francisco, the stupidly expensive hairbrush she bought when she freaked out that she might be losing her hair.

Lindy gathered it all up, and like a true pro, she began making plans, so this moment, this awful low point, was already behind her.

The manager at The Fig Tree would hire her in a nanosecond; she'd been trying for weeks to poach Lindy from TAO. And The Fig Tree was so hot right now, the tips would be better.

Angela was visiting her parents at their lake house this week and Lindy had her key so she could water the plants and feed the fish. So, she had a place to stay.

It was already a funny story she'd tell Angela over the phone tonight.

*No, I'm not kidding, Angela. All my stuff...out the damn window!*

She'd laugh and laugh and never let on how bad it was. Not even a little.

Her phone buzzed in her pocket and she fished it out, answering without looking because who else would it be but Ben apologizing for this next-level tantrum.

And the hope... God, it was embarrassing. Her relief that the man who just threw her underwear onto Third Street was calling made her mouth dry with self-loathing.

Lindy should be better than this.

She wanted to be better than this.

"I'm sorry, but I swear, Ben," she said past the stone in her throat. "I was talking to him about his girlfriend, who is a total—"

"Lindy? Is this Lindy McAvoy?"

*That voice. That...voice?*

"Ben?" she asked, even though she now knew it wasn't him. But she couldn't quite place that voice.

"No. Lindy. It's Garrett. Garrett Singh."

This...this was a joke. It had to be. Or a different Garrett

Singh, because there was no way the Garrett Singh she once knew was calling now. The world was not that cruel.

"Garrett Singh from high school?"

"The…ah…one and only."

*Look! Rock bottom has a trap door!*

Behind her a woman picked up Lindy's favorite pair of jeans, holding them to her body to see if they might fit. Lindy hissed at her like a stray cat. "Those are mine!"

"Then get them off the street, girl!" she hissed back, dropping the jeans and stepping on a T-shirt as she walked past.

"I'm sorry," Garrett said. "Am I interrupting something?"

"No. Nope. Not at all. What can I do for you, Garrett?"

"Well," he said, but then in the background came another voice. An older female voice saying something she couldn't understand. "Funny you should ask. Your mom asked me to call you."

"My mom?" She bent over, picking up her scattered jewelry. "How…?"

"Kind of a long story and I'm not sure how much you know about your mother's condition—"

She stood up straight.

"Condition?"

Garrett's silence was pronounced. "The stroke?" he finally asked.

"Is she okay? Where is she?"

*I have to get to Port. Keys… Where are my keys?*

"You know," he said, "I think this is a conversation you should be having with your sister."

Great idea. Except Lindy and Delia didn't have conversations. Not for seventeen long years.

"Garrett," she said. "Just tell me what's happening."

"I found your mom walking down the spit to the Fulbright House with a flare gun. She was clearly confused. Disoriented."

Lindy started kicking her clothes into a pile, searching for her purse. *Keys. Dammit.* "And what about a stroke?"

"It...it was three weeks ago. I think. They called it a brain event."

And Delia didn't even call her? Not even a message on Facebook or a text? It was easy not to be surprised. Impossible not to be crushed.

"I'm really sorry, I didn't mean to get in the middle of things."

"You're not, Garrett." There was the familiar rattle of keys and she dug through jean mountain to her purse.

"She's probably just been busy with the baby."

"Baby?"

More awkward silence on his end. "You're kidding. Right?"

That her sister had a baby and didn't tell her? Ha! Hilarious joke.

"Totally kidding." She even laughed along.

"So anyway, your mom asked me to call."

"Can you put her on, please?"

"Sure. Just a second—"

"Garrett?"

"Yeah."

*You were always so sweet. Far too sweet for the likes of me.* "Thank you."

"No problem, Lindy. It's...ah...it's good to hear your voice."

"You, too, Garrett," she said, but all she heard was the fumbling of the phone as he handed it to her mom.

"Linds?"

On another day, a day that hadn't already seen rock bottom, she might have been able to hear her mom's voice and not feel like curling into a ball and wailing, but this was not that day.

"Heya, Mom." Despite the smile she said them through, her words were strained and teary. "How's things?"

★ ★ ★

Lindy moved away from Port Lorraine seventeen years ago, but she never really left Lake Erie. Whenever she'd travel south and find herself landlocked, where the air smelled like cement rather than water, she would get twitchy.

Her father was in that lake, and if Lindy got too far away she forgot what he looked like. Stopped hearing his voice.

Erie was the shallowest Great Lake, storm prone and violent. Easily excitable. Remarkably unpredictable. For a few years everyone thought it was dying, unable to process the effects of the steel belt pollution dumped in by the cities of Cleveland, Cincinnati and Sandusky.

But it came back. Dead zone or not, it had fish. Beaches. Clean water.

A rock-bottom survivor. No wonder Lindy felt a kinship.

Lindy had planned to call her sister at some point on the drive, but somehow the phone stayed in her purse.

*I'm not scared. I'm not. She screwed up this time.* I'm *owed an explanation and an apology,* she'd told herself while getting into her car back in Cleveland.

But three hours later she still hadn't picked up that phone.

Highway 90 was in her rearview mirror, and she could smell the blue-green water on the edges of the breeze through her open window.

One thing she was sure of, she wasn't going to let Delia force her out this time.

Garrett said he'd found Mom walking. That was good. It meant she was still moving. Still mobile. Did she have a cane? A walker? Were there machines involved? That Mom had been disoriented was concerning—Meredith McAvoy was a lot of things but she wasn't disoriented.

And the flare gun? That was *really* concerning.

The road twisted past old filling stations and farm stands

selling the first of the season's tomatoes and peaches, sweet corn stacked in giant wheelbarrows. Gladiolas sat in buckets next to handwritten signs: a buck a stem.

The road got hilly as she neared Port, and as she came over the second-to-last hill, the glimmering blue of the harbor became visible. And in it—the old Fulbright House. The first thing anyone saw when they drove in from the highway. Port Lorraine's only landmark.

Something turned over in Lindy's belly, a prehistoric fish from the coldest part of her subconscious.

She couldn't look away, as much as she wanted to.

Everyone called it the Fulbright Island because it looked like it was floating in the lake, to the left of the harbor, just inside the breakers. But it really sat out on a thin spit. When storms blew in, the spit was submerged and you couldn't get out to the house.

And you couldn't leave it either. No matter how bad you wanted to.

In the day, the house was stunning, a three-story century house made of Erie slate and stone, ivy dripping down its turrets. The pure white gingerbread and elaborate widow's walk freshly painted every year. Its gardens fiercely manicured.

But now, that fabulous mansion, that floating castle, was a ruin. Half the house was overtaken by vines and weeds. The gingerbread, on the half Lindy could see from the highway, was dingy and peeling. The peaked windows were all boarded up, and the bright red door hung lopsided in its casing.

Behind her, a car honked. Lindy lifted her hand in apology and hit the gas down the hill into town, the now-decrepit Fulbright House lost behind the hills and trees.

She turned left at the stop sign, right at the next one, her Toyota's engine coughing into another gear as she headed up the steepest hill in town. It was all the same. Painfully so.

The Fosters' house, where she'd attempted her first sleepover but her dad had to come get her at midnight because she missed Delia so much. The Jackmans' lilac tree, where she and Jodi and Delia used to play dolls. May School on the corner. Nirosha's house next door. The bright purple door Lindy had gone in and out of as if it were her own.

As she got closer to Mom's, the changes came fast and furious. The old postwar bungalows had been torn down and replaced with giant three-story homes. All modern things with right angles and long narrow windows. One looked like it was made of stacked shipping containers.

Lindy wasn't sure why she was surprised at the changes. All the cities she'd lived in along the rust belt had seen some kind of boom lately. The people and industries that polluted the lake had all but died, and grandchildren were moving back to the beautiful beaches and clean water, bringing all their money with them.

Port Lorraine used to be a fishing town, one of the few commercial harbors left on the lake, but now it looked like a vacation town.

Every single house along the ridge was new and beautiful. The lawns as green as golf courses, cared for by hired locals and timed watering systems. They probably sat empty most of the year except for one week in the summer when the owners in Cleveland and Pittsburgh managed to take their vacations. The very same people Lindy had been serving at hipster bars in the cities for the last seventeen years. She'd muddled their oranges and sugared their rims and now they were *here*. In *her* town.

Mom's house, once blue, now gray, stood out at the end of the street. It was so out of place Lindy couldn't help but laugh. One story, sloping roof, the front garden wild with blooms. It leaned into the wind like it was looking for a fight.

*The neighbors must hate it.* She smiled at the thought.

Lindy parked her car in the drive. After the engine rattled its familiar sign-off, the quiet of the street she grew up on was absolute. There was only the wind and the gulls and a faraway wind chime.

*Home.*

On shaky legs she got out of her car and walked toward the back of the house.

The steps and wraparound deck were new, the wood blond. Crystal Gayle's voice filtered out through the bent and warped screens of the windows.

The stubborn bird still resisted air-conditioning.

At the back, the cats lolled in the sunshine, barely lifting their heads at Lindy's arrival.

She opened the squeaky screen door and took a step into the kitchen, with its familiar smells of coffee and toast. A bowl of blood-red tomatoes practically glowed on the tidy counter top.

"Mom?"

Through the kitchen was the living room with its shelves of books and crazy quilts thrown over the backs of comfortable chairs.

And there was Mom in hers. Eyes closed, head rolled to the side. Her white hair was a wild frizzy halo around her small face. She sighed and shifted the book she was holding open.

Meredith was wearing the shirt Lindy sent her for Christmas: What Would The Fonz Do? Printed over a smiling picture of Henry Winkler, thumbs up. The shirt was paired with beat-up chambray shorts and white athletic socks tucked into bright white New Balance tennis shoes.

Meredith used to visit Lindy, wherever she was living, at least once a month. Lindy would reserve the best seat in the house at whichever restaurant she was working in at the time, and the wait staff would spoil Meredith. Special desserts from the chef. A glass of wine on the house. Those monthly visits had slowed down over the years. It had probably been a year since she'd seen her mom. A year.

Lindy was relieved that Meredith looked the same as always— her amazing mother. And her unchangedness, after something like a brain event, was a gift Lindy wasn't expecting.

"Mom," Lindy said, now on her knees in front of the chair. Meredith's hand was warm and dry, the skin papery and soft at the same time. Lindy never met a woman who worked as hard as her mother and still managed to have hands so soft.

A life goal, for sure, though Lindy's were already shot to hell. Her hands and her life goals.

"Mom," she repeated, more loudly this time.

Meredith McAvoy snuffled awake, blue eyes wide and un-focused.

"Was I snoring?" she asked.

"No."

"Drooling?" She wiped her chin.

"No." Lindy laughed, her eyes watering.

Meredith took in Lindy in pieces. Over and over. Faster each time. Lindy wasn't sure she wanted to know what her mother saw.

Suddenly Meredith pulled Lindy against her. Her mother's body felt frail under that Fonzie T-shirt, but her arms were steel bands.

"You're here," she said. "You're back."

For better or worse the wild McAvoy sister was home.

# THREE

## *Delia*

"*H*ow's the bass?" asked Mrs. Muñoz, Brin's high school Spanish teacher. It was Friday just before five. Mrs. Muñoz always came in Friday just before five. Until the weekly fish fries started next week.

"No bass today. But the perch is fresh," Delia said. "So is the walleye."

"The perch looks great." Mrs. Muñoz's smile didn't quite get to her eyes. "I'll take a pound."

*I'm sorry,* Delia almost said. *I'm sorry about Brin. This year was hard. She's not a bad kid, she's just…acting that way.*

But Ms. Muñoz wasn't here for apologies, she was here for the fish Dan caught at dawn. Delia wrapped up the slick, firm filet, with its white flesh and silvery skin, in butcher paper and handed it over just as Ephie let out a little cry from the back room.

"Your daughter?" Mrs. Muñoz asked. This time her smile was real. Further proof everyone loved a baby but not so much a sullen teenager.

"Yes." Delia glanced at her watch, though she hardly needed

confirmation of the time. Her breasts ached. "Up from her nap. Five p.m., like clockwork."

*Please*, she prayed to her boobs, *please don't leak in front of Mrs. Muñoz, leave me some dignity.*

"She's here with you all day?" Mrs. Muñoz shook her head, and Delia wasn't sure if it was because she thought Delia was a modern marvel of motherhood, or an idiot.

Frankly, Delia wasn't sure either.

But she didn't have the luxury of choice.

"Most days," she said. "No mat leave for me." Delia tried to make it sound like a joke, but it came off bitter.

The bell over the door rang as Mrs. Muñoz left, and Delia darted past the fish counter and cash register to lock the door and flip the sign before anyone else could come in.

The McAvoy Bait, Fish and Lunch Counter was officially closed for the day.

In the back room, surrounded by boxes of paper towels and rolls of clear plastic bags, Ephie cried up at the mermaid mobile above the pack-n-play.

"Hey, hey," Delia crooned as she picked up her baby. Ephie was wet and hungry, but as soon as she was in Delia's arms she stopped crying.

And Delia's bitterness vanished.

After taking care of the diaper and sanitizing her hands, Delia dropped down in the rocking chair and put Ephie to her breast, wincing at the initial pins-and-needles rush. Delia rocked and stroked her baby's hair, and Ephie drained Delia dry.

The most straightforward relationship in Delia's life. And she quite loved it.

Delia wasn't going to say Ephie was a miracle, but she and Dan had stopped thinking it was possible. Ten years, after all, was a really long time to try. They'd given up. Dr. Alvarez said it was the hormonal change from perimenopause. Which wasn't a joke, but it sure felt like one.

It was a little over a year ago that Delia and Dan got pregnant, but it seemed like a decade. Actually, that wasn't true. It felt more like the happiness they once honestly shared was a decade old, a story someone told her.

About a couple who had been happy.

Because that wasn't them anymore. Not for the last year, really. They'd been together a long time and every couple went through rough spots—the late-night internet searches told her so. But that didn't always make her feel better.

She needed to apologize for the other night. That fight with Brin. Even though Delia was sure she was right, she shouldn't have yelled at everyone like that. She could admit to losing her cool. She would apologize and make everyone's favorite meatballs.

*Wait, is Brin eating meat this week?* Last time Delia had made meatballs Brin had gone on a rant about how cruel it was to eat things that had faces.

She could make that cold noodle salad thing Brin liked. *Do I have soy sauce? Or noodles?* God, she hadn't even made dinner and she was already exhausted.

Okay, she'd apologize and they'd order pizza. That was as good as things were going to get.

Ephie whimpered because Delia was holding her too tight. "Sorry, baby."

She closed her eyes and sighed, pushing out all the air from her body. Delia had taken a prenatal yoga class at the new rec center and she wouldn't say she loved it—she spent half the time thinking of her to-do list and trying not to fart—but the breathing stuff she learned was pretty good. She was supposed to be finding inner peace, which honestly was never gonna happen. But this, right now, these moments. This was pretty damn close.

The sound of the back door unlocking made her quickly snap up her nursing bra and arrange her shirt over her pouchy stomach, shifting Ephie so she could continue to eat but so that Delia wouldn't be sitting there half naked.

"Babe?"

"Back here."

Dan stepped in the doorway to the office, wearing his work boots and smelling like the lake.

"Hey," he said softly.

"Hey."

"How was your day?"

He leaned down and stroked Ephie's head, making her squirm. Her little fist knocked against Dan's and a smile ghosted over his face. He stepped back to the old desk, crowded with receipts and old pictures of long-ago fishing charters, turning yellow at the corners. Some Delia's father's, some her mother's, some Dan's.

Every day she meant to clean that stuff up. Every day she didn't.

"We sold out of perch. Walleye's got another day."

He nodded as if this was satisfactory.

"How were the charters?" she asked.

"Good." He looked tired. He probably *was* tired. They were *both* tired. He was on the boats every day at 5:00 a.m. And he woke up with the baby most nights. They were in this together. She tried hard to remember that. "One of the guys here from Cleveland booked another one for next week."

"That's great."

"Next week is full."

Dan hated turning away business. He lived with the lean years like a physical memory in his body.

"Friday fish fry starts next week." Friday fish fry was a blessing and a curse. They did it once a month through the winter, but in the summer they did it every week. It was a good moneymaker for them. But more important, it was tradition. For them and the town.

"Already?"

"Already."

He watched her through the flop of long blond hair in his eyes.

"You need a haircut," she said. He usually never let it go so long.

"It's pretty shaggy." He pushed his hands through his hair, making it all stand up. Delia used to cut it for him in their kitchen in their first apartment above the shop. He'd sit shirtless, a towel over his shoulders. She'd touch him more than was particularly necessary.

For a second the memory of his hands on the back of her thighs as she stood between his was so sharp she was lost in it.

Dan had been a handsome boy and now he was a handsome man. Blond and square. Sturdy. Tan, the lines around his eyes growing whiter every summer. He was strong from his work pulling nets over the shallow sides of the boat, fit when other men his age were growing beer bellies.

On a good day, when she'd had four hours of sleep in a row and managed to put on clean clothes that sort of fit, Delia looked five years older than her age.

"We need to talk," he said, and the way he said it, looking right at her... He was nervous.

She hated that he was nervous and she hated that she'd made him feel that way. But she didn't know how to stop. How to recalibrate her reactions.

"Shoot," she said with a smile.

"I ran into Garrett down at the harbor."

"Yeah? How he's doing?"

"Fine. He's fine. But he caught Meredith walking down the spit and said she was all confused."

"My mom?" She sat up, not caring so much about her rolly stomach anymore. "What? Where was Tiffany?"

"She got past Tiffany, I guess. Garrett said she had a flare gun with her."

"Is she okay?"

"Fine."

Anger swept up the sides of her face. "Tiffany is in so much—"

"There's more." He flattened the curled-up edge of an old receipt. "Your mom wanted him to call Lindy."

"Well, of course she did but—"

"He did."

"He did what?"

"Called Lindy. Your mom asked her to come home."

"Home? Here? Is she in Port?"

"I don't know. I just talked to Garrett like five minutes ago."

None of this made any sense to Delia. Lindy. The Fulbright House. It was word salad. She closed her eyes, and in the dark she reached out for her sister. Like they were girls again, sharing a room. A hand stretched over the narrow chasm between their twin beds.

Lindy. Home.

She took a deep breath, and the relief was a surprise in and of itself.

*I don't have to do this by myself anymore.*

"Delia?"

She opened her eyes and did her best to shelve the relief so Dan couldn't see it. Admitting she was relieved was too much like admitting she needed help. "I'll... I'll go up there."

"Do you want me to go with?"

She did. She didn't. How was she supposed to answer that question?

"You need to take Brin to work. Make sure she doesn't run off with Jenny again."

"Dee," he said, implored really, as if begging her to see reason. "It's Lindy."

Dan and Lindy had been friends years ago and they'd been…something…for a split second that summer, before everything went wrong. Before Lindy left. But Delia couldn't have him there the first time she saw her sister.

So she said nothing and her silence, sharp and hooked, did all the work.

He sighed and left without another word. That was their marriage these days: silences and sighs. Delia heard the truck start up, the familiar loud rumble.

Ephie pushed against her, full, and Delia glanced down into her smiling face. She had Dan's eyes, blue as the sky.

Delia did not skip over this feeling, she sank into love for her baby. Into gratitude.

Ephie was a miracle.

And for the moment, Delia felt prepared to deal with anything.

# Lindy

She expected coming home to feel clumsy. But she slipped right back into the house like she'd never left. She met Tiffany, the nurse, who continuously apologized for letting Mom escape. That was the word she used—escape. Lindy quickly forgave her. She knew how hard it was to keep a McAvoy from sneaking out. Tiffany filled her in on meds and fluid intake, and Lindy nodded, trying to absorb all the information.

"Don't worry, I wrote it down," Tiffany said before leaning down to Mom. "I'll see you later, Mrs. McAvoy."

"My daughter's here now. I don't need you," Mom said in a biting tone that was so not at all Meredith McAvoy.

Lindy blinked, flat-footed with shock. "I... I'm sorry, I'm—"

"It's all right," Tiffany said, in a low murmur like Mom couldn't hear her. "It's part of the condition. You'll notice the changes."

Despite having seen her mom get older over the years, whenever she thought of her mother, or her sister for that matter, they were the same as the night she left, brittle and tight-lipped. But life had moved on here and she needed to catch up. There was fluid intake to worry about.

And escape attempts.

The old house was unchanged, like stepping into a time machine to her girlhood. The shell lamp they made in Girl Scouts still sat on the table by the couch. The dining room table where Lindy shoved Delia and she fell (pretty overdramatically, if you asked Lindy) from the chair—still sat cluttered and unused off the kitchen. The door to their old bedroom was shut and she wasn't brave enough to open it yet. To see their twin beds with matching quilts. The sparkly rainbow stickers, faded but still stuck to the door, were enough for the moment.

She pressed her finger against them and felt the old rough glitter and remembered the night she left. The way she'd begged Delia to talk to her.

*Go away*, Delia had said. *Just…go away.*

"Lindy?" her mom said with just the thinnest thread of panic in her voice.

"Yeah, Mom?" She stepped back out of the hallway and into the living room.

Mom smiled. "I thought maybe I'd made you up."

It was a cover. A smart one, using her health like that. And it squeezed Lindy's heart so tight, this fear over her absence, but she, too, put one foot in front of the other, just as her mother taught her.

"You hungry?" she asked Meredith.

"Starved."

Perfect. Food was easy.

The industrial-size jar of mayonnaise was where it had always been in the fridge door, the blue cap not screwed on but set in place for easy access. Meredith McAvoy ate mayonnaise on anything that would sit still. Apple slices, toast, crackers. Old pork chops. Tonight's mayonnaise usage was as God intended.

Tomato sandwiches.

Lindy sliced up the tomatoes and served the sandwiches on chipped china out on the back porch. The sun was slipping down behind the front of the house, a cool breeze coming up from the beach. The mosquitoes were still a month away.

"Here, Mom," Lindy said, placing the plate in front of her. She was in total control, until Mom grabbed her wrist and squeezed.

"Should we wait for your sister?"

"Is she coming?" Lindy asked casually.

"Well, she's done at the beach at five."

"The beach?"

Mom looked at Lindy like she was the one who'd had the brain event. "She's managing the lifeguards this year. She works too hard if you ask me, but you know your sister. There's no telling her that."

Lindy blinked and Mom blinked back.

"That was years ago, Mom. When she was a teenager. She doesn't do that anymore."

In fact, Delia only worked at the beach that one summer. She worked at the beach and at the shop, and any place in town that would pay her a couple bucks for odd jobs. She and Dan had been saving every penny to travel Europe.

"Of course," Mom said. "I forgot." She shifted her attention to the open-faced sandwich. "Look at these tomatoes! Aren't they something."

Lindy wasn't fooled by her delight, but she also didn't know what to say or how to say it. So instead she smiled, big and bright. They could both pretend nothing was wrong. After all, that was the McAvoy way.

"Yes, they are, Mom." And they both took a bite.

Lindy had worked in high-end restaurants for the last ten years, and she'd eaten some pretty amazing food. But a perfect tomato with a smear of mayo on toasted sourdough bread—it was hard to beat.

"Where are the potato chips?" Mom asked.

Tiffany had been terrifyingly clear about Meredith's low-salt diet and the dire ramifications of straying from it, so instead of chips, Lindy had pitted cherries and sliced peaches, dressed them in lime juice, honey and mint from Mom's wild garden.

"You want some fruit?" Lindy gestured to the purple bowl she made one summer at art camp.

"Oh, honey, we both know you can't have a tomato sandwich without potato chips."

She pushed away from the table and Lindy stood up to stop her. "No, Mom, I'll get them. Are they still in the cupboard over the dishwasher?"

"No. I had to hide them from your sister and that Tiffany woman. I'll get them."

"Just tell me—"

"I've had a brain event," she said, dry as Lindy's favorite martini as she headed toward the door. "Not a body event."

The screen door slammed behind her, and Lindy sat back down in the slightly warped chair in her old spot around the table. She picked a cherry from the bowl and rethought the amount of lime in the dressing. Her phone buzzed in the back pocket of her jeans and she fished it out to find a text from Angela, her friend back in Cleveland.

Everything okay?

Fine, Lindy wrote back. Mom is... She paused. What was Mom? Certainly better than she thought she'd be. But also not great. Good.

Talked to Dante at Bola. He's looking for a new head bartender, told him you were looking for a new job. He got really excited.

Bola! Holy shit. Bola had been written up in *Esquire*'s Best 100 Bars in America and it was absolutely *the* spot in Cleveland. And with summer coming, its rooftop patio would be hopping.

Here's his number. I'll tell him you're interested.

"Hello?" a voice called out from the front.

A warning Lindy barely had time to register before her sister turned the corner.

# FOUR

## *Lindy*

On instinct, she got to her feet. Suddenly, after so long, there was Delia, Lindy's dark-haired sister with the broad shoulders and piercing eyes. The baby carrier in her hand swayed back against her legs, the baby inside shrieking like she was having a good time.

"Delia." Lindy's voice cracked when she wished it wouldn't.

"Lindy." Delia smiled, the cheerful, bright girl she'd been revealed herself, so familiar and so beloved it hurt.

"It's good to see you."

"You, too. You look—" Lindy braced herself as Delia's eyes skated over her, raked really, as if trying to pull at her clothes, finger through her hair. Like when they were kids and Lindy would climb into Delia's bed and Delia would put down her book and in the light of her little reading lamp brush out Lindy's hair, all matted from the water and sand. On that bedside table, Delia'd make a little stack of the stones and shells she'd find in Lindy's curls. Summer relics of a life lived by the lake.

"Totally the same," Delia said.

"So do you."

Delia rolled her eyes, her hand going to her hair. She looked like she could use some sleep. And some sun. A drink or six. But where it counted—she was still Delia.

"You had a baby," Lindy said.

"I did. I...didn't tell you."

Lindy laughed, a hard bark. "I noticed."

"I didn't know...how."

"I get it," Lindy said, waving it off. Forgiving Delia before she even had to apologize, an old skill resurfacing.

"Where's Mom?"

"She's inside, getting chips."

"Chips!"

"We're having tomato and mayo sandwiches and you know how she is—"

"She's not supposed to be having chips!" She set down the baby carrier. "Or mayo for that matter."

"It's a couple of chips—"

"Sodium intake is really important for stroke victims."

"Well, maybe I would know that if I had known my mother had a stroke."

That slowed Delia's roll and she had the good grace to look guilty.

"Were you going to tell me?" Lindy asked.

"I was," Delia said. "But the baby and then Mom, and Brin's been in so much trouble. I can't..." She stopped talking midsentence. Like her batteries had just run out.

It had been a long time since Lindy had seen Delia and she couldn't claim to be the expert on her sister that she once was, but this version of her sister was paper-thin and exhausted.

Lindy'd honed her anger to a fine point on the drive to Port, because for once in the life of the McAvoy sisters, the part of the righteous sister was going to be played by Lindy.

But jabbing at this version of Delia didn't seem very satisfying.

"Your baby. What's her name?"

"Ephie."

"I don't... Which garden is that?"

That had been her sister's plan since they were kids, lying stretched out head to toe on the couch, snowed in by an Erie squall. Delia was going to name her children after world-famous gardens. Brin was after Brindavan, a garden in India.

Lindy on the other hand was going to name her children after characters on *Days of Our Lives*. Bo, Hope and Adrienne were going to be beautiful little kids...

"She's named after the Jardins Ephrussi de Rothschild."

"That's beautiful." *It's ridiculous.* "Can I see her?"

"She's sleeping."

The baby let out a great squawk. Dee didn't even blink, or crack a smile.

"How's Dan?" Lindy asked.

"Fine."

"Brin?"

"She's...a teenager."

"Sounds ominous."

"She's a lot like you actually."

Lindy knew that was not a compliment. "Are you going to treat me like this the whole time I'm home?"

"Maybe. Depends on how long you're staying."

Lindy could tell her sister to suck it and drive back to get whatever was left of her underwear on Third Street, but she forced herself to hold her ground. "I'm here for as long as Mom needs me."

"Oh my god, so dramatic. Don't make promises you can't keep, Lindy."

Oh, that old barb. Delia used to wield that like a sword

when they were kids. You don't pick a sister up from band practice on a few occasions and suddenly a girl's untrustworthy.

"Nothing is more important than Mom right now. I would have been here weeks ago, if I'd known."

The screen door opened, and as Mom stepped out, a bag of ripple-cut chips fell from her fingers.

"Girls!" She pulled the collar of her Fonzie shirt to wipe at her streaming eyes. Lindy was struck dumb by the sight of those tears, and Delia's statue stillness seemed to imply she felt the same at their mother's display. "My girls." She smiled sweetly and lifted her arms to them, her hands fluttering like birds.

Mom's step toward them was awkward and her daughters darted to her side.

Lindy got there first, her arm around her mother's narrow waist, but Mom reached for Dee, too, pulling them both into her body.

A family hug.

Meredith's tears bathed Lindy's cheek, and when Lindy glanced over at her sister, she saw her suffering the same baptism by grief.

"Are you hungry?" Mom said into the silence. "You need to eat. Let me make you a sandwich."

"Mom," Delia said. "Where are you getting these chips?"

"Brin gets them for me."

"Brin!"

"Oh stop," Mom said. "Don't be mad at her. Let me get you some food."

"Mom," Lindy said. "I'll do it."

"The day I can't make dinner for my daughters is the day you can put me in the ground."

There was Meredith McAvoy. Brain event or not.

She headed back into the kitchen with a slight limp, but her shoulders were as square as ever.

"She shouldn't hold a knife," Delia scolded Lindy.

"The tomatoes are cut, so is the bread. She's just going to use the toaster."

The silence was thick like the smoke of a grease fire. Choking them both.

"She seems pretty good," Lindy finally said.

"Does she?"

"Well, when Garrett said *brain event* I expected to find her drooling and tied in her chair."

Delia was suddenly all smiles. "He's Chief Singh now. Police Chief Garrett Singh."

"He didn't say he was police chief." Though it fit. That earnest, stable kid growing up to be a cop—the head cop, even—made total sense.

"Well," Dee laughed. "He is. So…you know…try not to get arrested. Or, maybe do. Whatever."

"I'm glad this is so fun for you."

"Well, fun is pretty rare and if I can't laugh at your discomfort, what can I laugh at?"

Lindy recognized an old feeling. A willingness to be the butt of every joke if it made her sister's eyes light up like that.

"Anyway, I'm just saying Mom doesn't seem that bad."

"The left side of her body is a little delayed. But mostly it's her memory. Time is fluid and sometimes she knows what's going on and sometimes she thinks Dad's alive. Or you still live in town. It's unpredictable."

"Why was she walking down the spit?" Lindy asked. "With a flare gun."

"You know why," Dee whispered.

*The Fulbright House.*

"Well, I'm staying," Lindy said, with no doubt. "Right here. With Mom. As long as she needs me."

"Don't you have a job you need to get back to?"

Once upon a time Lindy could have told Dee about Ben and her clothes raining down all over Third Street, and Dee would have packed Lindy up in a car and gone not only to get her stuff but to scold Ben into a sniveling little ball. Then she'd turn right around and scold Lindy for having such bad taste in men.

If Lindy told her now, it would only prove right the version of Lindy that Dee probably had in her head.

And to her shame that version wasn't too far off from the truth.

"Mom showed us that magazine you were in," Dee said. "The Cleveland one. You seem really...important."

A year ago Lindy had been on the cover of *Cleveland Magazine*'s Best Bars issue, wearing a sexy vest with the top button unbuttoned. There was a big spread on her as a bartender to watch, which really wasn't a thing you could be, but it gave her a few months of notoriety and that was how Ben poached her from McGuire's.

"I'm just a bartender," Lindy said, waving off her career like it was nothing. "They can get another one."

The baby fussed and Dee leaned down to unbuckle her from her seat. The baby had dark hair, thick and curly like Dee's. When they were in high school, Lindy had spent hours straightening her sister's hair for dances and awards banquets or whenever they were bored on Sunday afternoons.

"I missed you," Lindy said.

"If you're going to stay, you're going to have to take Mom's health seriously," Dee said as if she hadn't heard her. "And if you could help Tiffany so we don't have any more issues like we did today, that would be great."

"Dee," she said. "Did you hear what I said? I missed you."

Dee crossed the deck and opened the door. The bright light from the kitchen took a slice out of the darkened patio and illuminated half of her face.

"I missed you, too," Dee said and walked into the old house, the screen door slamming shut behind her.

# *Delia*

Delia had done something called a dream feed—woke Ephie up to eat, hoping it might buy Delia a few more hours in a row of sleep. It never worked, but Delia couldn't stop trying. Which was her experience with motherhood in a nutshell.

As she left Ephie's room, she noticed the guest bedroom door was open and the bed empty, which meant Dan was in their room. A rarity these days.

Exhausted, she climbed in bed next to him. She got as close as she could—a few inches away from his freckled shoulders—without waking him up. He was a light sleeper and his schedule was so rigid. She'd long grown used to protecting his sleep as best she could.

He had a scar on his back, a mole that had been removed and he'd torn the stitches so what should have been a little mark was a defined round scar. She used to fall asleep at night with her lips pressed against it.

Dan rolled over, facing her, his eyes blinking open. "Hey," he said with a sleepy smile.

"I didn't mean to wake you up."

"No. I wanted to hear how it went."

She didn't have an answer, or if she did it was buried so deep she couldn't find it.

"Is Lindy back?" he asked and she nodded. Dan's hand touched her face, pushed hair off her forehead. "You okay?" he whispered.

If she said *no*—or even *maybe*—Dan would try to fix it. And she and Lindy weren't fixable. They were broken. When Lindy left home at twenty-one, she'd cracked them in two, and when Delia had kicked her out that Christmas five years ago, they'd cracked again. Every day apart wore the edges away so there was just no way they would fit back together.

"Fine," she lied and smiled. "She looks the same. Like time stopped for her."

"Hmm. Brin was asking about her," Dan said, his eyes shutting. Sleep settled over his features and then he forced his eyes back open.

"Uh-oh."

"Maybe Lindy will be good for her."

"A cautionary tale?"

"Someone who understands her might be just what we need."

*I understand her. Brin's my baby and I know her down to her toes.* "Go to sleep," Delia said. "We can talk tomorrow."

But they wouldn't talk tomorrow. Tomorrow would be full of chores and work and plans and talking would get pushed aside.

Delia stared at the water stain in the corner of the ceiling. The roof leaked but not bad enough for them to do anything about it. With unsaid agreement, they were waiting for calamity because there was no room in their lives, or money in the bank, for preventative measures.

In the dark and in the quiet, her relief at Lindy's return

was threatened by worry that things might spin even more out of control. That had always been Lindy's effect. She was gasoline on fire.

Delia closed her eyes but calamity was still there, heavy on her lids.

Waiting.

# Lindy

*So. That didn't go so bad.*

She and Delia got bonus points for not fighting. But then again maybe negative points for not really talking. She didn't know how to keep score anymore, she was seventeen years out of practice. Delia had left after explaining Mom's bedtime routine. The shower. The pill to help her sleep. Five minutes of the news and then tucked into bed.

Lindy did all of it, surprised at how willing Mom was to be managed.

She found herself standing outside her bedroom door. Their bedroom door. How had they done it? she wondered, staring at those stickers. Teenage girls sharing a room. It seemed impossible in hindsight. Some kind of miracle.

How had they not fought incessantly?

Well, she knew the answer to that. She let Delia win because winning was important to Delia.

And Delia was important to Lindy.

But Delia let Lindy have more than half the space on the desk and the bookshelves. She let Lindy's clutter and life spread right into hers. And Delia was always the one to turn off the lamp at night.

The door opened with a whine and there was the room exactly as she remembered. Matching quilts. The mermaid lamp on the table between their beds. A desk in one corner. A bookshelf in the other.

They'd loved each other, which was the real secret to how they lived in this room. That was what hurt the most.

She shut the door. The couch would be fine for tonight, because the memories in this room were too sharp. Her skin too thin.

# FIVE

## Brin

Saturday afternoon, Brin stopped in front of the Baumgartner Jewelry store. No idea why, her feet just stopped.

"What are you doing?" Jenny looked up from her phone for a microsecond and then went right back to texting. Brin's phone got put in "phone jail" the other night, so Jenny had been making all their plans. A job she took super seriously.

"You want to go to the bonfire tonight? Eric and Danny are gonna be there. So you know the weed will be good."

"I can't."

"Oh, that's right. Your mom is the worst," Jenny said.

Brin used to defend her mom, because she wasn't always the worst. She used to be fun. And kind. She used to take Brin out of school to go for lunch. Or drive over to York to get pedicures. She used to laugh and make delicious dinners and plan trips. When Brin had a problem at school, Mom would actually listen to her. She and Dad used to make out in the kitchen when they thought Brin wasn't around.

It was gross.

And Brin totally missed it.

But lately—yeah. Mom was the worst.

The jewelry store was right in the middle of Port Lorraine. Between the Drunk Duck and the Cypress House flower shop, it was where the people of Port Lorraine bought tiny diamond engagement rings and got their watch batteries replaced.

Directly across the street was the McAvoy Bait, Fish and Lunch Counter. Brin tried to see if her mom was in there with Ephie, but the windows were too dark. She was probably watching Brin, wondering what she was up to. Assuming the absolute worst. The other night Mom'd been super clear she thought Brin was capable of just about anything. As long as it was bad.

*Is this the kind of person you want to be, Brin? Sneaking around and lying?*

"Have you ever been in here?" Brin pointed to the jewelry shop.

"No," Jenny said with pure scorn.

Brin and her dad came here a few weeks ago to pick up a Mother's Day present, a necklace with garnet and peridot, Brin's and Ephie's birthstones.

Basically, a weird red and a weirder green.

Seriously, it was kind of ugly.

But points to the guy for trying. Dad was not the best gift-giver on the planet. Over the years it had been a lot of slippers for Brin and Mom.

Brin pushed open the door to the jewelry store, making the little bell above it ring. Baumgartner's didn't look anything like the jewelry store in the mall. It was dimly lit and the cases were wood, not chrome. It smelled nice though, like lemon Pledge.

Brin didn't have a plan. She wasn't entirely sure why she was there.

But the other night's total screamfest was still in her head. Since Ephie had been born, Mom had been super focused on the negative, while totally ignoring the things Brin was doing well. Like her grades, which were…fine. Her third place finish in cross-country. She had even been first chair violin in the orchestra. Until the baby was born and she couldn't practice in the house because the most important thing in the world was Ephie's sleep schedule, and Justin Schultz took her spot.

She even had two jobs lined up for the summer.

Two!

Jenny had like…none. Most of her friends didn't either. But Mom didn't care about that stuff.

*We are not that kind of people!*

Jenny, still on the sidewalk outside, rolled her eyes. "Seriously? You're for real going in there?"

"You don't have to come."

Jenny made adults nervous. Mom said when she first met Jenny that she didn't like the way Jenny slouched. Jenny's slouch was epically indifferent. It was like her superpower, because she didn't care what adults thought about her. Like at all. And Brin needed a little of that today. Because what her mom said the other night—it hurt.

*Is this the kind of person you want to be, Brin?*

Jenny slouched her way into the jewelry store after her, and Mr. Baumgartner, a trimmer version of Santa Claus with a beard and rosy cheeks and a green sweater vest, looked up at them like they were the best thing he'd ever seen.

It wasn't special, he did that with Brin and her dad, too.

He was just a really nice guy.

"Oh my god," Jenny breathed, stifling a laugh. Probably the sweater vest.

"Hi!" Mr. Baumgartner said cheerfully. "You were in here last week, weren't you?"

"Yeah," Brin said with a rusty smile. "With my dad."

"Yes! The birthstone necklace for your mother. Is everything okay with the necklace?"

"Totally fine. I just..." Brin gestured over at the watches. "I wanted to look at a watch for my dad."

"What a lovely idea," he said with a twinkly smile. He walked around the glass cabinets to the one with the watches. "Any idea—"

"That one," Brin said, pointing to the gaudiest watch.

"The Rolex?"

"'All I ever wanted was a Rollie Rollie,'" Jenny sang under her breath.

"Yes, please," Brin said, ignoring Jenny.

Brin could see what Mr. Baumgartner was thinking: the Rolex and her dad with his sunburned neck who'd had to pay for the birthstone necklace in installments didn't match up.

She put her chin up and itched with shame.

"It's very expensive," he said, trying not to show his doubt.

"Jeez, we're just looking at it." Jenny leaned back against the case, her thumbs flying over her phone. *Superpower unlocked.*

"Of course." He pulled a set of keys from the retractable ring clipped to his belt and opened the case. The Rolex glittered even more outside of the glass and Mr. Baumgartner went the whole nine yards, pulling out a blue velvet pillow and carefully laying down the watch.

"Holy shit," Jenny breathed, no longer so interested in her phone. "Are those real? Like real diamonds?"

Mr. Baumgartner's mouth went tight at Jenny's language, but he nodded.

Real diamonds. And when Brin had asked Dad how much he thought it cost, he'd told her if you had to ask that meant it was too expensive. For one second, the thought of Dad made Brin wonder what the hell she was doing.

Dad was not living his best life lately. But no one in Brin's house was living their best life.

Except maybe Ephie.

"Can I?" Brin asked, and then without waiting for him to say yes or no, because it was obvious he'd say no, she grabbed the Rolex. He flinched and reached up like Brin was holding a baby she might drop.

"It's so heavy," she said with a wild little laugh, more nervous than she thought she'd be.

"Let me feel," Jenny said, and Brin handed it to her.

"Girls?" Mr. Baumgartner was practically levitating with stress and he held out his hand for the watch.

"Wow." Jenny lifted the watch up and down in her hand, her eyes wide.

When Dad and Brin were here, Dad—holding the necklace—stepped too close to the metal detectors at the door and the alarm went off. Dad and Mr. Baumgartner had a big laugh about it.

The sensors were really sensitive and you only had to be about a foot away from the door and they'd go off.

Just a foot.

*Is this the kind of person you want to be, Brin? Sneaking around and lying? Because we are not that kind of people.*

When Mom said it the other night, she'd pointed to herself and Dad as if to make it real clear that Brin was not a part of the *we* she'd been talking about. And Brin got it—she was trying to inspire Brin to be more like them. Family pride and all that. It was a thing that might have worked on her when she was younger.

When her mother was the kind of person Brin wanted to be. When her mother had paid attention to her and cared.

Brin stepped back toward the door.

Jenny perked up and stepped away from the case. Brin wondered if Jenny thought they were actually going to do this. Of course she did. And of course she was excited.

Flushed with adrenaline, Brin, for a moment, was mad at Jenny. That she thought this was some kind of wild prank. But this wasn't fun. It was scary.

She was trying to make a point!

"Excuse me?" Mr. Baumgartner said, reaching for Brin.

To Brin's total stomach-clenching embarrassment, she met Mr. Baumgartner's eyes. He smiled a little, probably thinking of the sweet girl he met with her dad. *That* girl wouldn't steal a Rolex. Delia and Dan Collins's daughter wouldn't do that.

Brin took another step back.

And the alarm went off.

It was so loud and shrill Brin flinched and nearly dropped the watch. Mr. Baumgartner made his way around the case faster than she anticipated and Jenny breezed by Brin, hit the door and escaped.

"You are crazy, bitch," she laughed as the door closed behind her.

Mr. Baumgartner opened a panel on the wall by the door and the alarm stopped. He locked the front door and it was just the two of them.

He held out his hand and Brin put the watch in it.

"The alarm notifies the police," he said. "They'll be here soon."

On cue there were sirens in the distance.

Brin swallowed down what might have been vomit.

*This is who we are, Mom.*

# Delia

Delia's life had taken plenty of unexpected turns. But picking her daughter up from the police station felt like a turn too many. It was no balm either, that Brin sat in Chief Singh's office looking pale and scared.

*Good. You should be scared.*

"Mr. Baumgartner's not pressing charges," Garrett said, and Delia, long since immune to the guy's good looks, managed to both stare him in the eye and nod. There were women around town who could not manage that.

Ephie in her car seat squealed with delight at the star attached to the handle above her head. It was entirely the wrong soundtrack for this moment.

"Is there any way I can convince him to change his mind?" Delia asked.

"Mom!" Brin whispered in horror, and Delia's anger nearly got away from her.

"You tried to steal a watch, Brin."

"I wasn't going to steal it."

"No?"

"The alarm is just super sensitive."

"You're blaming the alarm!"

Garrett, leaning against his desk, held up a hand. "I have a suggestion."

Delia would take anything she could get at this point.

"I have a program I run on Sundays," Garrett said. "Community service—"

"Yes," Delia said. "Sign her up."

"Mom! Shouldn't we find out what it is first?" Brin asked.

"Yeah," she said seriously. "Chief Singh, is the community service hard?"

"Well, it's not easy. And it can be pretty gross."

"Sounds perfect," she said right to Brin, who tightened up her whole face and looked away.

"It's also really early in the morning on Sundays and if kids show up hungover I've got extra gross things for them to do."

"Even better. Is there anything else you need Brin to do? Wash squad cars? Walk the K-9 unit?"

Garrett shook his head, grabbed a card from his desk and scrawled on it with a Sharpie. "Here's the information. I think a special apology to Mr. Baumgartner would be appreciated. He was kind of rattled by the whole thing."

Of course he was. Of course dear sweet old Mr. Baumgartner was rattled by having two impudent teenage girls play chicken with a Rolex and his alarm system.

God. She was embarrassed even thinking about it.

"Of course and thank you," she said, the anger receding, leaving her grateful and shaky. She gave Brin a look and she stood up on cue.

"Thank you, Chief Singh. And I'm real sorry," Brin said without prompting. Which in these dark days Delia took as a glimmer of hope.

"See you Sunday morning," he said, putting on a stern face

for Brin. Her throat bobbed as she swallowed, and Delia could tell Brin recognized she'd gone too far.

It broke Delia's heart and made her happy at the same time.

Delia and her daughters were nearly at the door when Garrett cleared his throat and said, with completely unconvincing casualness, "I understand Lindy's home."

"She is," Delia said with equally false casualness. "Got in yesterday."

Delia felt Brin's sudden and keen interest. She didn't know what Dan told her about Lindy, probably a highlight reel. Maybe showed her that magazine picture of Lindy looking wild and sexy in a vest with nothing on underneath it.

"I'm sorry," Garrett said. "I didn't mean to get in the middle—"

*Of the McAvoy sisters' drama. No, I imagine you didn't.*

"It's all right," Delia said. "It's good she's home. She's staying up at Mom's. You should go on up and visit her. They rise and shine early up there. I'm sure she'd appreciate it."

It wasn't kind. It was in fact a bit dastardly.

And it felt so good.

"Maybe I will," he said.

The man might be an adult, but if there was one thing Delia understood all too well, it was that as adult as everyone was, they never got very far from the kids they'd been.

She glanced over at Brin and wondered what that would mean for her.

Ephie's carrier was clipped in the back and Brin was sitting in the passenger seat, radiating nerves and a cheap bravado.

The keys in Delia's hands weighed a hundred pounds. *How did this happen? How did we get* here?

"Mom?"

She hummed a sound, a kind of "go-ahead" but "be careful."

"On a scale of one to ten, how mad are you?"

"Seven thousand." She glanced at her daughter but had to look away.

"I'm sorry," Brin breathed.

Finally, Dee started the car and drove down past the store, just to see if Dan was back yet, but the shop was closed and the sign she'd put in the window was still there. There was no sense in opening the store back up for an hour. She turned left on Main Street and headed for home.

When she and Dan first got married, right after graduation, they'd lived in the apartment above the store. Before she left town, Lindy had been planning on moving up there and she'd done a ton of work cleaning the place up. She'd hung curtains and painted the walls, scoured yard sales for second-hand furniture that wasn't god-awful. She'd made it into a beautiful little space.

And then she'd run away in the middle of the night.

So, Delia and Dan moved right on in. He worked with Mom running charters and Delia worked in the shop until Brin was born. They'd been so happy above the store. Everything smelled like fish and they were poor as mice, but they'd had Brin and they'd had each other.

It wasn't perfect.

But if she had a couple good days in a row she'd been young enough to believe that she was *better*. And when the anxiety and fear came back, she was able to hide it and pretend. She'd force herself out of bed. Force herself to smile.

She'd got so good at it, had so much practice, the pretending became real enough. A kind of shell she could live in.

When Mom finally retired and Dan took over the whole of the charter business, they moved out south of town, a few blocks away from the harbor. They'd been happy there, too, but they'd also become adults there. With property taxes and sore knees, raccoons that got into the garage and a leaky roof.

Sometimes she wished they could move back to the apartment. To that simpler time. To those people they'd been.

"Aunt Lindy is back in town," Brin said.

"Yeah. She's helping with Gran."

"When can I see her?"

"I don't know," Delia said. "I haven't really thought about it."

Which was a lie. She'd spent half the day trying to figure out what was the best way to introduce her rebellious daughter to her rebellious sister. Wondering with some seriousness if she could just...not. Avoid the situation altogether. No official decision necessary.

"She's my aunt, Mom. She's not like a serial killer. Is she?"

"No. Of course not."

"Does she hurt animals?"

"Brin."

"Litter?"

That made Delia laugh and she turned and caught her daughter smiling, and for a second everything was all right. The moment spun out golden and happy.

# SIX
## *Lindy*

Sunday morning Lindy woke up on the couch, sweaty and annoyed by house flies. The sound of the lake outside the windows didn't even cheer her up. Seagulls were fighting and her head pounded.

"Shit," she said with a long exhale, and tried to rub the grit out of her aching eyeballs.

It felt like a hangover, but it was so much worse. A dread-over.

Mom did not sleep last night. At all.

Lindy'd been lulled into a false sense of security on Friday. Tiffany had made everything seem rather easy. Mom had been clearheaded, if not curmudgeonly. Saturday had been one of the best days she could remember. They talked on the porch and sipped iced tea. She repotted Mom's basil plant while Mom told her she was doing it wrong. When Mom napped in the afternoon, Lindy made pasta salad with some of the basil and a can of chopped-up artichoke hearts.

As per the instructions, Lindy tucked Mom into bed after the news, but she kept wandering out, waking up Lindy to ask about people long dead and events she couldn't remember. And Mom seemed...nervous, about all of it. She rubbed the hem of her nightgown until the seam frayed. She puttered. Fretted. Slipping back and forth in time. Looking for things and then forgetting them.

The hall closet had been emptied at about three in the morning. Mom'd been relentlessly looking for Lindy's and Delia's birth certificates, and the hallway was now cluttered with old photobooks, boxes of letters and business taxes from 1986.

The McAvoys' entire history on display.

Lindy felt old. And scared. She thought she was coming back home to something she understood. But she didn't understand anything. Not about Mom post–brain event, anyway.

About twenty times last night Lindy'd contemplated calling Delia. Once she even had the phone in her hand. But she'd talked herself off the ledge every time.

As Lindy put the coffee on, she noticed a pill left in the bright yellow compartment of Mom's weekly pill box. The top of the pill was blue, the bottom was white.

It was the one that was supposed to help her sleep.

*Crap.*

Last night had been all her fault. All her mother's agitation and distress could have been avoided if she'd just done what Tiffany had told her. And Delia. Twice.

She stared out the window at the gray day building over the lake. It was going to be humid, Lake Erie like a wet washcloth in their faces all day long. She closed her burning eyes.

*Two days back and you're already screwing this up.*

Maybe this was a mistake. Coming home, thinking she could help? She wasn't a nurse. Or even a particularly good daughter.

Her phone lay dark and charging on the counter. She grabbed

it and scrolled through the messages and found Angela's with Dante's number.

Dante, she texted him. This is Lindy McAvoy, I understand you're hiring for Bola. Consider this my application. When can we talk?

She wasn't expecting Dante to respond so early on a Sunday, but his reply hit her screen in just a few seconds.

Lindy McAvoy! Look at you, early bird. I was just thinking about you. We're closed for reno for two weeks. Come in and talk to me on the 3rd. You'd be a perfect fit.

June 3 was two weeks away.

Her thumbs paused over the screen. Two weeks. It seemed both impossibly long and far too short.

"Lindy?" Mom shuffled out of her room, dressed in an old Public Library T-shirt, hair pulled back into a tidy knot at the back of her head. She didn't look like she'd spent the night trapped between now and 1986.

Lindy put the phone down, Dante's text unanswered.

"Good morning, Mom," Lindy said gently.

"I worried I dreamt you," she said with the smile Lindy remembered from her childhood. Calm. Capable. Gruff at times. Reserved more often than not.

Meredith McAvoy wasn't warm. She wasn't the mother who smothered her girls with kisses and praise. In the city, Lindy's friends with kids took their eight-year-olds to get pedicures and something called baby cappuccinos. They spent afternoons in museums and art classes. They signed up for reading enrichment classes and kindergarten tutoring.

Growing up, Delia and Lindy had the bait shop. They had each other. A mother, whom they loved and who loved them, but who worked fifteen-hour days to keep them on tomatoes and meat three times a week.

The McAvoy sisters also had Mom's grief like a long dark shadow in the house, keeping the corners cold and silent.

"I'm here, Mom." Lindy poured her a cup of coffee and refreshed her own, then pushed the pill case toward her. "And while I'm here, and I'm supposed to be looking after you—"

"I don't need looking after," Mom said predictably.

She took the pills one at a time, washing each down with a sip of coffee. Lindy stopped her from taking the little blue-and-white one.

"Do you remember last night?" Lindy asked, and an expression flickered over Meredith's features. There and then gone, but Lindy caught it.

Fear.

"I didn't sleep well."

"That's right. You were really…anxious, Mom. Because I didn't give you the pill to help you sleep."

Meredith put her hand to her forehead, hiding her eyes, and Lindy gave her her privacy, turning away to the fridge for the cream.

"I can't believe I forgot," Lindy said, knee deep in this spiral of shame. "What if I…accidentally hurt you? Or make things—?"

"Lindy." Mom sighed. "You won't do that. It's some pills. I forget them all the time."

"Delia would kill me if she knew."

"Delia has always been good at making you feel dumb."

Lindy nearly dropped her mug. That was something the Mom she knew never would have said.

"I'm pretty good at making myself feel dumb," Lindy said. "That's not Delia's fault."

"You're not dumb, Lindy."

She thought of the night and her screwup.

"Let's drink our coffee outside before it gets too hot," Mom said, calming them both down.

Lindy followed Meredith out to the porch, where they sat in the morning sun, drinking their bitter coffee. "It's gonna be hot today," Mom said and she rolled up the edge of her shorts, her knobby knees in the open air.

"It already is." Lindy's feet were propped up on the chair beside her, her legs stretched out in her cutoff sweatpants. She'd had half a bottle of bad chardonnay when she'd cut them and the legs were lopsided. She'd never had the wherewithal to fix them. Out there on her mother's deck in the Lake Erie sunshine, it hardly mattered.

Lindy could smell last night's stress sweat, the odor of her unwashed hair. The unshaved hair on her legs glinted in the sun.

Officially, she was gross.

"Hello?" a voice called out from around the side of the house. A heavy boot took the first step on the stairs of the deck and Lindy barely had a second to put her legs down, to feel incredibly keenly her lack of a bra, before Garrett Singh was standing in the backyard.

Tall and rawboned, he wore dark blue pants and a dress shirt, a wide brown leather belt around his trim waist. Lindy watched, dry-mouthed, as he hitched the belt up like a spaghetti western cowboy. It should have been ridiculous, but it wasn't.

It *really* wasn't.

His thick brown curly hair was trimmed short, as if to keep those curls in line. But they were stubborn and not at all gray. Not even a little. His nose, broken a time or two as a lacrosse-playing teenager, now fit his face, and he looked... Well, he looked good.

He'd been a kid the last time Lindy saw him. A smitten teenager.

But now Garrett Singh—*Chief* Garrett Singh—was grown all the way up.

# *Lindy*

*I*t should be made clear that nothing *really* ever happened between Garrett and Lindy. In the wide spectrum of teenage
drama and heartache, they fit just on the other side of innocent.

He'd been a sweet, handsome kid with a crush on the
troubled McAvoy girl, and she'd liked how he looked in his
lacrosse uniform and the way he watched her with his deep
brown eyes. Like he was seeing a different version of her than
everyone else.

Garrett didn't hang around Lindy's crowd or go to the
parties she went to. But almost every summer evening, he
came with his sister to get ice cream at the shop where Lindy
worked.

Lindy flirted. He blushed.

She'd kissed him once or twice when he helped her take
the garbage out.

Or a dozen times. A dozen dozen times. Who counted?

He never pushed for more.

*A real gentleman*, Delia would say as part of her ritualistic teasing of Lindy every night from her side of the bedroom. *That's why you don't like him. Because he's a real gentleman.*

Sometimes Delia sounded like a character in a BBC drama.

Lindy'd thought maybe Garrett was gay. Because the boys she knew and went to those parties with, they were a constant barrage of *more*. They were a pack of hounds. Their unchecked privilege. Their football-player masculinity that required them to outdrink and outscrew each other. To top each other's ridiculous dares. That had been Lindy's impression of what men were like. How they behaved with women. How—in the end—she knew they wanted her.

Their harassment and lewdness was far more straightforward to her. Understandable. They pushed, and Lindy pushed back. Or didn't, depending on her mood.

But not Garrett.

At the time she'd thought, if this boy didn't want *that*, what could he possibly want from her?

And now, in her own backyard, the cats all coming out from their hiding places to watch, Lindy was the one blushing, trying to pull the legs of her cutoffs down, just to the edge of decent.

"Chief Singh!" Mom cried, all wide-eyed delight. She even clapped her hands. "What a pleasure. Would you like a cup of coffee?"

"No, ma'am," he said with a charming smile in Meredith's direction.

*Ma'am. Really?*

"You remember my daughter Lindy," Mom said, clearly having forgotten the walk on the spit and Garrett calling Lindy on her phone.

Lindy braced herself for the brush of Garrett's gaze over her revealed leg, but he locked eyes with her and only nodded, his lips twisting just a bit at the corner, like he was trying to keep that smile under control.

"Of course," he said. "Lindy McAvoy is a hard girl to forget."

It might be a sign of how the years had messed up Lindy's wiring: the compliment, their incredibly innocent past, the way he'd never hidden his crush but also never pursued it, should have simply made Lindy smile. Perhaps return the compliment. Something respectful. Maybe with a small undercurrent of flirtation. Of possibility. Lindy was in fact the queen of those compliments. She handed them out like fliers from behind every bar she worked.

But there, braless and exhausted, seagulls overhead—she rolled her eyes.

And that wry twist to the corner of his lips vanished. His face hardened right up.

"What can we do for you, Garrett?" Mom asked.

"I've got to get down to Ferris Beach by 8:00 a.m. to sort out the community service kids." He paused, watching them, and Lindy felt like she was supposed to say something. Or know something. But she was barely human at the moment. "But since I know how early you get up, I thought I'd swing by and check in on you here," he said, giving Mom another smile. "Make sure you were all right."

"Well, that's real nice of you, Chief Singh. But I'm all right. Lindy's home." Mom's beaming smile was strangely embarrassing. Her faith in Lindy's presence felt excruciatingly misplaced.

"I see that. I'm glad for you. Must be nice to have all your family around you. I'll leave you two to your coffee." He nodded at each of them and Lindy couldn't help but think, if the man was wearing a hat over that thick dark hair, he'd have taken it off and bowed.

"Garrett," she said as he slipped around the side of the

house. "I mean Chief Singh. Just a second." She ran and caught up with him by the blue hydrangeas blocking the front door.

"Lindy?" he said, his voice cool.

"Sorry," she said. "I was rude. It was a long night and I'm… well, I'm off my game, I guess. Thank you for calling me the other day to tell me about Mom. I really do appreciate it."

His smile came back briefly and she could smell him on the breeze coming up from the lake. Something cedary and Head and Shoulders shampoo. The combination shouldn't be special. Shouldn't even register. But somehow it did. It pulled at the knot in the low part of her belly.

"Hardly. Nothing to worry about." His thumbs found the edge of his belt and hung on. "She seems much calmer with you home."

Lindy laughed, a maniacal weird bark she immediately regretted, and the words covered in apprehension and guilt tumbled out of her mouth in an awkward jumble. "I forgot to give her her pill last night and she didn't sleep. She just wandered around. Took apart the whole closet looking for something that wasn't even there. And then this morning, she doesn't remember? I don't think. I don't… I'm rambling. I'm sorry. This is—"

*So much harder than I thought it would be. Not that I thought about it at all. Classic Lindy.*

He leaned forward, just a bit, and she sucked in a breath. "My grandfather had dementia. My mom took care of him as long as she could. It's not easy, Lindy."

She swallowed down about twenty different things she could say. Or wanted to say. Self-defeating prophecies. She was so proud of herself when she simply stepped back. "Thank you," she said. "For checking in on her."

"Doing my job," he said.

"Police chief, huh?" she asked, finding her own smile. "Look at you."

"At your service."

She took another step back. "It suits you. You always were a white hat kind of guy."

He bowed his head again and she rolled her eyes, but it wasn't at him, it was with him. A dangerous distinction.

"Can't help it," he said with a smile. "Comes with the badge. How long are you sticking around?"

"I'm not sure," she hedged.

"I guess I'll see you around."

"Probably." She couldn't linger by the hydrangeas flirting with Garrett all day. But she also couldn't turn around and flash him her butt cheek. So she stood there and he, being polite, stood there as well.

"Everything all right?" he asked.

"Yes, I just... I need you to leave. First. Before I turn around." Too much information, but she was exhausted, and cool eluded her.

# SEVEN

## *Lindy*

"Why?" he asked. "Is there—?"

"My cutoffs are cut off too short and I don't want to flash you."

His mouth dropped open and she remembered how easy he was to surprise. To delight.

"Lindy McAvoy," he said, and that was all. Just her name, his voice warm with affection and something she was not familiar with. Respect. Appreciation, maybe.

He crossed the street to his car, and she watched him go before turning and running in bare feet back to Mom.

Mom wasn't in her spot on the back deck. Her coffee cup sat on the table, steaming into the air.

"Mom?"

Silence.

The panic was instant and knee-quaking.

Her back turned for a minute, while she talked to a man, and Mom wandered away.

*How predictable can I be?*

"Mom?" Her voice shook.

No answer from the trees behind the house. She opened the screen door and stepped inside the cooler interior of the kitchen.

"Mom?"

"Back here," came the muffled reply.

*Get a grip. She went inside, for crying out loud.*

"Whatcha doing?" Lindy asked, feigning casual as best she could.

"Looking at this mess." Mom stood at the front of the hall-way closet, where the pictures had been spread across the floor. "What happened?" she asked.

"I... I was looking for something."

Mom wasn't buying it. She stood there shaking her head. Her white tennis shoes looked so big at the ends of her thin legs. Once upon a time Delia called her an ostrich, and it was so perfect of a description they laughed and laughed. Well, Lindy and Delia had. Mom had let them, even did a goofy bird dance to keep it going. "I don't... I don't remember doing this."

"It's nothing. Nothing. We'll clean it up."

The breath Mom pulled in lifted her shoulders up to her ears, and she held it so long it was like she was frozen.

"Come on." Lindy tugged on her hand. "Let's have some breakfast and then we'll clean this up."

The tangible proof of all their past mistakes was too much to take for the moment. So, there was only one solution...

Peach pancakes.

# Brin

"You've got to get up," Mom said, standing in the doorway of Brin's bedroom, bouncing Ephie in her arms.

Unbelievable amounts of snot poured out Ephie's nose. Like how could one baby produce that much snot? And why was she smiling?

"Chief Singh is expecting you."

Right. Community service.

Brin rolled over and buried her head in her pillows. It was waaaaaaay too early in the morning for baby snot and Chief Singh and her mom all angry in the doorway.

"Did you think you could steal that watch and not...not have to pay the consequences?" Mom asked in the Did I Raise You To Be Like This? tone.

On Brin's list of Top Three Least Favorite Tones, it was number two.

Number three was This Is For Your Own Good.

Number one was I'm Fine. Everything Is Totally Fine.

"I didn't steal it. I walked with it *toward the door*."

"Don't be cute. You have a choice right now. Take the consequences from Chief Singh. Or take consequences from me."

Brin sat up, because Mom's consequences involved the shop. And lots of time together. Neither one of them would survive that.

"Which beach are we cleaning up? Potter's?" Potter's was the public beach where Brin worked as a lifeguard in the summer and the worst she'd have to touch would be some bottles, cans and half-eaten hot dogs.

*Please say Potter's.*

"Ferris," Mom said, and Brin fell back in the bed.

Dead fish. Tons of them. Beach glass. Probably a million condoms. Once a dead body washed up in town and which beach did it wash up on?

Ferris.

"You're also grounded from Jenny."

"What?" Truthfully, Brin expected this one. Mom had been trying to get rid of Jenny for a long time. Which was part of the reason she hung out with her. But it would be suspicious if Brin didn't put up a fight.

"And your cell phone is gone. For another week."

"Wait. No Jenny *and* no cell?"

"Shoplifting, Brin. I still can't get my head around it. It's like I don't know you."

*Because you don't.*

Mom turned around, her green robe flaring out behind her. "You have five minutes. I'll give you a ride."

A ride. That was pretty much the best Brin could hope for these days.

Ferris was a west-facing beach on the far side of town. There was a rocky break that went out into the lake about twenty feet, and that break caught all the garbage from York-ville. Yorkville was a garbage town.

"There's Chief Singh." Mom pointed over at two people standing by the faded wooden sign that had been vandalized in truly imaginative ways over the years. "Who is that with him?"

A tall, lanky kid in jeans and a black T-shirt stood next to the chief, and Brin was about to say she didn't know when he turned.

*Oh. Shit.*

"Troy Daniels."

"You know him from school?"

"Know of him."

Troy Daniels had been kicked out of school for fighting with teachers, and once the principal found drugs in his locker. And there was a rumor that he knocked his own dad unconscious over a girl.

She didn't want to do this. Like *really* didn't want to do this.

"Mom—" *I'm in way over my head.* Those were the words in her mouth. She could taste them, the sharp sweet taste of the truth. And if she released them, her mom would be forced to talk to her. To turn off the car and listen like she used to.

"Come on, Brin. I need to get to the grocery store."

This problem—like all Brin's problems since Ephie was born—was her own.

"How do I get home?" Brin asked, one foot out the door.

"Call me and I'll come get you."

"You have my phone, remember?"

Mom dug in the cup holder and pushed a bunch of change into Brin's hand.

"What's this going to do?"

Mom pointed at the bank of pay phones at the edge of the parking area.

"Are you kidding?"
"Shoplifting, Brin."
Then Mom left Brin with all her consequences.
And Troy Daniels.

# EIGHT

## Lindy

Lindy and her mom—their stomachs full and happy, the breakfast dishes drying on a tea towel laid out by the sink—sat in the hallway, their backs against opposite walls, making piles of things to throw away and things to keep.

They decided since the closet was empty, it would be criminal not to clean it out.

Well, Mom had decided. Lindy pushed hard for the criminal behavior but predictably lost.

Now she had a lap full of mismatched single mittens and gloves all ready to be tossed.

"Work on those?" Mom said, pointing to the photo albums.

"You want to throw those out?" *That* seemed criminal.

"No. I just want them organized."

"I can organize," Lindy said, though she didn't want to. Those photo albums seemed like landmines she wasn't brave enough to deal with this morning.

Lindy glanced around for any other kind of distraction she could find. The floor of the closet was clean for the first time in a million years, give or take, and in the front corner she noticed a fragile chain stuck between the floor and the base-boards. With one finger she teased it loose, pulling from its hiding spot a long chain with an oblong pendant.

"Oh my god," she breathed. "I thought this was gone."

She flipped over the medal so St. Christopher and his staff were staring up at them.

Mom gasped. "Dad's medal! Oh, remember how we looked for it?"

He'd worn it every day, every damn day until about a year before he died, when the chain broke and it had been Lindy's job to get it replaced.

Which she had, and then immediately lost it. Dad had said it didn't matter. But they all knew it did.

Twice, they'd torn the house upside down looking for the damn thing. Once when she first lost it and then again when Dad died. Since his body was never found, they'd wanted to bury the medal beneath his memorial stone in the cemetery.

Lake Erie fishermen were a superstitious lot, and Dad had had his fair share of seemingly nonsensical rules. No fishing on Sunday (Mom and then Dan both broke that one). No bananas on the boat. No one on board could drink a beer until the first fish was caught. There was something about locks being tossed in the water. They should do it? Or shouldn't? She couldn't remember.

And of course, the St. Christopher medal. For a safe return.

Lindy slipped the chain over Mom's white, pillowy hair and rested it against her neck. The medal fell down to her knobby breastbone. "So you can find your way back," Lindy whispered.

The landline rang and they both jumped because it sounded like a 1985 tornado drill.

"Hold on." Lindy stood and leapt over the stack of banker boxes to grab the cordless from its place by the shell lamp.

"Hello?" Lindy said.

"Aunt Lindy?"

Lindy blinked. Her body still as could be. "Brin?"

"Hey." Her voice was low and muffled, and wherever she was it sounded like there were a ton of cars nearby.

"Oh my god," Lindy said, paralyzed with surprise and a cloudy kind of joy. "Brin."

"Right," she said with a laugh. "We established that."

"What... Where are you?"

"Ferris Beach."

"Why?"

"Long story. But...do you think you could come pick me up?"

"Of course." Lindy was already reaching for her keys. "But what about your mom?"

"What about her?"

"Does she... Does she know you're calling me?"

"Am I not supposed to?"

It certainly felt like she wasn't supposed to.

"Of course not," Lindy lied. "I just—"

"Don't want to cross my mom?" Brin asked in the dry tone of someone who had crossed her mother plenty of times and had the scars to show for it.

"Something like that."

"Well, I called her and she's not answering her cell. I'm running out of coins and Dad has a charter, so I can walk home or—"

"Gran and I are on our way."

Lindy hung up and clapped her hands, the joy was so real.

"What's happening?" Mom asked. "Who's on the phone?"

"Brin."

The silence from the hallway was thick, and Lindy imagined her mother trying to recall who Brin was, why she should know her and not being able to connect the dots. Lindy didn't know how to make that better for her. Or easier.

So instead Lindy said, "Let's go for a ride."

Ten minutes later Lindy pulled into the parking area that ran along the long rocky shore of Ferris Beach. It was the wild beach in town, with craggy, scrappy trees and bushes full of trash. Twisted bits of rebar and yellow bricks, worn down on all the edges, washed in from the clean fill dump twenty miles away. The towns west of Port Lorraine had ferries to the Lake Erie islands: Kelleys Island, Put-in-Bay on South Bass, North and Middle Bass. And all the junk from those places washed up on Ferris Beach, before it could float into town. As far as beaches go, it was about as ugly as it got. It stunk like dead fish and engine oil.

Ferris was also the trouble beach. Where kids went to make trouble. Where trouble washed up.

"It's Lindy." Mom pointed to a long, leggy teenager standing beside the graffiti-covered wooden sign.

"It's Brin," Lindy corrected. But it was eerie how much Brin looked like Lindy had at that age. Her hair was the same deep red. Long, with thick bangs. Brin had to keep tossing her head to shake them out of her eyes. Lindy remembered that move. Ankles crossed, eyes squinted against the sun, Brin wore a red tank top, cutoffs and black Converse low-tops. Her vibe said she didn't care that she was standing alone on this rocky wild beach. The carefully cultivated indifference, a lie seen through from a mile away.

At this assessment of her niece, Lindy felt the sudden sharp bite of embarrassment. Lindy had wanted to be this girl on the beach her whole life. She'd known this of course, but there was something about coming face-to-face with her niece that made it bitterly clear.

Lindy was supposed to chase other things now. Biology should have forced her to, and if not biology, then common sense. Or shame, maybe. But here she was, soon to be thirty-eight, jobless, without real relationships.

Practicing the indifference.

Never fully realizing that that moment was only for youth. For girls on the edge of everything.

Lindy parked a few spots away and turned off the car.

"She's in trouble again," Mom said. "I don't know how to make that girl care about anything but boys."

"Brin?" Lindy asked.

"Lindy." Mom shook her head. "Always sniffing out trouble."

*Yeah. Don't I know it.*

As Lindy turned to get out, she noticed a boy in jeans and a black T-shirt walking up to Brin.

Brin looked at him and then away, her shoulder lifting to hide her smile.

*Uh-oh.*

"Brin!" Lindy yelled, waving her arms, making as much of a scene as she could. A method Mom never ever would have used when Lindy was making her own teenage trouble, because she was too busy and maybe too embarrassed by having a daughter who needed such watching. But family and lots of it was an all-natural, bad-boy repellant. "Brin! Come on! I got Gran in the car. Maybe we'll go see your mom."

Brin's face turned a very satisfying shade of red before she gave the boy a casual wave from the hip.

When Brin came to a stop right in front of Lindy, she didn't know what she was supposed to say. Or do, really. How to be the person she'd like to be to this girl.

Brin had blue eyes, like Dan.

*She looks like us. Me and Dan.*

Because Brin was, after all, Delia's daughter, raised, no

doubt, on lists and schedules and chore charts, Brin took control of the moment.

"So you're Aunt Lindy?"

"So you're niece Brin?"

Brin smiled with half her mouth as if committing to joy would be too much.

"Lindy," Mom said from the passenger seat. "Who was that boy?"

"No one, Gran," Brin said with ready practice, having not noticed the name mix-up.

Meredith scoffed in her throat. "Doesn't look like no one."

Brin went a little pink but rolled her eyes, and Lindy laughed.

She couldn't help it.

She laughed and laughed.

*My sister has a daughter just like me.*

# NINE

## Meredith

*T*here were two Lindys in the car

And that wasn't right, but it was true.

Meredith's brain could do that now, make the impossible happen, and some days she just let it happen, because fighting it was too dang hard. Two Lindys, one young, one old. One driving. One in the back seat.

"Wait a second. Ferris Beach on a Sunday morning?" Driver Lindy asked, glancing in the rearview mirror. "You're doing community service."

"Something like that," Back Seat Lindy said.

"Not something like that. *Exactly* that. What did you do to earn it?"

"It was just a misunderstanding."

That made Driver Lindy raise an eyebrow, but when Back Seat Lindy was silent, she finally said, "Sounds serious."

It did. It sounded like Lindy got in real trouble, and the embarrassment of being the mother of a girl she couldn't control was a hot flush up her neck.

"You hungry?" Meredith asked Lindy in the back seat, focusing on what she could control. The girl was looking out the window at a boy as they pulled away from the beach. "Lindy?"

"We just ate," Driver Lindy said. "Are you hungry?"

"I'm asking her." Meredith pointed to Back Seat Lindy, who smelled her hands and wrinkled her nose.

"I can't eat anything until I clean up," she said.

"Should I take you home?" Driver Lindy.

"There's nothing at home." A long-suffering sigh. "Mom's like completely given up on groceries."

"You can clean up at my house," Meredith said, settling the matter. "And we'll have some peach pancakes."

The boy and the beach were vanishing in the distance, the black T-shirt reduced to a speck and then a smudge and then gone.

But not gone.

That, too, happened somehow at the same time.

He was in Lindy's head. In the corner of her eyes and the way she'd dress for the rest of the summer. The way her shrugs and evasions would turn to half-truths and then outright lies.

And then disaster.

"Who is that boy?" she asked again. Determined, suddenly, to get this part right. To not turn away from the hard things.

"Mom?" Driver Lindy asked. "Are you okay?"

She was breathing too hard. She knew that. Lindy in the back looked nervous.

"I asked you a question," Meredith said, pleased with how the words came out of her mouth with just the right tone.

"He's just a boy," Lindy said, with a shrug and wide eyes.

"They are never just boys."

"Amen," Driver Lindy said.

Meredith ignored her. Her eyes were on the girl in the back seat, fresh and ripe for trouble.

"He's from school. He has to do community service, too."

"Why? What did he do?"

Lindy looked down at her hands, picking at her nails. Which was different. Lindy didn't pick her nails. She had no nervous telltale habits that gave away she wasn't as confident as she was pretending. She was nothing but bravado and an upthrust chin.

"He's been breaking into the Fulbright House," she said in a soft voice.

Meredith wasn't sure she heard her right. "Breaking in *where*?"

"The Fulbright House."

The back of Meredith's head pulled tight. "You stay away from that house." Panic was a bird in her throat. "That boy—"

"You don't know him," she said. "*I* barely know him."

"That Fulbright boy is trouble—"

"Mom?" Driver Lindy said, and Meredith realized she had gotten this wrong. There couldn't be two Lindys in the car. That was more magic than was possible.

But the Fulbright boy was trouble and that house was one the McAvoys didn't go to. Not for any reason. Meredith clung to that belief with all her might. With every bit of strength in her fingers. The way she should have years ago.

"Tell me you'll stay away from him." She turned almost all the way around in her seat so she could look the girl in the eye.

"Mom?"

Meredith shushed Driver Lindy.

Lindy shrugged. "Yeah. Sure."

Meredith could have predicted that response like the weather. For all her trouble, Lindy was always predictable. Her summer storms blew through fast and violent only to turn sunny hours later. She'd only been agreeable because Delia made her that way.

Meredith was suddenly tired. Too tired to explain that there was something very wrong. And there always had been.

*And it's my fault.*

Because she knew that boy was trouble and she didn't stop it when she should have.

# Brin

## W.T.F.

Brin tried to be cool and not stare at her aunt as she made pancakes.

But she couldn't stop.

Lindy looked like Brin in some other universe. A universe where Brin would be allowed to wear tight tank tops with barely there lacy straps and long skirts that hugged her hips before flowing down to her ankles. Where Brin didn't wear a bra and her long hair was wild around her head. Not pulled back in tight ponytails. Not hidden under hats so she didn't get a sunburn. Aunt Lindy had so many freckles on her nose and shoulders she probably never even wore sunscreen much less a lame hat.

Aunt Lindy looked the way Brin *wanted* to look.

"What?" Lindy said.

"Nothing."

"You're staring at me."

"We...look alike," Brin blurted. "Right?"

Lindy smiled and nodded, tipping one of Gran's metal bowls

and whipping the batter with a whisk until it was all bubbly and creamy. Dad made pancakes some mornings in the winter and he used a mix and there were always lumps.

"We do."

Brin touched the small mole on the side of her nose, the mole she hated. Lindy had the same one.

Brin and her mom shared none of those things. Mom was short and round. She had curly brown hair that got frizzy in the summer. They didn't act alike. They didn't like the same food or music. Jenny and her mom were both allergic to strawberries, and when they sneezed, they sneezed in threes. And they were both afraid of heights. And spiders.

All Brin and her mom had in common were sixteen long years of living in the same house.

"Is that weird?" Brin asked.

"No," Lindy said with a laugh. "It's genetics. The mole. The hair. Your height." She shrugged and dropped tiny circles of batter onto the hot skillet. They watched the circles puff up and bubble on the edges. "Silver dollars okay?"

The tiny pancakes cooking in the melted butter smelled so good. After the last dead carp she'd bagged up at the beach, Brin thought she'd never be hungry again.

"You want to talk about community service?"

"You sound like my mom."

"Do I?"

"There's nothing to say. I got in trouble but not serious trouble, and this is Chief Singh and my mother's idea of *consequences*."

Aunt Lindy nodded. "And the boy?"

"Oh my god." Brin made a super weird sound that was part laugh, part shriek and totally embarrassing. "I barely talked to him. We picked up rotting fish together."

"You feel free to tell yourself that." Lindy turned back to flip small pancakes onto one of Gran's old china plates, chipped along the pink-rose edges. "But I am the wild McAvoy girl and that whole situation…" She spun the spatula in her hand in a slow circle. "It looks familiar."

Brin wondered if what Gran had been saying in the car—about the Fulbright boy being trouble, if that had anything to do with Aunt Lindy.

*I'd bet a Rolex watch on it.*

"Take this out to the porch to eat," Aunt Lindy said, putting the plate in Brin's hand. "I'll be out in a second. I'm just gonna check on your gran."

"That stuff she was saying?" Brin asked, the smell of the pancakes and peaches making her nauseous with hunger. "She thought Troy was—"

"Brain event stuff," Lindy said and got busy cleaning up.

"But did the Fulbrights have a son?"

"'Fraid so."

"The house…?"

"What about it?"

Troy went there almost every weekend. He said there was a whole party situation happening there.

Brin knew her mom hated that house. She drove the long way out of the neighborhood so they didn't have to see it, and when they did drive by, she turned her face away. *It's ugly*, she always said. *An eyesore.*

Which was totally true. But it was an eyesore Brin was so used to she never even noticed it anymore.

"Have you ever been there?" Brin asked.

Lindy nodded.

"Like inside?"

Lindy nodded again.

*When?* she wondered. *Why?* "What's it like?"

"Fancy. Well…it used to be. Looks terrible now."

"What happened?"

"I wish I knew," Lindy said as she put the skillet in the sink and cranked the water. The hot skillet released a cloud of steam.

# TEN

## *Brin*

Brin sat out on the porch, in the tiny corner of shade near Gran's mint plants.

She'd lied to Aunt Lindy earlier. She had called Mom from the beach and told her she was done with community service but catching a ride down to Potter's Beach to put in a few hours stripping paint off the lifeguard chairs.

Lying to Mom was second nature at this point. It was just so much easier than telling the truth. For both of them. Delia didn't really want to know where Brin was because then she'd feel obligated to do something about it. When what her mom really wanted was a nap.

The lying was for both of them.

It was *kindness*.

But lying to Aunt Lindy felt a little wrong. Not wrong enough to stop. But wrong.

Halfway through her last pancake—they were totally delicious, a million times better than what her dad made—Aunt Lindy came out, arms stacked high with photo albums.

"You need help?" Brin asked, getting halfway out of her

seat. Lindy made a funny face at Brin, and she sat back down. "What's that face for?"

"You're polite."

"You want me to be rude?"

"No," Lindy laughed. "I just don't know any teenagers, I guess. I expect you all to slouch and sneer and mumble stuff under your breath."

Brin slouched and sneered. "Whatever," she sighed in her best Jenny impression.

"There it is," Lindy said.

Lindy set the books down with a thunk that made the old glass tabletop wobble.

"What are those?" Brin asked.

"Gran went on a scavenger hunt last night." Lindy blew a piece of hair out of her face. "And now I'm going through the items to see what we can get rid of, and since you're here…"

"I don't know what to do with that stuff," Brin said, shoving the last of her pancake in her mouth.

"That makes two of us. But I think we can probably throw out half of it. And while we're doing that—" she sat down and grinned at Brin, the way Jenny grinned at Brin when she had convinced some stranger to buy them beer at the gas station in Yorkville "—you can tell me everything."

"What everything?"

"Everything everything. Friends. School. Summer jobs. Summer boys."

"Aunt Lindy," Brin groaned as if she were reluctant, when in reality she had been dying to talk about that stuff. She just hadn't had anyone to talk to.

Lindy's expression went soft and kind of shocked.

"What?"

"I just… I've been an aunt for sixteen years and until today I've never been called Aunt Lindy."

Brin could tell how robbed she felt, partly because Brin felt robbed, too. It would have been nice to have had Aunt Lindy in her life all these years.

"My mom made you leave, didn't she?"

"No." Lindy shook her head. "I left. Drove away in the middle of the night without saying goodbye."

"She kicked you out that Christmas, though."

Christmas Eve, five years ago, Gran apparently called Aunt Lindy and told her to come home. Brin had been at Gran's while her parents did some last-minute Christmas shopping and Aunt Lindy walked into the house like some kind of Ghost of Christmas Fun. She had presents and bells in her hair. She had tons of this wild food the Collinses never ate, like octopus and Spanish cheese covered in rosemary, green olives with almonds stuffed inside. There had been bottles of red wine and Aunt Lindy let Brin take sips when Gran wasn't looking.

Lindy had long red hair and an armful of bracelets that jingled as she danced around the kitchen. She laughed really loud and sang off-key to the Bing Crosby Christmas album Gran always played. She was the most glamorous thing Brin'd ever seen in real life.

But then Mom had walked in and Lindy yelled "surprise" and went to hug Mom and… Oh god, it was awful. Mom went into full porcupine mode.

Dad tried to smooth over Mom's radioactive silence at the sight of Lindy, because that's what he did. But it was an epic fail and Gran went to her bedroom and Mom and Lindy had a whisper-fight on the porch and Lindy left without even a goodbye.

The few times they'd talked about Aunt Lindy, Mom called her trouble and left it at that.

*Pure trouble, Brin,* she'd said. *Nothing for you to worry about.*

Brin loved the way those words sounded. She'd lie in bed

and listen to her mom walk past her bedroom door down to
Ephie's room, not even stopping to say good-night, and Brin
would whisper those words up to the ceiling.

*Pure trouble.*

"She did kick me out at Christmas, and she had her reasons.
But," she said in that super bright, super fake way of adults
trying to change the subject, "I'm here now. And so are you
and I want to know everything."

Brin didn't have any experience telling an adult anything,
let alone everything. She wasn't sure where to start.

*I drink warm beer even though I hate it.*

*Jenny thinks I should give Damen Gorke a blowjob, just to get
the first time out of the way.*

*I hate my baby sister and I'm pretty sure that makes me evil.*

*I hate my mom and I'm pretty sure she hates me, too.*

All of it felt too big to say. The words didn't fit in her
mouth.

"Start with something simple," Lindy said. "How's school?"

"Fine. Easy."

"Easy? Look at you, hotshot. What about colleges?"

"What about them?"

Lindy laughed. "Are you looking at them?"

"I'm only a sophomore."

"A junior next year. And that's when people start looking.
You're not interested?"

Brin shrugged. The truth was, she didn't know. She didn't
have an answer for that question and she wasn't sure why
everyone thought she should. Her mom hadn't gone to college, after all. Jenny wasn't even thinking about college. She
wanted the two of them to move to Cleveland and get jobs
in a bar. Make a ton of money because they were young
and hot.

"Why don't you tell me about your life," Brin said instead, and Lindy laughed. Lindy laughed a lot. It was a nice change.

"My life is not that interesting."

"You're a bartender."

"Mixologist," she said, all fake snooty.

"Do you like it?"

"I'm good at it."

"That... Is that the same thing?"

"Sometimes."

Lindy placed a thick photo album in front of Brin. Pages stuck out, the holes for the binder rings ripped.

Brin flipped it open only to find Gran as a young woman in white gazing up at her.

Gran looked so young. Pretty. Her dress was plain but lovely and her arms were full of lilacs. Mom and Gran really looked alike, she realized. Same curly hair. Same smile. No mole.

"I've never seen this," Brin said. "We have a picture of them on our wall at home, but I didn't know they had an album."

"Look at that handsome fella," Aunt Lindy said, pointing to Brin's grandfather in his tux. His sleeves were too short and he was kind of skinny as a whole, but Brin could see how he'd be considered handsome.

Troy was kind of skinny like that, too. His wrist and the way it turned and shifted into his forearm. His elbow. The muscle of his arm as it pressed against his black T-shirt.

"Life goals, kid." Aunt Lindy tapped one of the photographs. "Don't settle for anyone but a guy who looks at you just like this."

Lindy stroked her thumb over his face.

"They got married late," Lindy said. "Had us even later. Mom was almost forty when she had Dee. But they look like kids here."

"Mom talks about him sometimes," Brin murmured.

"Yeah?"

"She told me the story about the cats in his boat. How he had to jump overboard to save them."

"Classic Dad."

"She told me he died a hero."

"Also classic Dad." Lindy smiled but it was dim. "Answering another ship's distress call during a storm."

Brin's grandfather drowned when his boat was capsized by a wave. Though no one ever told her that until she did her fifth-grade health report on what happened to your body when you drown. The carbon dioxide levels build up in your blood until you can't resist trying to breathe even though you know it's not air you'll be pulling in. The need and instincts of the human body override the brain. It kind of made the victim an active participant in the whole thing.

It had been fascinating to Brin.

Mom got totally freaked out by the project and told Brin to pick a different topic. Any other topic. There'd been a big fight and Dad stepped in and explained how Grandpa had died and it was painful for Mom to be reminded of what her dad's final minutes must have been like.

"Why doesn't anyone talk about him much?" Brin said.

"Because it makes us all sad. You know something," Lindy said. "I'm not ready for this one. Let's start with a different one."

Lindy shut the book and shifted it to the bottom of the pile. The next album was newer. White with gold letters that spelled *Wedding*.

It was Brin's parents' wedding album. Now Brin wanted to close it and pick another.

Aunt Lindy said, "I've never seen these."

Aunt Lindy hadn't come back for the big day.

"So what should we do with these? Just like take out the blurry pictures and consolidate the duplicates?" Brin asked.

Lindy laughed. "Oh, you are your mother's daughter, that's for sure."

Mom looked stern-faced in all their wedding pictures, Dad like he was trying hard not to appear too happy. Mom's stomach was still flat, her face young and thin. When she got pregnant with Ephie, her cheeks were like chipmunk cheeks.

She wore a tea-length white dress. Lilacs from Gran's garden in her hands and tucked into her hair.

"Mom told me they got married at city hall," Lindy said.

They'd had a party back at Gran's. A fish fry and kegs of beer with their friends. Dad always said there'd never been a better party.

Brin went through the album fast and then set it aside.

"You have a boyfriend you need to tell your aunt Lindy about?"

"No," Brin said and pulled the next dusty album to the table in front of her. This one was bright red and kind of puffy. It said *Summer* in big block letters. The edges of the plastic had lost their stick and most of the pictures had fallen and gotten trapped in the corners of the book.

"Oh wow," Brin said, pulling out the pictures, smiling at the young faces smiling back at her. "Look at you."

As Lindy leaned over, her earrings jangled just slightly. "Oh my god, I remember this," she said.

"When is it?"

"My last summer at home." She took the pictures from Brin, who grabbed another set. "Look at your mom," Lindy said, holding up a photo. Mom posed with a plane ticket, her face radiant.

"What's the ticket for?" Brin asked.

"Their Europe trip."

"What Europe trip?"

Lindy stared at her. Jaw slightly agape and then she shut it and went back to the pictures.

"Seriously. What Europe trip? Mom and Dad never went to Europe. Can you even picture my dad in Europe?" With his sunburned neck and his white-soled shoes and the faded foam gators around his glasses. He was the least European person Brin could imagine. He was Port Lorraine through and through.

"She and your dad were going to go to Europe after that summer. Three months from September to December and then she was starting college—"

"College?"

"University of Ohio. She...didn't tell you? She had like a scholarship and everything. Full ride."

"No, she never told me."

"Well, I guess it doesn't matter," Lindy said quietly.

"She didn't go because of me."

Brin could see Lindy formulating some bullshit about how Brin was better than a trip to Europe and a scholarship to college, but for the eighteen-year-old girl in that picture, Brin was a life-changing mistake.

Everyone could dress it up or, even better, never talk about it, but they couldn't change the truth.

Brin ruined her mom's life.

She turned the pages of the photo album and landed on a picture of Delia and Lindy behind the counter at Ed's Big Scoop, the ice cream shop in town. They were wearing matching blue T-shirts and holding mops. They had their arms around each other. No space between them.

Brin handed the photo to Lindy, who smiled but tossed the photo aside.

"You guys were really close," Brin said.

"We were," Lindy agreed.

"What happened?" Brin handed Lindy another picture, the two of them dressed up for a dance, Delia in a tame black dress, Lindy in bright red sequins, both wearing wrist corsages.

"It's hard to say."

Lindy's voice was quiet, and when she looked up, Brin met her steady gaze.

"I fucked up," Lindy said.

Brin felt a little small in the face of Lindy's swearing. Adults didn't swear in front of kids, at least not in Brin's world. Except the one time Mom dropped a bunch of pans and yelled "Shit!" and then apologized profusely to Brin.

"But so did Dee," Lindy said.

"My mom? My mom doesn't...fuck up." Using the word in front of a grown-up felt super weird.

"Everyone makes mistakes," Lindy said. "Not just me."

They each grabbed more pictures. Blurry ones got tossed in the throwaway pile. Good ones tucked back in the album. She knew everyone in this one—Mom, Lindy, Dad. Mom's friend Nirosha with her hair in long braids, Dad's friend Victor who worked for the coast guard.

Until the last few in the pile. "Who is this?" Brin asked Lindy, who had been silent and serious, no longer full of fun questions about Brin's life.

Mom, Dad, Lindy and a tall guy, super hot with black hair and a smirk. They were inside someplace fancy. Wood on all the walls. Maybe the golf club?

"That..." Lindy jabbed at the picture with her finger but didn't actually touch it "...is garbage. You can toss it."

"Who is the guy?"

"No one."

*"Lindy,"* Brin admonished. "Don't treat me like a kid."

They caught eyes for a second, and Lindy seemed to get it. What it was like growing up with Mom and Gran who never talked about anything. How it was kind of like being put in a box and everyone trying to keep her there.

"It's Eric Fulbright."

"And that's the Fulbright House?"

Lindy nodded.

The hair lifted off the back of Brin's neck.

Jenny would say it was cosmic. She would it say it was the universe pointing to something, but Brin never felt like that. The universe didn't care what happened.

"And...this is the guy Gran was talking about?"

Lindy nodded again. In the picture, Lindy's head was cocked toward the guy.

"Were you guys like...a thing?"

"Nope."

"You're doing it again," Brin said.

"What?"

"Treating me like a kid."

"You are a kid."

Brin rolled her eyes.

"He wanted to be a thing with every girl in town," Lindy finally said.

"He's hot."

"Toss the picture before Gran comes out here and sees it."

Troy might be interested in it. In seeing whose house he was breaking into every weekend. And what it used to look like. Brin imagined surprising him with the picture, how his green eyes might light up. She tucked it into the back pocket of her jean shorts when Aunt Lindy wasn't looking.

The next picture was at Potter's Beach. It was the Fourth of July—Brin could tell because the city still used the same banners across the bathing stations and lifeguard chairs. Mom was in front, smiling nice and wide, dreaming of Europe no doubt. Behind her, Lindy's arm was around Dad, and Dad was looking at her like she must have just said something crazy.

It was the three of them before whatever went wrong went wrong. Before Europe and college got canceled.

Before Brin happened.

When her mom smiled with her whole face.

She tucked the picture in her pocket with the other.

"I've gotta go," she said.

"Where?" Aunt Lindy asked.

"Home."

"Okay... I'll drive—"

"You stay with Gran. I'll take the shortcut."

Lindy stared at Brin hard, as if she was looking through her skin to her bones. "You didn't tell your mom you were here, did you?"

Brin rubbed a drop of syrup from the table's edge and then wiped it off on her jean shorts.

"Brin."

"You know she wouldn't like it," Brin said. "She'd be up here and this whole nice little afternoon, it wouldn't have happened."

Aunt Lindy was quiet.

As Brin walked across the deck, the pictures in her back pocket felt like weights, throwing off her stride.

"Hey." She turned back around. "Do you mind if I come back? I can help with the pictures and stuff."

"When?"

"Whenever I can?"

"What about school?"

"I'll come after. Work at the beach doesn't start for another week."

"You going to tell your mom?"

"Will you?"

Aunt Lindy looked up at the blue-gray sky, squinting into the sun. "We can't keep it a secret forever."

# Meredith

*I have my mother's hands.*

When the heck did that happen? Meredith wondered, looking up at her hands as she loafed in bed. In the middle of the day no less.

Her mother would not have approved. *Sleeping in the middle of the day is for layabouts and drunks.*

In the afternoon sunlight the liver spots near her wrists looked like bruises. Her knuckles were big and swollen like knots in a dock line, and the veins stood out against the skin. The skin was fragile, too. Cuts turned into weird tears she had to tape to get them to stop bleeding.

At the end of her life, her mother's hands had been exactly the same.

Meredith curled them into fists and clenched them, hard as she could, feeling her power and her strength.

Mother was the one who kept the house going. The lights on. She wrung money out of that old lunch counter until the day she died—nickels and dimes mostly.

Daddy was mean and drank too much. Meredith never told

anyone about what happened under their roof. Mrs. Newson, her PE teacher in high school—until Meredith dropped out—would ask if she wanted to talk, but Meredith kept her mouth shut and changed her clothes in the bathroom stall.

*We don't tell Pastor Frank what happened. Even if he asks. It ain't nobody's business what happens under our roof. Daddy takes good care of us. And that's the only thing that matters. Right, Mer?*

Meredith was surrounded in that hard shell of her mother's silence.

She blocked out the sun with her hands, making the tips of her fingernails glow. There was that joke that women are destined to become their mothers at some point. And she never found that joke very funny. But…was that what had happened?

When William McAvoy walked into the lunch counter that Thursday afternoon, it was the very best thing that had happened to her. She was thirty-five. Officially on the shelf and resigned to it. He was a long and thin string bean of a man, with hands and an Adam's apple to match. But his voice had been calm and his smile the easiest in the world. Like he had a million smiles to give away. He'd ordered a turkey on rye and a milkshake, and when his eyes met hers she blushed all the way up from her belly. Every inch of skin pink and hot.

When he came in the next day, it happened again. And the next. And the next.

Daddy hated him, which had been all the proof she needed that William McAvoy was the one for her.

"William?" she asked. She glanced over at his side of the bed, the pillow fluffed and fat like he'd never laid his head there. Heavens. That man. Why he insisted on trying to make it all the way through the news was a mystery. He barely stayed awake long enough to see Dan Rather's face.

The day started for them at 5:00 a.m., earlier if there'd been weather in the night. The nightly news was for people with jobs that didn't start until 9:00 a.m. Dabney Peabody didn't open up the Cypress House until ten.

"William," she said. "Can you even imagine? What would we do with all that sleep?"

Meredith pulled herself out of bed, wondering what she did to make her body hurt so bad. All the aches and pains were settling in her back; she felt like a chair that had been folded up all wrong.

*I need to find the heating pad. Delia took it for her cramps last month…*

No. She stopped. Her fingers on the edge of the bed, the old knots of the quilt her mother made for her wedding gift against her knuckles.

No, that wasn't right.

She couldn't have William sleeping in front of the nightly news and Delia with her monthly. William died before the girls were old enough for their periods.

She crawled back into bed, the tears seeping out of the corners of her eyes. Believing for just a moment that William was here, still alive, created a grief as sharp as ever. It was hard to breathe with the pain of losing him all over again.

Meredith rolled to her back and wiped her eyes. It wasn't even nighttime. The afternoon sunlight came in through the window. Her hands looked old.

*I have my mother's hands…*

# ELEVEN

## *Delia*

Delia parked the van in front and grabbed Ephie from her carrier in the back seat.

When she'd called Mom earlier to remind her about the doctor's appointment, Lindy had answered, surprisingly eager to come along.

She expected Lindy to be mid-shower and Mom to be doing the crossword and unwilling to leave, but they were both sitting on the back porch, handbags in their laps.

"Hey!" Lindy said and got to her feet. She wore a pretty flared skirt and a loose-fitting pink top that slipped off her shoulder. It was the kind of thing that looked amazing on a thin woman and would just look messy on Delia.

Delia pulled her green shirt down low to cover up the stretchy panel on the maternity pants she was still wearing four months after giving birth.

Mom grumbled as she stood up. "I feel fine. I don't know what we need to go to the doctor for."

"It's just a checkup," Dee said. Though the checkups since

the brain event had been more in-depth and frequent. The family doctor interspersed with specialists in Yorkville.

"Why are we all going?" Mom asked, which wasn't a bad question.

"Because if I'm supposed to be taking care of you I need to know what's going on," Lindy said.

"You know what's going on. I forget things sometimes." Mom shrugged like it was all no big deal.

"The closet?" Lindy said, and Mom sucked her teeth and looked away.

"What about the closet?" Delia asked.

"I'll tell you later," Lindy said.

"Still, I don't understand the fuss," Mom said.

The two sisters followed her to the van.

"Shotgun!" she shouted.

Lindy and Dee shared a laughing look, and before Dee could stop it, the past rose up in a giant wave. The mundane nature of the three of them getting into a car shouldn't seem so loaded. So fraught. But it was. It just was. Those moments they took for granted growing up. When they'd pile in the car to go for groceries. Or the rare ice cream. One of them calling shotgun. The end of summer trip to Yorkville for school shopping. Those were the memories that hurt the most. The big ones surfaced every once in a while. Memories of Christmas morning or camping birthdays. But these little ones, the day to day memories of who they'd been. To each other. To their mother. As a family.

The McAvoys.

These memories just arrived from whatever place she'd kept them all these years. Put away so she could get on with her life.

Put away so they didn't hurt.

# Lindy

*A* million years ago, when Chef Gilmore let Lindy into his kitchen, he had told her to bring a notebook. She didn't understand how a notebook would help; wasn't her role to stir and chop?

"You won't touch a knife today," he'd said and pointed to milk crates stacked in the corner. "You're going to sit over there and take notes."

The next morning she came armed with a brand-new notebook and a two-pack of Bic pens in her purse. She sat in the corner until the hatch marks of the milk crate were imprinted on her butt. For every day and job after that, she showed up with her notebook. Some days she didn't need it. A lot of days she did.

"You must have been a really good student," her Cleveland friend Angela said one time, and Lindy had burst out laughing.

In the waiting room with her mom, sister and baby niece, Lindy pulled the notebook and pens from her purse and held them on her lap. Dr. Alvarez was part of a group of family doctors in a new building near the highway exit, and the reception desk was absolutely buzzing.

"Is that Tony Bell?" Lindy leaned over and whispered to her sister. Delia, never cool in these situations, turned her head and craned her neck to get a glimpse of the balding doctor behind the desk, going over a file with a nurse.

"Dr. Anthony Bell," Delia corrected.

Lindy slouched a little in her seat, trying to conceal herself behind her sister.

"What are you doing?"

"Nothing."

"Are you hiding?"

"I just…don't need a reunion with Tony Bell before Mom's doctor's appointment."

"What did you do to him?"

"Why do you think I'm the one who did something to him? Maybe he did something to me?"

Delia shot her a look that wasn't entirely unwarranted. Lindy had gone to freshman year homecoming with Tony and at the end of the night ditched him for a senior with a mickey of vodka. Part of the origin story for the wild McAvoy girl.

Mom sat in the chair beside her, her fingertips running over the St. Christopher medal around her neck. She and Lindy had decided to dress up for the doctor's appointment. Lindy wore a skirt. Mom wore a button-down shirt. They were very fancy.

Lindy put her hand over her mom's, giving her something of flesh and blood to worry, and Mom turned her hand so they were palm to palm. Holding hands.

"You found Dad's St. Christopher medal?" Dee whispered from the other side of her.

"Yeah."

"Where?"

"Caught in the floorboards of the hall closet."

Dee's interest was pointed and Lindy felt it right between her ribs.

"I forgot to give her the pill that helps her sleep the other night," she confessed.

"The melatonin?"

"Yeah. She was…kind of a wreck. Spent most of the night emptying out the closet." Lindy put her chin up, ready to take her sister's recriminations. But Dee was quiet.

"You're not going to lecture me?"

Dee shrugged with one shoulder. "You want me to?"

Something was sincerely off with Dee this morning and if scolding Lindy would make her right, then Lindy was ready to accept it.

"Meredith?" the receptionist said. "You can go into exam room two."

Dee, Lindy, Mom and Ephie in her carrier filled exam room two to the brim, but they got themselves organized and within seconds the door opened back up.

"How are you feeling, Meredith?" Dr. Alvarez swept into the room, her calm and cheerful vibe immediately putting everyone at ease.

"I'm good," Mom said in a diligent student's voice.

"How are you sleeping?"

"When I take that melatonin, it helps."

Lindy nodded. Every night since, she had been on top of that 3 mg pill.

"And food?"

"Tastes as good as ever. Lindy's a good cook."

Dr. Alvarez smiled. "Lovely." She asked a few more questions and all the answers Mom gave seemed to be exactly what she wanted to hear. Her blood pressure was good and so were the cognitive tests.

"Things look positive," Dr. Alvarez said. "Do you have any questions?"

"Nope," Dee said and stood up.

"I do," Lindy said and Dee slowly sat back down. Everyone was looking at her, but she was watching Dr. Alvarez. "How do I make this better?"

"I'm sorry, make what better?"

"This whole thing. Mom. Her memory. The effects of the brain event."

Dr. Alvarez's brow wrinkled just enough that Lindy's buoyed hopes plummeted. "Considering the series of strokes and seizures your mother has had, her recovery has been amazing. But there is no making the whole thing better. She will continue to have good days but there will also be bad days. And that's the new reality."

Lindy looked over at Dee and then back at the doctor.

"So...what are you saying?"

"I'm saying, continue her course of medication. Continue the beautiful care you're giving her. But understand that she should not be left alone. That her memory will be fluid. That her temperament will also get fluid and perhaps volatile. Cherish the good days and prepare for the not-so-good days."

Dr. Alvarez spoke with a soft smile that suddenly didn't feel so reassuring. Now it felt like a lie.

"I'm sitting right here, you know," Mom said like a rather ornery cat, and Lindy loved it so much she was able to smile through her dread.

"Keep doing what you're doing."

Lindy looked at her mom and her mom looked back at her.

"Who are you again?" Meredith asked, and Lindy's stomach dropped.

"Mom..."

"I'm joking, kid. I'm joking!"

# Delia

Lindy was mad at her. She didn't say it outright, but Delia remembered what it felt like to have her sister mad at her. It didn't happen often when they'd been growing up, but enough that this feeling of rubbing up against steel wool was familiar.

And Delia couldn't blame her.

They were shuffling themselves out of the tiny exam room, Delia trying to figure out how to apologize to her sister for robbing her of all the good years with their mom, when Dr. Alvarez stopped her at the door.

"Delia," she said in that calm doctor's voice. Dee used to love that voice; now it made her nervous. "How are you doing?"

"I'm fine. Ephie's doing great. We have a doctor's appointment with her pediatrician this week."

"That's wonderful...but how are *you*?"

Oh. "I'm good. Fine, really. Much better than I was."

Dr. Alvarez dropped her voice to a murmur. "You know the treatment has gotten much more sophisticated since Brin was—"

"I'm fine," she said, all too aware of Lindy pretending not to be watching from the hallway. Jesus. What happened to doctor-patient confidentiality? What happened to privacy? "Thank you, Dr. Alvarez."

She walked down the hall, Ephie's carrier banging against that spot in her calf that was always bruised.

"What was that about?" Lindy asked.

"Nothing."

"You're not acting like it was nothing."

They burst out of the building and into the parking lot. Mom was a few paces ahead and Dee, with the baby carrier, hustled to catch up.

"Shotgun," Mom cried. This time there was no amused look between the sisters.

"Are you going to talk to me?" Lindy asked from behind her.

Nope.

"Hey!" Lindy shouted, and Delia turned. "I'm here," Lindy said. "And you can be as grumpy as you want to be but I'm here!"

"Okay."

"That's it? 'Okay'?"

"What do you want me to say?"

"How about I'm sorry? How about I should have called you about Mom the second it happened?"

"I'm sorry," she said. "I should have called you."

"How hard was that?" Lindy asked.

Delia forced herself to breathe. It was a crap apology. The kind of sorry Brin would offer that would make Delia's head explode.

"Really hard."

"You need a drink? A nap?" Sarcastic Lindy was the worst Lindy and brought out the worst in Delia.

"You're hilarious."

"You know something." Lindy crossed her arms over her chest. "You don't get to be pissed. I do."

"Oh, I think if I work really hard I can find something to be pissed about."

"Go ahead." Lindy stepped back, held out her arms. "Have your say."

How like Lindy to invite a fight in the middle of the medical center parking lot.

"I don't have anything to say."

"Don't do that," Lindy breathed. "Don't lie. Don't pretend. I've missed you so much there are days I couldn't get out of bed. Don't try to tell me you haven't missed me."

Delia kept her mouth shut. It was hard, but she managed it.

"What was I supposed to do?" Lindy pushed and pushed because that was what Lindy always did.

"Not leave," Delia spat. There. It was out. She'd said it.

Lindy gasped. "You kicked me out. That Christmas—"

"I know," Delia whispered, but the words wanted to be shouted. They wanted to be screamed. "Before that. You didn't even say goodbye. You sneaked off in the middle of the night."

"It was the only way I could leave. If I said goodbye—"

"Then why go?"

"Delia," Lindy gasped. "We were killing each other. You, me and Mom. I couldn't stay and let you *hate* me. I couldn't stay and be your whipping post."

"How cruel of me to forget that you are the victim. That everything is about you!"

"That's not fair!"

"Fair! You do not want to get in a discussion with me about fair!"

"Girls!" Mom snapped, her face appearing over the top of the van.

"Sorry, Mom," Lindy said and got into the van, leaving Delia with the last word.

She usually loved having the last word. But this felt hollow and awful.

"I'm sorry, too, Mom," she said when they all got settled into the van.

"I would think so. Fighting in a parking lot, I taught you both better than that."

Lindy, in the back seat, muttered to herself.

"What was that?" Mom asked.

"Nothing," Lindy said.

But Delia heard her. Lindy had said, *You should have taught us to fight.*

Instead of swallowing their feelings and smiling when they wanted to scream. Silence hadn't gotten the McAvoy sisters very far.

"Let's go down to the shop and get lunch," Mom said as Delia pulled out of the parking lot. Delia's heart was still beating like she'd just avoided an explosion.

"I'd love to see the shop," Lindy said softly from the back seat.

Delia had taken the shop over a few years back, when their mom retired, but it was always supposed to be Lindy.

Delia wondered how Lindy would react when she saw it after all these years. She had tried to make updates but life had gotten so busy. And her ideas were never as good—or as fun—anyway. The shop had never been her choice or her passion. But with a baby on the way, choice and passion had been luxuries she couldn't afford.

The problem, Delia realized, was not that Lindy was home. It wasn't her irreverence and cute flippy skirts. It was the memories she brought with her. Memories of the girl Delia'd been. And the plans she'd had.

And how everything went wrong.

# Lindy

Delia took the long way to town, driving almost out by the highway. Lindy almost raised the point, but then she realized it was the route that kept the Fulbright House hidden until the very last turn.

Ephie in her car seat stared up at Lindy with big dark eyes.

"Hey," Lindy said, and the baby had a little spasm of joy in her car seat. "It's good to see you, too," Lindy whispered and rested her hand against Ephie's belly. Feeling her whole little body rise and fall with her breath.

It was a beautiful May day and the harbor was busy with people putting in sailboats that had been in storage for the winter. Teenagers hung out in the gazebo in the town park, smoking like they were daring someone to come and tell them to stop.

On Queen Street, the main strip caught between the beach and the harbor, all the old shops were still there. The CutNRun. Cypress House. Monty's Diner with the all-day breakfast.

Lindy practically tossed herself out of the van. The sidewalks had the same cracks. The rooflines cut into the blue sky with all the same shapes. The squawk of the seagulls. The smell of diesel from the harbor and a grill full of cheeseburgers from Lucky's. Under everything—the evergreen smell of the lake. If her childhood had a scent, this was it.

The Drunk Duck, Baumgartner's across the street, Ed's patio of picnic tables all painted pink. "It hasn't changed," she said and wondered how it was possible that some chain—a Starbucks or a dollar store—hadn't moved its way in and put small stores out of business.

"Sure it has," Mom said, slamming the passenger side door.

"How?"

"We've got a McDonald's now. And a streetlight."

"Big changes."

"You're telling me."

Lindy couldn't wait to see the store. It had been their second home growing up and for as much as she'd hated it as a child, it was where so many of her best memories lived. Dad coming in from the lake, Mom behind the counter. Dee and Lindy with coloring books in the back room until they were old enough to help out.

It was where she learned the foundation of her job, anticipating the needs of a customer and trying to surprise them all at the same time. She walked faster, her heart in her throat, anticipation making her eyes burn.

And suddenly there it was: the McAvoy Bait, Fish and Lunch Counter. Looking like it had seen better days. A lot of them.

The bright red paint had gone beige and was chipping off. The blue sign had faded to gray and was largely unreadable. The windows were dark, not just because the store wasn't open, but because they were grimy.

Delia used her key and opened the front door.

"You want to come in?" she said, half in and half out of the dark murk of the old store.

The invitation stung. The sight of the place stung, like salt in a wound.

The smell, vaguely fishy, never overt, mostly like lake, filled her up. *At least that is the same*, she thought.

The front of the store was split into two counters. One was the sandwich counter, the other for preparing fresh fish. A door in the middle led to the back room, which had been part storage, part office.

Inside, the place looked the same as seventeen years ago. The walls and floor and ceiling were all pine plank, and when the sun came in just right, the place glowed yellow. It was the warmest room in the world in those days—not sweaty warm, but a comforting warm. Safe. The walls and floor weren't grimy like the windows on the outside, but they were gray, the wood soft in places. The floorboards bounced under her feet.

*That's not good.*

There was still a white cooler in the corner with night crawlers for kids to use for fishing off the pier. When Lindy and Delia were really young, Dad used to sell fishing poles, and it was nice to see a small rack of them next to the cooler.

All the old trinkets still covered the walls. Fishing art. Fishing jokes framed as if they were art. Jarred tartar and cocktail sauce and boxes of fish fry sat for sale on the same old shelves. Some of the boxes, covered in a thick dust, looked old enough to have been there when Lindy was a kid. There were also newer delicacies, supposedly for picnics. Granola bars and candy. Juice boxes.

Were third-graders planning these picnics?

*Delia*, she thought, *what have you been doing all this time?*

Nothing, was the answer. Or if not nothing, the bare minimum.

It broke her heart to see the shop this way. Unloved.

"You want a sandwich?" Delia asked, setting Ephie's carrier down on the table of the small booth in the front window. People had been invited to eat their lunches there for years, but few ever did. Everyone did takeaway. It was where Delia and Lindy used to do their homework.

"Yes," Mom said. "Use that good bread you got now."

"Whitefish?"

"Yep."

"Lindy?"

Lindy wasn't sure what her face said. What anger and hurt and disappointment she wasn't able to hide. But Delia must have seen something. Her face tautened and her jaw clenched. "I'll make you a sandwich," she offered through tight lips.

They were rusty and out of practice, but they were still sisters. And her sister always knew what she was thinking.

Lindy recalled, briefly, her plans for the place. The curtains she was going to make. Fresh bread and cookies. Baskets full of produce. A takeout salad case. An espresso machine. Breakfast sandwiches on the weekends. Craft beer and local wine. She remembered what she wanted this place to be. Imagined it like Ed's—a community favorite, a tourist's hidden gem.

She met her sister's eyes.

*I had so many dreams for this place. So many plans and this is how you took care of them?*

"You left," Delia said, low enough so Mom couldn't hear. "You don't get to come back and judge." Then she walked behind the old counter to make Mom's sandwich.

The door opened and the bell rang out and a vaguely familiar woman stuck her head in the door.

"Hey, Jeannette," Delia said with a wan smile. "It's Monday. We're not open today."

"You sure look open," Jeannette said, but she was looking right at Lindy.

"What do you need?" Lindy asked with a smile. "I can get it for you."

"That's not—" Delia said but Jeannette walked on in.

"Two pounds of perch would be great," she said with acidic sweetness.

When the shop was closed the fish was kept in refrigerator units built into the fish counter. Lindy took a gamble that that hadn't changed either.

"You don't remember me, do you?" Jeannette asked, standing at the edge of the fish counter.

Lindy pulled up the plastic tub filled with Dan's freshly caught and beautifully cleaned fish. Really, the filets were gorgeous. Way better than Mom used to cut them.

"Should I?" Lindy asked.

"I'm Jeannette Bracker."

*Oh shit.*

"Good to see you again, Jeannette."

"Never thought we'd see you back here," she said.

"No?" Lindy said with false brightness.

"Not after your mom kicked you out."

Lindy focused on the task at hand, wrapping two fillets of perch in white butcher paper. "She didn't kick me out."

"No? You just left without saying goodbye to anyone?"

"Yeah, I just left without saying goodbye," Lindy said, pressing the wrapped and bagged fish into Jeannette's hands.

"You haven't changed a bit." Jeanette laid it on thick.

"You haven't either," Lindy said, not even pretending to be fake about it. "Enjoy that fish, it's on the house, and say hello to your husband for me."

Jeanette turned bright red and was out the door, no doubt eager to turn this little exchange between them into today's news.

Delia and Mom both stared at her as Lindy put the tub of fish away.

"She doesn't like you," Mom said.

"In high school her boyfriend liked Lindy," Delia said. "A lot."

She wasn't that girl—the one who went after other girls' boyfriends just because she could.

*Well, just that once.*

But no one wanted to listen to the wild McAvoy sister defend herself. And why should she? It had been almost two decades. She was a woman now. Back in the city people she worked with admired her. They listened to her ideas and valued them.

That's when Lindy realized there wasn't room for her here. Not really. Everywhere she turned she would run into the ghost of the person she'd been. With the town. With her sister.

She put the fish away and then took out her phone and found the message from Dante. It would be different, this time. She was only a few hours away. She'd come back a few days a week and stay with Mom. It wasn't exile, it was just her getting back to her life.

Sounds perfect, she wrote back. I'll see you in two weeks.

# TWELVE

## *Brin*

$M$onday, Brin grabbed her lunch tray and walked around the edges of the cafeteria, trying to avoid being noticed. As expected, Jenny had told everyone about the jewelry store and the news traveled fast.

Mrs. Weidmann, the guidance counselor, tried, again, to convince Brin to join the teen counseling group that met at lunch. She'd been trying pretty much since Ephie was born and Brin had that freak-out in chemistry class.

*Change is hard*, Mrs. Weidmann had said. *And everyone needs help sometimes.*

Yeah, well, Brin didn't need help from a bunch of stoners on probation and Melissa McCue who'd had a miscarriage last year when she was a sophomore and couldn't stop eating her hair.

Jenny rushed up to Brin near the windows. "Hey!" she said, all wide-eyed and whispery. She smelled like weed and Damen's Axe body spray.

"What's up?" Brin took a step sideways out of range of the cologne.

"Damen and Jay are skipping and I'm going with. We're heading over to the mall in Yorkville. Come on."

"I can't."

"What? Of course you can."

Finals wrapped up last week and school was basically over on Friday, so most kids weren't bothering to stick around for afternoon classes, let alone lunch. They got marked present in the morning and hoped no one noticed if they were gone in the afternoon. It didn't hurt that Ms. Sheer, the administrator who handled all the tardies and absences, had had her baby early.

"I'm already in so much trouble, I'm not going to add skipping to the long list of things I'm being grounded for," Brin said. "There's only a few days to go."

"I told Damen about the watch," Jenny whispered. "He thinks it's hot."

"He thinks it's hot that I set off the alarm at Baumgartner's?" Brin couldn't help laughing.

"Yeah, you're officially bad ass. Come on. Let's go to the mall. We need new bikinis."

"I don't have the money for a new bikini."

"Who says you need money?" She waggled her eyebrows and suddenly Brin was so...over it. So done with sitting in the back seat of some football player's truck, getting hotboxed and hoping they didn't crash.

Besides, she had other plans for this lunch hour.

"I can't, Jenny," she said. "Seriously. Shit is serious at my house."

Mom had legit freaked her out this morning. Brin had found her in bed, staring at the baby monitor while Ephie fussed. It had been deeply weird. Mom was always up before everyone. Sometimes even Dad.

"Okay," Jenny finally relented after a series of ridiculous pouty faces. "I get it. I'll steal you something nice."

"Don't—"

But she was gone. Racing off with two boys in letterman jackets. Damen waved at Brin as he headed out the door. All she felt was relief. Hanging out with Jenny wasn't as fun as it used to be. All that stuff was getting old.

The cafeteria was mostly empty.

Except for *him*.

Sitting in the corner at a table closest to the far window.

She figured he'd be skipping, too. But there he was, earbuds in and a book in front of him.

Troy Daniels.

It occurred to her that he might have been sitting there every day all year long and she never noticed. But after yesterday at Ferris Beach, she couldn't stop thinking about him.

Why, she had no idea. It was something in her belly that was connected to something in her brain that woke up at the sight of the bones in his wrist, the brush of his leg against hers when they both knelt for that dead carp.

"Hey," she said, stopping a few feet from his table. Close enough he knew she was talking to him, but not so close that she couldn't walk away like she never wanted to sit down.

He didn't look up at first and Brin considered leaving, pretending she hadn't approached him. And had never wanted to.

But the picture was burning a hole in the back pocket of her skirt.

Her best skirt, too. The new one barely long enough for dress code requirements. The one Mom didn't call her out on this morning—also deeply weird.

Brin bent sideways at the waist, revealing a whole lot of thigh, and waved her hand in his periphery vision.

Finally, he looked up and she was struck again by the green

126

of his eyes. The hard, sharp angle of his eyebrows. For a breathless second she wasn't sure if he was going to pull out one of the earbuds and ask what she wanted or look back down at his book and ignore her altogether.

He pulled both earbuds out. "Hey."

"Hey," she said back. Too bright. Too happy. Too cheer-leader.

*I want to die.*

"You...want to sit down?" he asked, clearly baffled.

"Sure!" Again, too bright.

His eyes grew squintier.

Brin put down her tray—French fries and an apple—next to his, which was the full hot lunch. Turkey swimming in gravy with potatoes. One side compartment with corn. The other with a brownie. He'd eaten most of it. Brin wasn't sure she'd ever seen anyone eat the full hot lunch before, except for the welfare kids—

Brin's brain went cold and she sucked in a breath. *I am an awful human.*

"What do you want?" he asked, pulling his tray away like he could tell what she was thinking.

"I, ah... I was going through my gran's stuff and I found a picture I thought you might be interested in."

"Why?" He actually laughed at her and Brin felt like the stupidest girl in the entire world. She wished more than she could say that she hadn't sat down.

"It's... Well, it's the Fulbright House. The way it used to be. And Eric Fulbright."

"Who the hell is he?"

She finally got the picture out of her pocket and slapped it down on the table. But it was the wrong picture. It was the one of her mom, dad and aunt Lindy on the Fourth of July.

"Sorry, wrong one." Brin pulled out the other picture. "Here."

"Who am I looking at?"

"Him." Brin pointed to the dark-haired stranger next to Aunt Lindy. "That's Eric Fulbright. Son of the Fulbrights who owned the Fulbright House. And that is like…the living room of the Fulbright House? Maybe?"

"Holy shit," he said, no longer squinting at her. "The kid in the painting. And that looks like the den. It's kind of hard to tell. All the rooms in that house look the same."

"I guess." She had no idea. She was just going along with it.

"They have a big portrait of the kid up at the house. All fancy. Your mom knew him?"

"Yeah, my mom and aunt. My dad, too, I guess."

"Your mom is hot," he said, looking at Brin and then back at the picture. He was smiling now. Well, he wasn't frowning, and that felt like a smile. "You look exactly like her."

Brin laughed, too loud. "My mom and I don't look at all…"

*Did he just say I was hot?* She tilted her head so she could hide behind her hair, an old habit she still hadn't grown out of.

He put down the picture and pointed to Aunt Lindy. "You're like twins."

"Oh no, that's my aunt."

"Get out."

Brin pointed to her mom in the picture. "That's my mom."

"No way."

"Why would I lie?"

"Are you sure your dad and your aunt didn't get it on behind your mom's back?"

"Stop!" She swiped the photo away. "Don't be gross."

"Jesus. Okay." He sat back with his hands up like Brin had suddenly pulled a gun. "You just look an awful lot like your aunt is all."

Brin felt jittery and hot all of a sudden, and she stood up, leaving her apple and fries untouched on the table. She shoved the pictures back in her too-tight pocket, unable even to find the words to say goodbye. Or screw you. She just left, her brain buzzing.

She headed to the office where Nancy, the secretary, let her use the phone since Brin's was still in jail.

"Whatcha need, honey?" Nancy said. She called everyone honey, which was probably against the law, but no one complained.

"Need to call my mom," Brin said through numb lips.

"Dial nine," she said like it was news to Brin.

She called Jenny.

"What up, bitch?"

"I changed my mind," Brin said. "Can you swing back and grab me?"

"Hell yes!" she said.

And it was nice that someone was genuinely happy to see her.

It didn't feel right. But it did feel good.

And that was enough.

# Lindy

While Mom took a nap, Lindy made an after-school snack for Brin. Graham crackers and buttercream frosting with three drops of the ancient green food coloring she'd found in Mom's lazy Susan. All arranged on a plate at the kitchen counter.

Like Brin was four.

It was as if the green frosting screamed "love me, please love me." But Lindy wanted her niece to love her. There was a lot of time to make up for. Brin was still the child she never got the chance to know. The kindergartner exhausted by endlessly having to share her blocks. The fourth-grader coming home full of the small defeats and victories of grade school. The seventh-grader with her period and awkward feelings for a boy in eighth grade.

Lindy imagined herself the wise aunt full of no-nonsense advice. The aunt with life experience and pockets full of stories to relieve her niece of all her fears.

Silly, maybe. But she couldn't help herself.

Lindy had been so confident Brin would show up that when she didn't, Lindy thought for sure the worst had happened.

A car accident.

Detention.

Kidnapping.

She managed to get a hold of herself, but when 4:30 came and went, Lindy had to face facts: Brin wasn't coming. She'd just found something better to do than hang out with her aunt.

"What's all this then?" Mom asked, looking down at the plate of graham crackers and homemade frosting.

"A snack," Lindy said with a smile for her mother, who was already making her way through one of the graham cracker sandwiches.

"Remember when I used to make this for you?" she asked, her eyes bright.

"I do." Lindy threw caution to the wind and ate one of the seven-million-calorie snacks.

"They were your favorite. You and Delia. You used to try and make it yourself."

"We put in too much milk. Every time."

"It was like soup." Mom laughed. "Came home and caught you girls trying to suck it through straws."

The way the butter and powdered sugar coated the roof of her mouth was such a happy memory.

"I'm worried about that girl," Mom said.

*Yeah? Which girl? At what age and in which time period?*

"Delia had some baby blues after Brin. I thought maybe it was on account of all her plans changing." Mom gave her a loaded look. "She got better, but she's not getting better with this baby."

Lindy didn't know if she should be worried or relieved that Delia wasn't always this prickly.

"What about Dan?" she asked. "Doesn't he help?" It seemed outrageous that the sweet and utterly devoted boy he'd been would change as an adult, but humans were inconstant creatures at best.

"Oh," Mom said. "You should have seen him when Brin was born. You'd think she was the second coming the way he cared for that baby. But all the help in the world doesn't matter when you're low after having a baby."

"Did you have postpartum depression?" Lindy asked.

"They didn't call it that. They didn't call it anything. But enough gossiping about your sister." Mom waggled her eyebrows at Lindy. "What are you making me for dinner?"

Lindy glanced at her watch. "Since Brin isn't coming, Mom, I'm going to have Tiffany come up and stay with you for a bit so I can run some errands—"

"Nope," Mom said. She squeezed the graham cracker sandwich down flat so the frosting squished out the sides, then ran her finger around the edge, scooped it up and put it in her mouth.

"We are out of groceries. Toilet paper."

"I'll go with you. I don't need a babysitter."

At the moment it seemed true. She was sharp and present.

"All right," Lindy said and gathered up her keys and purse. "Let's hit the Giant Eagle."

Mom snagged another graham cracker and followed Lindy out the door.

The Giant Eagle was a new monstrosity just outside of town between Port and Yorkville. Lindy had hopes that no one there would remember her. After Jeannette Bracker, she wasn't exactly ready for a trip down the Lindy McAvoy mess-up memory lane. The morning's trip to the doctor had kind of been fraught enough.

She parked in the football-field-size parking lot, as close as she could get to the doors without using the handicapped spot.

"I'm not that bad yet," Mom had muttered.

They grabbed a cart, Mom resting her elbows on the handles, steering it with her body, just like always, and for the moment Lindy was flush with pleasure. A trip to the grocery store with her mom. Who would have guessed how pleasing something so simple could be?

"Oh my god!" a voice yelled out and the happy feeling wobbled. "Is that Lindy McAvoy?" There was a gasp and the shuffle of trotting feet.

Smiling, Lindy turned, braced for the worst, only to see Nirosha Mendis running up to her from the open door of the store, three kids strung out behind her, the oldest pushing a cart with a mountain of bags and the youngest, a boy with black curls, eating a cookie.

"Is that Nirosha Mendis?" Lindy said with a smile. The good memories were really good with this girl. Of course some were hazy from drinking and smoking. The summer between their junior and senior years was basically one giant hangover, made sustainable by frequent trips to Taco Bell in Yorkville.

But Nirosha had been a good friend. A perfect companion for a girl who wanted to live her life on the edge of her small town. Nirosha had been Lindy's check-and-balance system. Up for a good time, but ready to pull Lindy off the steepest of cliffs.

Their hug was more like a collapse into each other.

"You look amazing," Lindy said, holding her old friend at arm's length. The long black hair, bronze skin. Lips she religiously painted a deep red. She'd been a knockout seventeen years ago and still was.

"You look exactly the same," Nirosha said. "Skinny bitch."

"Introduce me to your kids." Lindy was vaguely familiar with the kids from Nirosha's infrequent Facebook posts of her messy house or her youngest covered in marker and mud and once—memorably—dog poop. They had once messaged each other often enough, and every few months Nirosha had come to visit and they'd do it up like the old days. But the last few years, Nirosha would make a plan and inevitably a child emergency or an emergency at her husband's dentist office would derail it.

"You coulda said something about coming home," Nirosha said.

"It was quick," Lindy said.

"Right. Of course. Hey, Mrs. McAvoy!" Nirosha said loudly.

"I'm not deaf," Mom yelled back and Nirosha's oldest kid laughed but quickly swallowed it when Nirosha gave him the mom death glare.

"It's really good to see you out and around," Nirosha said. A minor squabble broke out between her youngest and middle child and the chitchat was over.

"We'll need to catch up," Lindy said.

"Girls' night out!" Nirosha agreed, her brown eyes wide and excited at the prospect. Lindy had been on the other side of the bar for enough girls nights out not to want to have anything to do with it, but Nirosha's enthusiasm was contagious.

"Oh my gosh." Nirosha sighed. "Wait until they get a load of us again."

Lindy promised to call her later and waved as they walked away.

"That girl was a good friend," Mom said.

Lindy laughed. "That is not what you thought in high school."

"I knew she'd never leave you alone someplace. And you wouldn't leave her. And her mom was a tough cookie. I liked that about her. I liked that a lot."

This talkative version of Mom would still take some getting used to.

They weaved their way through the produce and meat department with an eye out for what looked good and might be local. Lindy was uncomfortably aware, standing in front of the field cucumbers, that she was getting a lot of attention from two women by the fresh salsa.

It was an act of will, but she didn't turn to look right at them. As she put a field cucumber in the basket, out of the corner of her eye she recognized Vanessa Pilkey and her little sidekick whose name Lindy could never remember. They still didn't have anything better to do than worry about what Lindy was doing.

Mom, leaning against the grocery cart, was walking over to the two women, gradually increasing her pace like a battering ram. She got close enough without slowing down that Lindy thought she might do it. She might actually charge at Vanessa and what's-her-face. But they scattered like crows.

"Sorry," Mom said to the women, grabbing a package of premade guacamole. "But I had a brain event. Just can't control myself."

"What's gotten into you?" Lindy asked once the women were gone.

"Seems people should be able to buy cucumbers without having to be gawked at."

Lindy was having a hard time reconciling the mom who just defended her honor with the mom of her childhood who would routinely miss parent-teacher conferences because they were too confrontational.

Brain event, maybe.

It might be too many years too late, but it felt good to have Mom stand up for her in this small way.

"Put this away." She handed Lindy the guacamole. "And get the hot salsa, I like it with my eggs."

Twenty minutes later they were finishing up in the frozen food section.

"Mom," Lindy said. "I got brownies. We don't need ice cream."

"The ice cream is *for* the brownies."

"Can't argue with that logic," said a voice from behind her. She heard the gasp of a freezer door and the cold brush of air against the back of her thighs.

When she turned, there was Garrett smiling at her through the glass of the freezer, his face becoming obscured by the fog as he placed items in his basket.

She felt the familiar combination of a giggle and blush climbing its way up her body and gave herself a stern talking to.

*You are nearly thirty-eight years old. Thirty-eight-year-old women don't giggle and blush at a smile from a cute guy.*

To distract herself she glanced down at his basket of frozen dinners. The pasta and the chicken with broccoli, the burritos and butter chicken were an awkward glimpse into his life. She imagined him in his grandfather's old house, alone in front of the TV, peeling back the plastic cover of the packaging.

"You shouldn't eat that stuff," Mom said, looking at his selections.

"Apples?" He lifted a bag of apples from under a frozen beef stew.

"Very funny, smart guy," she said. "That frozen stuff. Doctor told me I had to stop. Too much sodium."

Lindy imagined her mother alone like that. The ding of the old microwave telling her dinner was ready. Sitting alone at the back deck, feeding bits of chicken to the cats who came out of the bushes.

Shame pinched her stomach. She should have been here

all those years, making sure her mom was all right. Eating properly. Not alone. She should have just ignored Delia and come back.

"Yeah." Garrett looked down at the basket. "I've heard that about these dinners. But I'm not much of a cook and I can't eat out every meal."

"Here." Mom pulled one of the fat organic tomatoes from their cart and put it in his basket. "And you need some of this." She transferred a smaller jar of mayonnaise. Lindy had managed to convince Meredith to downsize from the industrial size.

"Tomatoes and mayo?"

"Put it on one of those bagels with a big slice of tomato. That's a good dinner."

Garrett looked at Lindy and she shrugged. "We eat a lot of tomato and mayo sandwiches in my family. We were practically raised on the stuff."

"I heard you're a big deal chef in the city now. You're still eating tomato and mayo sandwiches?"

"Not a chef. And certainly not a big deal."

"That looks like a chef's cart." He gestured to the pork butt with its thick ring of creamy fat, the red flank steak, the frozen shrimp. The leafy green fresh herbs, the plug of good goat cheese and the wedge of excellent parmesan. The best olive oil the store sold. The six bright red tomatoes, the purple onion and small basket of local peaches. More garlic than any two people could ever need. Eggs. Asparagus. Peas and ramps. The sourdough loaf with the crusty shell. The bags of beans and pasta and the bottles of spices.

"I've worked in a lot of kitchens. I've picked up a few things over the years."

"I don't even know what you'd do with half that stuff, besides burn it."

"You should come over for dinner," Mom said. "Let Lindy cook for you."

"I'd love to," he said the same time Lindy said, "You don't want to do that."

Garrett shook his head, his dark hair blue-black in the bright lights of the frozen food aisle. "You always were hard to convince," he said.

Lindy wanted to know "of what," but her mom jumped in. "Don't listen to her. It's my house and I'll have anyone I like over for dinner."

"Then I accept," he said with a grown-up version of the grin he used to give Lindy in the ice cream shop.

"Great," Mom said. "Tonight?"

"Mom," Lindy said. "I'm sure he's busy—"

"Tonight, actually, is wide open."

# THIRTEEN

## Lindy

*I*t wasn't a date. She knew that. Her mother was going to be there for crying out loud. That was the furthest thing from a date. But her stomach was a little giddy, because it felt like there were stakes involved. Like things were in the balance. She put on her favorite skirt and her best bra. She put on lipstick, then wiped it off.

*Because it's not a date!*

Mom was looking mighty pleased with herself on the back porch with the crossword puzzle. Lindy snapped the paper away and placed a bowl of peas in her lap.

"Shell those, would you?"

"Sure," she said as Lindy spun back toward the screen door.

"And don't—"

"Don't what?"

"Don't go playing matchmaker," she finally said.

"I'm not playing anything. I invited the police chief over to try some of my talented daughter's cooking." Mom shrugged, but she did not wear innocent as well as she thought she did.

Lindy knelt and grabbed her mom's knobby, soft-skinned hand. "Mom," she said but found it hard to finish the sentence.

*I wasn't so nice to him. And I'm leaving in less than two weeks.*

"What, Lindy?" she asked. "Do you want to tell me how you didn't treat him very well in high school? And how he's probably not still interested in the wild McAvoy girl after all these years? That maybe you aren't all that interested in a police chief from your small hometown?"

Lindy blinked.

Mom patted her face. "Loosen up, Lindy. It's just dinner."

Lindy roasted shrimp with garlic and parmesan and made a fresh spring salad of Mom's shelled peas, sugar snap peas, asparagus, ramps and butter lettuce. She was making the lemon vinaigrette when headlights flashed through the house.

There was the car door slam and a man's heavier tread on the back deck. How strange that was, to hear a man's heavy footstep in this old home. It had been so long. The low rumble of his laughter sifted through the screen door.

*Relax. It's just dinner.*

The door squealed open and Garrett stood there in khaki pants and a green linen shirt that made his skin glow. He was clean and pressed and freshly shaved, his dark curls back off his forehead.

Lindy wished she hadn't removed that lipstick.

"Lindy," he said with a conspirator's smile. "Thank you for having me."

She bit back the words, the flippant, slightly cutting remark about not having a choice that would wipe off that smile. She didn't want that. So instead she allowed herself to smile. "It's our pleasure."

He lifted the two bottles of wine in his hands. "I wasn't sure if you wanted red or white."

"White is perfect." She took it and glanced down at the label. "Oh, Garrett. You didn't have—"

"I like good wine, too, Lindy," he said. "Tonight is a rare thing, let's all enjoy it."

And just like that, some of the weirdness in her stomach disappeared. *Let's just enjoy it…* How simple. How easy if you just let it happen. Not everything in Port was loaded with potential disaster.

"All right then, big spender. Why don't you open the wine and take out some glasses."

"Will your mom have some?"

"Not sweet enough for her."

She took out the shrimp and the homemade cocktail sauce and aioli she'd made to go with them. The grilled garlic bread and then the salad heaped on plates, topped at the last minute with a creamy white poached egg.

"My god," Garrett said, looking down at the meal.

"Told you she was a real good cook," Mom said.

"Eat, eat." Lindy shooed them down into their seats. Garrett at Delia's old spot and Lindy in her usual one. Mom at the head of the table.

The wine was perfect. The shrimp a little overdone, thanks to the ancient and unpredictable oven. But the salad, even she could admit, was amazing. The cats came out of hiding to twine around everyone's ankles. Garrett and Mom made sounds of delight.

"Okay, calm down, you drama queens," Lindy said, but inside her heart was a balloon filling up. "So, Garrett," she said, sitting back with a second glass of the crisp pinot grigio. "How is crime and punishment in Port Lorraine?"

"About what you'd expect," he said, using the last of his garlic bread to wipe up the traces of vinaigrette and egg yolk on his plate. She totally approved. "Though, if the rumors around town are true, I think my life might get a bit easier this summer."

"What rumors?" Mom asked, dragging yet another shrimp through the cocktail sauce and then the aioli.

*Delia would kill me if she saw Mom eating this.*

"The Fulbright House is going to be sold."

Mom coughed. Lindy brought her glass down on the edge of her plate and it made a clatter.

"Really? They're selling." Lindy's voice was pinched and strained.

"That's the rumor. Mrs. Fulbright has been in and out of town the last few weeks. She hired Jodi Reis. You remember—"

Mom stood up, her chair raking across the wooden planks of the deck. The cats headed for the bushes.

"I think it's about time for my show," she said and walked, plate in hand, into the house.

"I'm sorry," Garrett whispered. "I didn't mean to upset her."

"It's okay. Just give me a second." Lindy stood from the table and found her mom in the kitchen, rinsing off her plate.

"You okay?" Lindy asked, touching the soft hump of her mother's shoulder under her T-shirt.

"That damn house has been floating out there for years and no one says boo. Suddenly everyone is talking about it." Mom was washing other dishes now, soap and water spewing everywhere.

"Mom, stop," Lindy whispered. "I'll get this. Why don't you go sit down?"

"Has Delia come out of your room?" Mom glanced up and looked around, her face lost and unfettered.

"She's not here, Mom. She's in her—"

"You have to stop pushing her, Lindy. You have to. Give her some room. Some time. She's not like you."

*Oh*, Lindy thought. *Where are we now?*

"Everything will be okay if we just give her some time."

Lindy closed her eyes. This was right before Lindy left. When Delia wouldn't come out of her room if Lindy was in the house. When she stopped showering and didn't fill out the paperwork for college. Broke up with Dan and canceled Europe.

When it felt like the only thing Lindy could do to make things right was be gone.

Mom was winding herself up again, her fingers at the edge of her shirt.

"Mom, it's okay. It's all a million years ago."

"But it's not," Mom whispered. "It's not a million years ago."

Lindy stroked her face, skin that smelled the same as when she was a girl. Oil of Olay, the original formula.

"I should have done more," Mom said. "This is my fault. This is all my fault. Dan, you—"

"Mom!" she said sharp and fast, cutting her off. That was too far.

Mom blinked and looked away, and Lindy was paralyzed, like she'd been pushed to the edge of a cliff and if she even breathed wrong she'd catapult right over.

So many years and no one had said anything. There were times she'd convinced herself she dreamt it. All of it. That summer. The fight. The way she left. *Why* she left.

"It's okay," Lindy said, hoping those tears would dry. Meredith McAvoy didn't cry. Not in front of her daughters. Not in front of anyone. The tears of joy at Lindy's arrival had been a surprise enough. But this felt like the closet and birth certificates all over again.

Proof that Mom was different. Changed.

"I'm going to get you to bed."

★ ★ ★

Fifteen minutes later Lindy stepped out of Mom's room to find Garrett in the kitchen, drying the last of the dishes. His fine linen shirt had water drops down the front.

"I'm sorry," she whispered.

"Nothing to apologize for. I was just finishing up."

She waved him back outside where they could talk above a whisper. Their wineglasses were still there, the bottle sweating into the May evening.

"I should go," he said.

"No, please." She splashed the last of the wine into their glasses. "It's still early."

She never learned the skill of being alone in this house, how to be by herself with Dad's ghost and Mom's grief. They were weights she used to share with her sister. But without Delia, she found shallow friendships and flings to try to carry the load.

It never worked.

They settled back down in their seats, but she noticed he didn't pick up his glass.

"She okay?" he asked. "I didn't mean to bring up bad memories of your dad."

She hadn't mentioned her father or the night he died, but Garrett must have heard the story at some time. Maybe as a warning.

"She's fine," Lindy said, not sure if she was lying or not. "Everyone in town probably has some horror story about that family. Or that house. We're no different."

"Mr. Fulbright tried to have me arrested once," Garrett said with a tight smile.

"What? Why?"

He shrugged. "Being brown."

She blew out a long breath. "Whoa. I'm sorry."

"It will be good if the rumor is true and we can get that place taken care of. Kids are out there all the time causing trouble."

"I remember being one of those kids," she said wryly.

The silence between them expanded, but it wasn't heavy or awkward.

"Can I ask you something?" he said.

"Sure."

"Why did you leave?"

"Wow, you're not beating around the bush."

"Sorry. You can tell me to shove it. But it was so surprising. You, your sister and your mom… You were so close."

Lindy nodded, looking down at her wine. More was a bad idea, which of course was why she wanted it. "That's why I left," she said, which wasn't the whole truth, but it was a lot of it. "We were so close. But I needed to figure out another way to live. You know?"

He nodded. "So, did you?"

"What?"

"Find another way to live?"

Lindy thought of the string of not-great boyfriends. The jobs she traded up because they didn't mean much and she was just ready for a new scene.

She had left so her sister would come out of that room.

She left so she could grow up to become something besides the wild McAvoy sister.

And she realized, with some pride, that both had happened.

# FOURTEEN
## *Delia*

*T*he world smelled like a campfire.

Someone in town had started his big burn pile and the smell of wood smoke was coming through the front doors of the shop, reminding her of the camping trip her family had taken every summer for her and Lindy's birthdays (Dee's was in June, Lindy's in August). They'd book a campsite way out on the beach and Dad would build a bonfire. They'd have s'mores for breakfast.

Such a small thing, really. But it had been so special. Camping Dad had been the most fun Dad. Telling ghost stories around the fire, letting them stay up to see the sky full of stars. Mom kept up the tradition after Dad died and managed to be pretty fun herself. They went every year up until Lindy left.

It had been so long since Delia had thought of those trips.

In the baby carrier strapped to her chest, Ephie fussed and tried to spit out the pacifier. Delia held the pacifier to her daughter's mouth, bent her knees and put a little more bounce in her step to calm her.

*Come on, baby, just take it and go to sleep. You know you want to.*

Ephie had gotten her shots today, one in each of her fat little thighs, and she'd been letting the world know how unhappy she was ever since. It was panic-inducing, the sound of her crying. Delia wanted to close up shop and take her home, cuddle her to sleep.

Brin's appointments had been the same way. It had felt awful to hold her baby down so someone could hurt her. After the first appointment she'd come home and told Dan they weren't going to vaccinate Brin anymore. He'd stroked her hair, dried her tears and then pulled up twenty different articles about why the world was better when kids were vaccinated. And then he volunteered to take Brin to the doctor for the rest of her shots.

How easy it could be to forget the good memories.

Ephie's tears were drying up. She had taken the pacifier and was making the snuffling sounds of a sleeping baby, exhausted from the day's events. It was a crap time for a nap. If she slept now, the whole day would be thrown off, but shots trumped schedule.

She looked down and craned her neck to see Ephie's sleeping face against her chest. Her eyelids dark with sudden deep sleep. There was a bloom of sweat on her forehead. That's how hard she slept sometimes—she sweated like it was work.

"Okay, baby," Delia sighed, calmed by the sight of her baby at peace.

She walked back toward the counters, passing the shelves of dusty boxes of fish fry and fruit snacks. Yesterday had been awful, looking at this place through Lindy's eyes. How shabby it was, how little they'd cared for it, whereas Lindy had been so excited to turn it into something special.

*Stop*, she told herself. *You've been busy. Kids. Bookkeeping for the charter business. Mom.*

But those were just excuses.

The bell over the door rang and Delia swallowed the urge to shush whoever was coming in, only to find Brin standing before her.

"Hey!" she said in a happy whisper. Happy to be surprised. Happy that she felt happy. "What are you doing here?"

"Should I leave?"

"No! God, no!" Delia smiled. "I'm just surprised to see you is all. You hungry?"

"Yeah. I just came in to tell you about Spring Assembly at school on Thursday night."

"Oh!" Delia clapped her hands silently above Ephie's head. "I love Spring Assembly."

"I know, Mom," Brin said and rolled her eyes.

Band, orchestra and choir all performed at Spring Assembly—like one big high school talent show.

"Brin, I'm so sorry you lost first chair. I know that things being so crazy at home didn't help."

"Mom, it's fine." The way she said it indicated that it was not in fact fine. It hadn't ever been fine, but Delia kept apologizing, knowing full well it wouldn't make up for anything. "They're gonna hand out awards and stuff, too."

"Awards?" Delia beamed at her daughter. "Are you getting something?"

"I don't know. But I thought you'd want to know."

"Of course I do. We'll be there. All of us."

"Aunt Lindy and Gran, too?"

Her first instinct was to spew reasons why that wasn't a good idea, but Brin sounded so hopeful. "If you want them, sure. I'll give them a call. Anything else you need?"

"A sandwich?"

Oh! The spiky thrill that filled her, that her daughter had a straightforward need that Delia could meet.

"Turkey on whole wheat? Or just veggies?" She stepped

over to the lunch counter and opened the sandwich cooler. The tomatoes had seen better days, but the cucumbers and peppers were still fine.

"Turkey sounds good."

"You're eating meat again?"

Brin shrugged and Delia pulled out the fancy wheat bread Brin loved. "How was school?"

"Stupid."

"Ah, what every mother loves to hear. You got home late last night."

"Not that late. Before curfew."

"I'm not yelling, Brin. I'm just making an observation."

"There are extra orchestra rehearsals for the assembly."

Delia nodded and smiled wide, delighted. There was her girl. The girl she knew.

"Good for you. Do you need any money or anything for food?"

"My phone would be handy."

It would be handy for Delia, too, if Brin had her phone back. But she'd promised the other night that this time would be different. A few days wouldn't suffice. And then that whole thing with the watch… No, this was a battle Dee had to fight.

"Sorry, kiddo. Phone jail until next Friday."

Dan came in through the back, bringing the smell of lake and sunscreen and smoky campfire.

"Whoa," he said. "What's going on with all my girls in one place? There some kind of meeting no one told me about?" He smiled and kissed Delia's head, then Ephie's, then he jogged into the center of the shop to hug Brin.

And their daughter not just let him hug her, but returned the hug. Her hands with their bitten-down fingernails on his back.

"Seriously," he asked and turned to face her, his arm still over Brin's shoulder. "What's the occasion?"

"I don't know," Dee said with a shrug. "This stranger who looks like our daughter just wandered in. Maybe she got lost."

"Weird," Dan said.

"You guys are weird," Brin said but she didn't pull away from Dan.

It was a statement on how bad things were in their house that this moment felt like a reprieve. Being in the same room and not fighting seemed like an indication they might actually survive as a family.

"We should go camping," Delia said. "Wouldn't that be fun?"

Dan and Brin shared a look and burst out laughing.

"What?" she asked, smiling because they were smiling.

"You hate camping. You've always said that," Brin said.

"It's true. You've always said that," Dan confirmed.

*Have I?* A lie she told, probably, so she could put those Lindy memories in a box. Out of sight.


Delia cut the sandwich into triangles, the way Brin liked it as a girl, and handed it over on a paper plate.

"Sit down," Dan told her. "I'll get something and join you."

Dee started to make Dan a whitefish spread sandwich—still his favorite after all these years.

Brin took just half of the sandwich Delia had made and said, "I gotta go. See you later tonight."

"Hey!" Delia said. "Remember fish fry this Friday. We need you in the shop after school."

Predictably, Brin rolled her eyes.

"Will you be home for dinner?" Dan asked.

"I don't know. What's for dinner?"

Both Dan and Brin looked at Delia, and she blew out an

exasperated breath. Dinner was the bane of Delia's existence. She hated planning it, shopping for ingredients, cooking. And the monsters insisted on having it every night.

"You know Aunt Lindy is a super good cook. We should just go up and have dinner at Gran's," Brin said as she pushed open the door with her butt and disappeared out of sight.

It wasn't until she was feeding Ephie that night that Delia even thought to wonder how Brin knew Lindy was a good cook.

# Meredith

*B*rin was back again. First Sunday and then again, a few days later? Meredith hadn't seen this much of the girl since she was eight and Meredith got to spend afternoons with her while Delia worked the shop.

Not that she didn't enjoy seeing her grand-girl, but even an old woman who'd had a brain event could see something was up. There wasn't a teenager on this planet who wanted to spend so much time with adults.

Lindy came out the back door with another one of her after-school snacks. Grapes and slices of cheese.

Boo. Meredith had liked the frosting sandwiches a whole lot better.

Brin followed, her arms full of photo albums.

"Are we still doing this?" Meredith asked. "Cleaning up these photo albums?"

"There are a lot of them," Brin said.

"You want a drink or something?" Lindy asked.

"I'll have some of that iced tea you made."

Brin nodded. "That sounds good."

Lindy wasn't through that doorway back into the house before Brin was pulling a photo out of a red album like she'd just been waiting for the chance. "Gran," she said, innocent as pie, and placed a picture down in front of Meredith. The girls on some Halloween dressed up like black cats. Dan stood between them in a dog costume.

"Oh lord, look at them," Meredith said. She flipped the picture over because she used to be real good about writing down the dates and yep, there it was. Halloween 1999.

"What happened?" Brin asked.

"They handed out candy in the shop. It was Lindy's idea. Not one of her best ones, but we had fun."

"No...with them. Why they stopped talking. Aunt Lindy and Mom."

"Honey," she said. "I'm not sure I know anymore."

But she did. She knew. It was one of the secrets that lived down in her belly.

"But I don't get it. How are you so close with someone and then just...not?"

"'Cause you're young," Meredith said. "And you don't understand how some things are so painful you'd do just about anything not to remember, including push away the person who makes you think about them."

Her eyes flared wide and Meredith could see Brin putting her teeth into the idea that something real painful happened between Delia and Lindy.

"Did Dad and Lindy—?"

"All right, party people," Aunt Lindy said, her hands full of glasses with lemons and tea. "Which album is on deck? Please tell me it's junior prom because I have been thinking about Todd Ackermann for YEARS!"

Brin, the sneaky girl, pushed the Halloween picture back into a bottom album and opened the one on top. The girl was no dummy, though. And if her parents weren't careful, she'd be figuring things out soon enough.

"Brin," Lindy said, her face so serious after one look at the pictures. "Pick a different album."

"I'm sorry. It was just on top," Brin said. She was really pouring it on with this innocent routine.

Meredith reached out and grabbed the bottom of the album, tilting it so she could see what the fuss was all about.

"It's your wedding album," Brin said like Meredith wouldn't know her own face and that of her beloved.

"Oh." Meredith pulled the album closer to her. "Look at that man. Never could find a jacket that fit him, he was always showing off those bony wrists of his." She flipped a page and then another. Smiling down at the pictures like they were old friends. The pain wasn't sharp; it was dull and bittersweet.

"Can you tell me about the night he died?" Brin asked.

"Brin!" Lindy snapped, sounding just like Delia.

"What do you want to know?" Meredith said, turning another page.

"Mom," Lindy said. "Seriously. We don't need to remember—"

"You think I don't remember? I remember every day. Talking about it doesn't change that."

*Except we never did talk about it.* Those days after the storm when the girls were crying so hard she'd worried they'd make themselves sick. When she'd been so low and so sad she would have done anything to have him back—they'd been dark days. But she was the mother, the only adult left standing in the house, and she had to do something to keep them from all sliding into despair.

So she did what most people do when they don't know what to do—for good or ill—she did what her own mother would have done.

*Don't remember,* she'd told them, stroking the hair off their wet faces. *Don't remember that night. Remember the kittens. And his awful jokes. How much he loved Christmas morning and drive-in movies. How he sang off-key and how he'd tuck you in at night, rubbing the scratch of his beard over your chin. Remember how he loved you. How there was nothing he wouldn't do for you.*

And to herself she'd said: *Don't think about whether he was scared when he died. Or hurt. Or if he knew he was dying.*

And they did it. All of them. They put away the bad stuff. The pain they'd do anything to forget. And they only talked about the good.

Meredith pulled in a breath, a sharp fishhook of pain caught in her ribs.

"Gran?"

"Put the album away, Brin," Lindy said. And there was Lindy doing what she'd been taught. Keeping the secret. The silence.

"There was a storm," Meredith said, looking down at the pictures. She ran her thumb over her husband's face. *Those glasses, my goodness.* "A November Witch. Came through like a hurricane. So fast. So...so much faster than anyone thought. We'd had November storms before, but this was different. Everyone said so."

She remembered the air tasted like iron that morning. School was canceled and the grocery store shelves were emptied by noon. All the radio stations were telling people to bring their pets inside and turn off their gas lines. The girls had been laughing that morning, because every time they put a brush through their hair it stood on end like they'd been electrocuted.

"William went out to get the nets and was just about back at the harbor," Meredith said. "That's what the coast guard said. He was almost back. The boy who was manning the radio said he made a joke about the weather. And he told it to everyone else in the office and they laughed, too. It was a good joke, that's what the boy told me at the funeral. Everyone laughed."

"Dad was funny," Lindy said quietly. He wasn't really. He was too quiet for that. But he was a little corny and after a glass or two of rum he'd get silly. He'd probably made the joke because he was nervous. Another thing she never liked thinking about.

"There was a distress call from Dean Van Loan and...William went back out. Thought he could help them."

Brin would know that Grandpa wasn't able to help them. Dean Van Loan's name was on that plaque in town with the same date as William's. Port Lorraine's Brave Fisherman Claimed By the Sea.

"And we waited, didn't we?" she said, looking up at Lindy, who was white-faced and uncomfortable. "For as long as we could. But there wasn't any word."

Lindy shook her head.

"What did you do?" Brin asked.

"Mom took us out to the Fulbright House."

"Why?"

"Good question," Lindy muttered, probably thinking Meredith couldn't hear her.

It had been a fool's trip. So dangerous she could still give herself a scare imagining all the ways it could have gone wrong. But she'd been unable to sit in this house one minute longer. She dragged the girls along because she couldn't do it alone. They all could have been hurt. Or killed, and it would have been her fault. The guilt caught at her, years later.

"We wanted to light flares off the roof," Meredith said. "So he might see them out there on the lake and know which way was home."

"That sounds dangerous," Brin said.

"The spit wasn't washed out yet. It was treacherous, but it wasn't impossible." If William had known what she was doing, well, he would have had something to say about that. "The three of us drove up there, loaded down with as many flare guns as we could find. We went to the Zawislaks', too, didn't we?"

"Raided their fireworks stash," Lindy said. "We drove as far as we could down the spit until the car got stuck. Water started coming in, remember?" Lindy asked. "Soaked our feet."

Meredith nodded. The water coming through the seams of her good work boots had been so cold. It'd shocked her right into regret, but they'd been too far along the spit to turn back.

"You told us we'd be okay, that we just had to leave the car where it was. I thought for sure we were going to die. Your mom," Lindy said, looking over at Brin, "opened the door and immediately got knocked over by a wave. I screamed so hard I lost my voice for a week."

"You girls were so brave," Meredith said. "Your raincoats and backpacks full of wet fireworks that weren't ever gonna work. You were so scared but you kept going. We linked arms and bent our heads and made our way up to that house."

"When we turned around it was all water," Lindy said. "The car was gone. We never saw it again."

"Then what happened?" Brin gasped. "When you got to the house?"

Meredith's eyes met her daughter's and then they both looked away.

"It took them so long to get to the door we thought they weren't there," Meredith said. "Even though we could see the lights on in every room in the dang house."

"I wish they hadn't been home," Lindy said.

"Why?" Brin asked, her voice little-girl quiet.

"So we could break in and run onto their roof and shoot

those flares without worrying about them and what they thought." Meredith's voice was changing. She could hear it. Lindy offered her hand, and Meredith held on as tight as she could. "But they *were* home. And we had to ask them for permission to go up and shoot off flares."

"They weren't going to let us come in," Lindy said.

Brin's head swiveled to face her. "What?"

"It was late. They had guests there for the weekend. Thanksgiving and everything. And we were wet and desperate and armed with explosives," Lindy said with a shrug. "A lot of people wouldn't have let us in."

"My mom does that," Brin said.

"Does what?"

"Explains away other people's bad behavior. Like there's always a reason why someone is terrible."

"You don't think there is?"

"Some people are just bad people."

"That can be a real hard way to look at the world," Lindy said.

"Mom says that, too."

The Fulbrights had been the worst kind of people. It was proven over and over again. The McAvoy benevolence had been misplaced.

"We had to beg them," Meredith said, the taste of her pride sour in her mouth. In front of her girls she'd had to beg them. Promise them anything. Like the McAvoys had anything to offer the Fulbrights. It was years still until that Fulbright boy started sniffing around Lindy.

Lindy took a deep breath. "Mom, why don't we go back inside? It's getting hot—"

"I'm fine," Meredith said, though she wasn't sure that was true. It was like the spit in the storm all over again. All she could do was bend her head and keep going forward. Hope the ground would stay where it was supposed to. "They finally let us up on the walk and we stood out there for... I don't know. An hour. Flares were the only thing that worked. The fireworks were ruined. I dragged you girls out there for nothing."

"Not nothing, Mom," Lindy said. "At least we tried."

"By then the road was gone, not even emergency vehicles could get out to us. The coast guard wasn't letting anyone out. And the storm was so bad we couldn't...we couldn't get back," Meredith said. "We had to sit in that damn house with them watching us like we were gonna steal the silver. We had to apologize for our tears and our fear. And I tried to make you both stop crying so *they* wouldn't be so uncomfortable. We had to let them pity us and fetch us hand towels to sit on so we wouldn't ruin their couches."

"They brought us leftovers, remember?"

Delia had opened up that Tupperware of asparagus and nearly vomited. Never could stomach asparagus again.

"Finally, they let us have a guest room and some privacy," Meredith said. "And we sat on that bed and you girls tried so hard not to cry until the storm passed and the road cleared. We got out of there just before dawn while they were sleeping."

"You walked home?"

Waterlogged and in shock, they walked the whole way home.

"Town had this big service," Lindy said. "Bagpipes and everything, for all the sailors who died that night. And the Fulbrights didn't come. They closed up that house and didn't come back for years."

"That's why Mom drives the long way through town, isn't it? So she never has to see the Fulbright House? And if we have to drive by, she turns her head away and holds her breath. Like it's a graveyard."

"Maybe," Lindy said.

"And Gran..." Brin turned her bright eyes on Meredith, like she'd cracked some case. All the secrets out in the open. "That's why you were walking down the spit the other day with the flare gun, right? You were confused and thought you could go save Grandpa?"

Meredith looked at Lindy for a long time. Too long, maybe. Thinking about all the things she'd do anything not to remember. There were too many.

"You know," Meredith finally said, bracing her hands on the arms of her chair. "I think I'll go lie down and try a nap."

# FIFTEEN

## *Brin*

*W*ednesday, Brin skipped school in the afternoon. Again. It wasn't like a big deal, tons of kids were doing it. But still being new to it, she wasn't sure where to go.

After the mall trip Monday, she was avoiding Jenny. She was just so over that whole scene. Drinking and driving around. Shoplifting. She wished she could go over to Gran's and hang out with Lindy.

Aunt Lindy was cool, but she wasn't going to let Brin skip school and not tell Mom.

She was walking by the bus station when the bus that ran between Port and Yorkville pulled up, which was how she ended up at Ferris Beach.

She couldn't quite believe it herself.

It was perfect.

The beach was empty and the dead fish smell wasn't bad because she and Troy had picked them all up last Sunday. Brin stepped across the rocks, holding her hair back at the nape against the Ferris Beach wind, and headed down the breaker to the very end of the spit.

From there, she could see a side of the Fulbright House. The story Lindy and Gran told her yesterday was still stuck in her head, and she couldn't imagine being that brave, scared and sad all at the same time.

The story was absolutely terrible. But it was kind of epic, too, in a way. It made her feel really young and stupid. Like… her life was safe and she didn't know anything of the world.

Brin sat, tucked her hair into the back of her T-shirt and pulled her beaten-up copy of *The Hate U Give* from her backpack. Tucked into the pages were the pictures she'd swiped from Gran's photo albums.

By now she had quite the collection going.

There were pictures of barbecues. The first McAvoy Bait, Fish and Lunch Counter fish fry. Christmas mornings. Even a dog she'd never known a thing about.

*A dog!*

The three of them—Mom, Dad and Lindy—together all the time. Occasionally a different guy thrown in as Lindy's date for a few dances.

But all these pictures laid out like this told a new story. A different story. As much as Dad was looking at Mom, he often had his arm around Lindy. His head bent toward her. Yesterday she'd been about to ask her grandmother if Dad and Lindy had ever been a couple. Like maybe Dad and Lindy had been together first and Lindy got pregnant? That's why they looked so much alike?

It was a ridiculous idea.

But all those pictures were like secrets her family had kept from her. Tucked away into books that no one looked at.

The McAvoy Book of Secrets.

And she wanted them all. Every single one. She wanted an answer for every question and the secret behind every picture.

Because right now the silence in her house, the way no one talked about anything—all of that felt like lies.

"Hey."

Brin screamed and jumped, slipped off one of the boulders and landed hard on her butt.

"Oh my god. I'm sorry. Let me—"

It was Troy Daniels. Like a foot away. She looked behind him for Chief Singh, like maybe Troy had to do extra community service. But there was no one else in sight.

He held out his hand to help her up. Rattled, she got to her feet on her own. Her ankle hurt but she didn't wince.

"What…what are you doing here?" she asked, out of breath and panicky.

"I followed you."

She opened her mouth but she didn't know what to say. An awful feeling slithered through her stomach. "What? Why?" she asked.

"I tried to catch you at school. But I got caught up by Mr. Granville. And then I saw you on the bus and I just… I got off when you did. I can leave," he said, poking his thumb out behind him back to the shore. Where there wasn't a bus and wouldn't be for another hour.

"No," she said, deciding she was making too big a deal of things. "It's cool. I was just—"

"Skipping school?" he asked, his eyebrows going up over his eyes.

"So are you!"

"Yeah, but you're Brin Collins."

"So?"

"I didn't think skipping school was your thing."

"Well, I'm changing my thing," she said and sat back down on the rock. She gathered up her pictures and put them back in her backpack before he could see them. He settled in next to her, and she did everything she could to keep her body small so they didn't accidentally brush shoulders.

"I read this," he said, picking up her book.

"For real?"

"Yeah, Brin. I read."

"I didn't... I mean..."

"Relax," he said. "I'm just joking."

"So you didn't read the book?" She was so off-balance around him. Saying the wrong thing. Thinking the wrong thing.

"Nope. I did. It's good."

He was wearing black jeans and a Kendrick Lamar DAMN. shirt. On his wrist was a leather-and-silver bracelet. Just a thin rawhide strip strung through a long silver bead and then tied in a knot. It was big on him, dangling down past his wrist, and it seemed like if she tugged she could pull it right off his wrist.

Her face hot, she took the book and threw it in her bag. She pulled out her lunch because she just needed something to do with her hands. And then she realized if she kept going with her lunch she'd have to eat in front of him and there was no way she could do that.

So she shoved her lunch in her backpack.

"I'm sorry." He pushed the words into the silence, like they were difficult to get out. "For what I said in the cafeteria the other day. I didn't mean to freak you out."

"It's all right," she said and managed to gather herself enough to look in his face.

"My mom says when girls say that, they don't mean it."

"Okay." Brin made her voice cold. To push all this weird trembly excitement down. "How about I don't want to talk about it?"

"Cool," he said. "That I get."

His knee bumped into hers, and she realized in a whole

new way how alone they were. How she'd never quite been alone like this with a guy. There were guys she kissed in bedrooms at parties or in the shadows around the bonfires. But her friends were always close by, the moment could always be interrupted.

There was no one around for miles.

She shifted her knee away and immediately missed the contact. She was scared of him and attracted to him all at the same time.

"Are you still going out to the Fulbright House?"

"Yeah."

"Are you…going anytime soon?"

"My mom works third shift at the post office depot in Yorkville on Thursday and Sunday nights. I usually go then," he said.

Thursday night was Spring Assembly. "When do you go?"

"Late. After midnight."

"Next time you go, can…I go with you?"

He blinked at her and she could see him start to smile. Laugh at her even. Like it was a crazy thing she was asking. So she channeled her mom and gave him her best Delia Collins dead eye.

His grin dried right up.

"It's pretty bad, you know. There was a homeless guy living in one of the bedrooms for a while. A couple of racoons. There's tons of needles and shit from the druggies—"

"I'm not scared."

"Why?" he asked.

"Aren't I scared?"

"No. Why do you want to go?"

She shrugged. "I just want to see it." He said nothing. "You know, I don't actually need you as some tour guide. I can go alone anytime—"

"Give me your cell phone," he said.

"I don't have it right now." She barely managed not to begin a rant about the cell phone jail drawer.

"What's your number?" He pulled his phone out of his back pocket and plugged it into his contacts.

*Troy Daniels has my phone number.*

*What planet am I on?*

She was going to have to do something to bust her phone out of jail.

# SIXTEEN

## Delia

"She's where?" Delia asked, shifting her phone and Ephie at the same time. Sometimes she felt like she had eight hundred hands, each one occupied by some impossible task. It was the afternoon, Dan was late getting back to harbor, and Ephie had had enough of this place.

So had she, to be honest.

*Just one second*, she mouthed to Mr. Granville, who was waiting for his Wednesday whitefish spread sandwich.

"She's here," Lindy said. "Mom's house."

"She told me she was at the beach scraping paint off the lifeguard stands." Or was it orchestra practice?

"Ahhh…yeah. That was a lie. She was here after her community service on the weekend and yesterday and today."

Delia sighed and hung her head. *That's how she knows Lindy is a good cook.*

"Dee…" Lindy said. "It's not that bad."

"Not that bad?" Delia repeated.

"Is there a chance I can get my sandwich today?" Mr. Granville asked.

"Yes," she told him. "One quick second."

"It's been five minutes."

That was a stretch, but Delia only smiled and placed Ephie in the high chair behind the counter, where she immediately started to scream.

Delia put Lindy on speaker and set the phone down on the chopping block.

"You're on speaker," Delia said and returned to making Mr. Granville's sandwich.

"Heavy on the whitefish salad," he said, and she gave him an extra scoop.

"She just wanted to look through old photographs," Lindy was saying, "hear some stories."

"Instead of heading home. Or here?"

"I'm just saying on the wide spectrum of trouble, this is pretty tame."

"Well, as long as I have your expert opinion on my daughter I guess I'm totally fine. Tell her not to go anywhere. I'll pick her up when I'm done at the shop."

Without another word she hung up and smiled at Mr. Granville.

"Did you want anything else with your sandwich?" she asked over Ephie's screams.

"To pay and leave," he said.

*You and me both, buddy. You and me both.*

Mr. Granville, despite Delia giving him the sandwich on the house, left with his nose in the air—over her customer service and perhaps the smell of Ephie's diaper, which needed to be changed *again*.

She braced her hands against the cutting board and hung her head. Tears burned behind her eyes. It was all just...too much today.

"Dee?"

Dan's voice cracked Delia open and she sobbed, once, not looking up.

*Come on, Dee. Get it together.*

"Honey? What's happened?"

Delia could feel him behind her, and she waited, her breath held, for him to touch her. Comfort her.

"We're going to get closed down because Ephie keeps pooping while I'm making sandwiches."

"Is she pooping on the sandwiches?"

Delia laughed, but it turned into another sob when Dan's warm arm wrapped around her shoulder.

She actually flinched.

The perverse wanting of what she couldn't actually tolerate was pulling her apart.

Her skin was too thin for his touch. For any touch.

His kindness felt like too much.

And it wasn't just today that she'd felt this way. Sure, some days were better than others. But ever since Ephie had been born, Delia had been different. It wasn't the same as what happened after Brin and she couldn't explain it. How it felt some days like her feelings and thoughts were being translated by someone who spoke only gibberish. What should be joy could feel like grief. What should be love felt like anger.

"Talk to me, Dee," he whispered.

All Delia could do was stare at the yellow plastic cutting board.

His arm lifted off her shoulder without further comment, and she was grateful that even if he didn't understand, he didn't push. Dan had always been that way. Always. So understanding. Decent and kind. Empathy out his ears.

So why did that make her feel like scratching his face off right now?

It didn't make sense. *She* didn't make sense.

Delia couldn't lift her head yet. She stared at the yellowed plastic cutting board and wondered if it was full of salmonella.

"Well, hello, stinky," Dan cooed to Ephie when Delia didn't respond.

"She's been fussy all day," Delia said, but the baby's shrieks had stopped and turned to laughter.

"Well, let's see what we can do about that," Dan said, and he took their baby into the back room.

Pulling herself together felt like a superhuman task. But what choice did she have?

When Brin was in middle school, she'd been the kind of student who was so diligent and worked ahead and tried her hardest, and all the effort would sort of climb to a fever pitch. Delia had grown attuned to the signs of her daughter's stress— she'd stop eating, except for her nails which she bit down until they bled. Her sleep would get erratic. There'd be more tears than laughter. That was when Delia would call a blanket-fort day. She'd keep Brin at home and Delia would get Mom to run the shop and the two of them would build an epic fort in the living room. They'd stay in their pajamas and eat Oreos and Twizzlers and read books all day.

And the next day—things would be better for Brin. And for Delia, too, she had to admit.

*When did I stop doing that?*

*WHY did I stop doing that?*

*I need a blanket-fort day.*

*A blanket-fort week.*

But since that wasn't an option, Delia cleaned up the shop, flipped the sign and turned off the lights.

In the back room, Dan had Ephie cleaned up and smiling, making wild grabs for his hair and his sunglasses. Hanging over her face by his gators.

He was laughing and blowing his mouth against her stomach and Delia just felt empty.

"Brin is at my mom's," she said.

"Yeah?"

"Apparently she's been showing up there every day after school."

"I thought she was scraping paint off the lifeguard chairs?"

"That's what she told us."

"She's been lying?" He sighed. "Have you been up? To your mom's?"

"A couple times. You?" She tried to be casual, but it didn't work.

"You clearly don't want me to go. And I've been respecting that." His face was completely unreadable. Was he angry? Frustrated?

"There was a time," Delia said with a small smile, trying to pretend she wasn't worried, scared even, "when I could tell what you were thinking just by looking at you."

"And now?"

"I don't know what you're thinking."

"There was a time I *didn't* know what you were thinking," he said. "You were this mystery I got to unravel every day."

"And now?"

"Now it just feels like we're always disappointing you."

Her heart sank.

"Go on home. Draw a bath. Take a nap. Whatever you need to do. Ephie and I will go get Brin and we'll pick up some burgers on the way home."

"You don't have to—"

"Go home, Dee," he said. "I can take care of our family, too."

# Lindy

Lindy could feel Brin's attention like a heat lamp.

"How mad is she?" Brin asked.

"Your mom? Pretty mad."

She was sitting at the counter, eating the banana bread Lindy had made this morning, managing to look both guilty and proud at the same time.

Lindy only felt guilty and stupid. She should have told Dee right away that Brin was sneaking up here. Keeping that secret only gave Dee ammunition against her.

"Did you tell her I skipped school?"

"No, my friend. That one is all yours."

"Is she like…coming to get me?"

"I imagine, yes."

"She's coming here?"

"It's where you are. Tell me something, why did you call me today?" Brin had been out at Ferris Beach and called from the pay phones again. She'd clearly been skipping school and Lindy, who'd been so ready to be the cool aunt, reached her limit. "Are you hiding something?"

"You sound like my mom."

Lindy made a noncommittal sound.

She'd been enjoying this time with her niece. These secret hours going through the picture albums and getting to know each other. Brin had a seemingly unsatisfiable thirst for the McAvoy family history. Which worked because Lindy had an unsatisfiable need to talk about it. After seventeen years of exile she was soaking it in through parched skin.

But she was starting to feel complicit in something bigger that she didn't quite understand.

"What are we going to do while we wait for her?" Brin said.

The photo album project was finished. All those old photos of fresh-faced girls in matching sweaters, posing in front of Christmas trees year after year, back in the right albums. And the albums stacked up neatly in the hall closet.

Lindy walked over to the old record player covered in dust in the corner of the room. Her parents used to play records all the time. On Sundays and vacation days, snow days and holidays. During dinner and while they cleaned the house. Neil Diamond and Kenny Rogers. Crystal Gayle and Loretta Lynn. Some Dolly Parton every once in a while if Dad pulled out the old bottle of rum from over the fridge. They'd drink it with Sprite.

Thinking of how her hipster clientele might respond to that combination delighted her.

"We're going to listen to some music." Neil Diamond. On vinyl. The perfect punishment for a teenager. And the perfect pick-me-up for Lindy.

She found *Love at the Greek* and cued it up to the third song.

"Oh!" Mom said from her chair as the first big chords of "Sweet Caroline" filled the room.

"What is this?" Brin cried, her face the picture of teenage disgust.

Lindy gasped. "That is a travesty."

"This song? I couldn't agree more!"

"This is the best song ever," Lindy yelled as Neil launched into the first line and Mom sang along. "That you don't know it by heart is the travesty.

"You're not impressed?" Lindy cranked the volume for the chorus.

"Turning up the volume doesn't make it better," Brin yelled, but she was laughing.

Mom was in her chair, eyes closed, smiling and humming. Her fingers tapped against the worn armrests—as close as she got to dancing.

"It's better if you dance!" Lindy pulled Brin off her stool, holding her hands, forcing her into dancing, which she did with plenty of eye rolls and heavy sighs. Lindy put her arm around Brin's waist and led her in a polka from the living room toward the open area of the kitchen and back again, until her niece had stopped eye rolling and was laughing along.

"One more time!" Lindy cried, and she spun them back around toward the kitchen, and suddenly there was a man in their path.

Dan.

Lindy stumbled them to a halt.

"Don't let me stop you," he said with a smile directed entirely at his daughter.

"Hey, Dad," Brin said, out of breath and flushed. She pulled strands of red hair from her lips.

"Neil Diamond, huh?" he asked.

"Aunt Lindy thought it was a… What was it?"

"A travesty," Lindy supplied.

"Right. A travesty that I've never heard of him."

"Well," he said with a nod. "I guess it is. Thank god Lindy was here to correct that."

He was looking right at Lindy now, and he was so the same as he'd been. A little older. A little more sunburned. But him—the sweet kind Dan who moved to town in the ninth grade and started working on the boats for Mom. The Dan who fell so hard for Delia.

"Hi, Dan," Lindy said, affection like sweet thick syrup filling the chambers of her heart.

"Hi, Lindy."

Lindy hugged him carefully, as if Delia were in the room. He smelled like the lake and fish and motor oil. Exactly like Dad used to.

And that was no small part of his appeal to the McAvoy sisters. He reminded them of their father. Because he was the same kind of man.

Solid. Steady. Quick to laugh. Slow to anger. Patient. Capable.

"Dad," Brin said. "Aunt Lindy is making steak with something called chimichurri. Can we stay?"

"No, your mom is home waiting for us."

"She won't care," Brin said.

"She will because I promised her burgers from Lucky's."

"Dad, we can have burgers any night," Brin said. "Call her. You know she's probably eating popcorn and watching *Grey's Anatomy*. Or she's already asleep."

Dan smiled. "You're probably right. How about you call her?"

"She took my phone away, remember?"

Dan fished his phone from his pocket and handed it over to his daughter, who grabbed it and spun away.

"It's good to see you," he said to Lindy.

"You, too. Congrats on Ephie." She leaned against the counter. The potatoes roasting in the oven made the kitchen about seven hundred degrees, but they stayed right there, sweltering.

"Thank you." He rubbed the back of his neck. "Can't say I thought I'd be the father of a newborn and a teenager all at the same time, but I'm not complaining."

"How about sleeping?"

"Not doing much of that either."

Lindy pressed her finger down on the counter and watched her nail turn white. "She hasn't been up here much."

"She's at the shop every day," he said with a shrug. "As far as I know you haven't been there either."

Right. The thing she'd forgotten only one other time in her life. Without fail Dan was always on Delia's side. Always.

"She didn't answer, Dad," Brin said, coming back into the kitchen.

"She probably fell asleep on the couch."

"So? We can stay, right?"

"We can stay for a half hour," he said. "And then we need to go get your mom some food." He looked at Lindy. "Does that work for you?"

"Totally works."

It had been a long time since Lindy pretended that Dan was hers. A long time. It was only a second. A blink. A terrible blink. But when he took the baby out of the car seat and handed her over, a curled-up bean in a green-and-yellow-striped onesie, she couldn't stop herself.

It's not that she wanted Dan, or these kids. That life.

It was Delia's. Completely and utterly.

What she really wanted was something *like* this. But all her own.

"Aunt Lindy?" Brin asked. "You okay?"

She realized she'd been standing there, her nose pressed to Ephie's head, her eyes shut tight.

"I think this baby is defective," Lindy said.

"What?"

"She smells like fish. Not baby."

"That's because she's my baby," Dan said and winked at Lindy as he walked into the living room.

Lindy glanced up at Brin, ready to make another joke, but she was already watching Lindy intently.

"What?"

"Nothing."

# SEVENTEEN

## *Brin*

*D*ad didn't use the air-conditioning in the truck.

"Can't smell the weather," he said, like there weren't professionals hired to predict the weather for them. Old-fashioned didn't even begin to cover it. He'd literally *just* gotten a cell phone. Mom and Brin were pretty sure it was only so he could play Words With Friends with them.

As they were driving home from Gran's, windows down, Ephie squawking away in the back seat, all Brin could think was that this was the first time she'd had a chance to talk to Dad since she'd found the pictures on Sunday.

"You want to explain why you've been lying to your mom and me about what you're doing after school all week?" he asked.

"Not all week. It's only Wednesday."

"Brin."

Internally she rolled her eyes. "If I asked to see Aunt Lindy, Mom would have said no. You know she would have."

"We don't know that and it certainly doesn't mean you lie. You didn't give her a chance."

This wasn't what Brin wanted to talk about. She looked out the window at the place in the middle of the lake where the water and the horizon met, where the world was one color. The same still blue.

"Why didn't Mom go to college?"

"What?" He looked over at her, startled.

"I know she was accepted and had a scholarship and everything. And she could have gone, right? Gone back to school when I was older and everything."

"Sure. But we were busy. You. The shop."

"But if she *wanted* to, she could have. Right?"

"What's this all about?" Dad asked.

"What did she want to study?" she said instead of answering his question.

"She wanted to be a teacher. High school English. Actually, I think she wanted to be a principal. But teacher was the first step."

"Mom would have been good at that."

She could feel Dad's attention on the side of her face. "Yeah, she would have."

Brin turned back to the window. They were driving by the harbor and the masts were all lit up. Jenny said they looked like haunted trees, but she was usually high when she said that. Still, Brin thought they were beautiful. She liked how they were magical and industrial at the same time. Totally Port.

The bridge was up and traffic was stopped so a sailboat could pass through from the lake to the harbor.

When the bridge was back down and traffic was moving again, Brin asked, "Did you know Lindy in high school?"

"Of course."

"No, I mean…were you friends?"

"I was actually friends with Lindy first. I got a job with Gran and met Lindy at the shop."

"And you liked her?"

"Everyone liked Lindy. Lindy was impossible not to like. She was…magnetic."

Brin scowled, feeling protective of Mom, which surprised her.

"Don't," he said, laughing. "I met your mom three days later and that was it for me."

This was a familiar story. Mom walked onto one of Gran's boats, didn't see Dad there, got startled and nearly fell into the harbor, but he pulled her back, knocking himself off-balance and falling instead.

*I fell for her*, Dad always said.

*Literally*, Mom always continued.

And then the two of them would smile at each other.

They hadn't done *that* little routine in a while.

She missed those times. When they went to parties and stayed late. She would hang out with other kids, listening to the adults get loud in the kitchen. She remembered the sound of her mom's laughter, brighter than the rest.

That seemed like a million years ago.

Brin knew it had been long enough and bad enough that those happier memories were slipping away. She wanted to just point to Ephie and say, she's the problem. That ever since Ephie came along, things had been bad.

But she was scared, like for real scared, that it was her. Brin. Who caused the problem.

And what if it was all a lie anyway? What if they'd actually *never* been a happy family, and that story about Dad falling in the lake was made up, because the truth wasn't as rom-com cute?

"Why did Aunt Lindy leave?"

He shrugged.

"Dad!"

"What?"

"You're lying. You're totally fucking—"

"Brin!"

"Lying."

He swerved to the side of the road.

"Why don't we ever talk about her?" she asked. "Why have you guys pretended like she doesn't even exist? Aunt Lindy is real. And she's nice and fun and—"

"First of all." Dad turned off the car and faced Brin. "You use that language toward me one more time and you'll understand what consequences are."

He silently waited, and if it was Mom, Brin might have started a fight rather than apologize. But this was Dad.

"Okay," she said. "I'm sorry."

"Second, we didn't pretend she doesn't exist—"

"Uh…yeah, you did. And you know it!"

When she was a kid, like eight or something, she and Dad had gone swimming one weekend down at Potter's. They had the ropes up between the shallow water and the drop-off for safety. She'd just passed Level Two swimming and felt like a pro and she'd edged out to the rope.

She'd ignored Dad's pleas not to and bobbed away.

She got to the buoys, lifted the scratchy algae-covered white nylon rope up over her head and went under. The drop-off made the water colder, immediately. As soon as she couldn't feel the sand under her feet, it was like she just forgot how to swim. She searched for the bottom with her toe, but all she felt were the tips of the weeds tickling her feet. Dad grabbed her wrist and pulled her under the rope, into the shallow end and into his arms.

The face he gave her now was the face he had given her then: *What are you doing, kid?*

And the answer was she didn't know.

But she had a pocket full of pictures that hinted at a story she needed to hear.

"No one is pretending anything," he said. "Your mom got pregnant, we got married and Lindy left. That's what happened."

He put the truck in gear and drove back up onto the road, the gravel spitting out behind them. In the back seat, Ephie was quiet, asleep, probably. "You gonna get bacon on your cheeseburger?" he asked.

Brin nodded, but the subject wasn't changed in her head.

It wasn't changed at all.

# EIGHTEEN

## *Lindy*

*M*om woke up on Thursday in the mood for a walk. She put on Dad's old hat and her walking shoes, same as her other shoes, just—unbelievably—a brighter white. She even found an old cane in the closet from when Delia sprained her knee in high school.

"Mom," Lindy said, shoving her feet into her tennis shoes without socks because Mom wasn't giving her time to find any. "You sure you want to do this?"

The doctor said exercise, supervised and light, was good for her. But she knew her mother wasn't the strolling type.

"What have I always said, Lindy?"

"Don't trust men who drive red cars?"

"Besides that."

"Don't trust men who use toothpicks in public."

"Lindy—"

"I don't know what you want me to say right now!" Lindy pulled the rubber band from her wrist and put her hair up. She was not wearing her butt cheek cutoffs and she had a bra on. So it was a victory.

"Exercise isn't just good for your body," Mom said.

"You never once in your life said that."

"Well, I thought it. Let's go."

Mom was out the back door and around the side of the house before Lindy managed to find her purse.

"Slow down there, speedy." Lindy caught up with her by the hydrangea bush. "Where are we going?"

"Shortcut."

The shortcut into town that dropped them at the bottom of the spit.

"Mom," she said, matching her mother's pace as they walked down the street to the edge of the ridge. The shortcut used to be a worn-out trail that disappeared into the grove of trees along the ridgeline. Sometimes it would wash out during a big storm and it could be seriously treacherous at night, but if you were a kid on a bike or on foot, the shortcut shaved twenty minutes and a giant hill off the trip into town.

In the last seventeen years, some genius had decided to make it a legitimate path, with concrete, a handrail and everything.

Meredith started down the staircase, one hand on her cane, the other on the handrail. She went slow and steady as if completely aware of her limitations.

At the bottom they stepped down into a small forested area on the side of the road. At the end of the road was the spit. And the Fulbright House.

They both stopped. Lindy didn't mean to, she was going to walk right on by, but Mom hadn't moved.

"Look at that place," Mom whispered.

"It's pretty ugly."

"It was always ugly. Ugly people lived there."

Lindy thought of Garrett's story about Mr. Fulbright trying to get him arrested because of his skin color. Why didn't anyone ever stand up to them? she wondered. What was it about all that money that made people keep their mouths shut?

"I never understood how you could go out there after your father died."

"You knew?"

Mom shot her a sideways glance.

"It's where the parties were," Lindy finally said with a shrug. "I liked parties."

Mom grunted and soldiered on.

For a moment, Lindy stayed in the shade of the trees. It was another beautiful day in Port Lorraine. Blue sky, puffy white clouds. All the flags were snapping in a nice breeze. Queen Street looked postcard perfect from this angle, except for the shabby eyesore of the McAvoy Bait, Fish and Lunch Counter.

"So, do you want to get a cone? Or stop by the shop—?"

"It's Friday fish fry, Lindy. We need to go help out."

"It's Thursday, Mom."

"No, it's not."

"Mom."

Her determined face crumpled. "Really?" she asked. "I could have sworn."

"It's not a big deal. Let's go see how Dee's doing anyway."

They continued walking toward the shop and Lindy realized she'd been avoiding it since they'd stopped there after Mom's doctor's appointment. It was just so hard to see what had become of the place.

"You guys kept the fish fry going?" Lindy asked. The fish fry had been Lindy's baby. Well, her and Dan's.

After watching the VFW rake in the cash every week all summer long, they'd decided to take a stab at it. She and Dan only got one under their belt before she left, but it had been a good one. The potential was there.

"Delia mostly. Every Friday in the summer and then once a month in the winter. It's real popular."

Mom had given her life to the McAvoy Bait, Fish and Lunch Counter. She'd run charters every day, just like Dad before he died. She'd be up and out of the house before dawn, do an hour at the shop, repairing nets mostly, before going out on the lake for another four to six hours. She hired more employees during the busy season. Nirosha's mom worked there every summer, a smiling, stout presence behind the counter, her own kids running wild in and out the door with Delia and Lindy.

"Your mom," everyone would say. "Hardest-working woman in town."

But now, on the other side of childhood, Lindy realized that Mom had been dealing with more than just exhaustion back then.

"Were you scared, Mom?" she asked when they were walking side by side again.

She stopped, looked out at Lindy from under Dad's hat. "When?"

"When me and Dee were kids. When you were doing the charter trips and running the shop."

"Scared?" She considered the word for a moment. "Maybe. Worried."

"About money?"

"Sure." She kept on and Lindy thought she was done talking about it. Moved on in her shifting brain. But then she said, "Mostly, I worried that I was a bad mom."

"For working so much?"

"For wanting to work. It was easier to fish and run the store than it was to be a mother on my own."

Stunned, Lindy blinked into the sunlight. It never occurred that her mother would feel that way.

"You should see your face," Mom said, watching Lindy over her rounded shoulder. She was smirking but not really.

"You weren't a bad mom," Lindy said.

"Wasn't I?" She was walking faster, that cane of hers stabbing at the ground. "Look at what's come of you two. You don't speak to each other. You barely speak to me."

"Mom. None of that—"

Lindy was about to say that none of that was Mom's fault. But...maybe it was. Some of it, at least. Mom missed a lot. Not just school assemblies and parent-teacher conferences. She missed when Delia wasn't sleeping nights in a row during finals week. She missed when Lindy went to Cedar Point with a shitty boyfriend who abandoned her there. It wasn't a condemnation. It was just fact. Lindy had known how to use that lack of supervision to her advantage. The wild McAvoy sister hadn't grown wild on her own.

And then there was the long list of subjects Mom didn't have time to—or want to—talk about. All the ways Lindy and Delia learned not to talk about things. And all the ways to talk about things they simply never learned.

"You know I'm right."

"Well, I'm here now." Lindy tucked her arm through Mom's. She felt clammy from the walk, and again Lindy wondered if she'd made a mistake not getting the car.

But Mom smiled, and the air smelled like the color green, and the sidewalk under Lindy's feet was one she'd known by heart her whole life. They glided in step past the CutN-Run with the old-school dryers in the window, down to the storefront.

It had not magically improved since the last time she'd been here.

*My dad would be so upset if he saw this.*

"Doesn't this bother you, Mom?"

"What?"

"The way the shop looks?"

"What's wrong with it?"

"It just looks...tired." Understatement.

Mom sighed. "She was never gonna do what you would have done. Or what I did. And we both walked away, honey. It's not fair to come back and judge her."

Chastened, Lindy pushed open the door to find a shop that was surprisingly busy.

Lindy could hear Delia discussing the whitefish behind the small line of customers at the sandwich counter, baby Ephie's coos and shrieks a happy soundtrack.

Mom sat down at the booth in the front.

"Do you need a drink, Mom?"

"Water would be good."

Lindy eased her way around the knot of people and grabbed a bottle of water from the cooler beside the sandwich counter. When she turned she caught sight of Delia, Ephie strapped to her chest as she cut a sandwich in two with a giant knife.

Just inches from her daughter's footy-pajamaed toes.

"Lindy?" Delia said. "What are you doing here?"

"Delia," a woman in line in front of the fish counter said. "Can I get a pound of the whitefish?"

"I'll be with you in just a second, Mrs. Bates," she said and shooed Lindy away with the knife.

Lindy was no authority on child safety. But this was shocking. And it was even more shocking that no one else seemed shocked. After dropping the water off with Mom, she went behind the sandwich counter. There was a good chance she wasn't welcome, but in her eyes, she was sure as hell needed.

At a small white enamel sink, Lindy washed her hands with the gray cracked bar of Dove soap that she prayed wasn't the same gray cracked bar of Dove soap that had there when she was a kid.

"Dee," Lindy said calmly, sidling up beside her sister. "Put down the knife."

"What are you doing here?" she asked again, bagging a sandwich.

"Mom thought it was Friday, wanted to help out with the fish fry."

"It's Thursday."

"Yeah. I know."

"How did you get here?"

"We walked."

"Should she be doing that?"

"She's fine," Lindy said. "Exercise is good for you. She always said that."

"She never said that."

"Put down the knife. I'll make the sandwiches."

"I don't need your help."

"*I'd* like some help!" Mrs. Bates said. "A pound of white-fish."

"It's you or me," Lindy said. "And I vote we get Ephie away from sharp objects."

Delia rolled her eyes and stepped over to the other service counter. Lindy put a big smile on her face and glanced out at the customers. Lots of faces, she was pleased to notice, that she didn't recognize.

It was this perspective, standing behind a counter ready to serve up something delicious for others, Lindy loved most. In her sleep she was good at this job. Hungover she was good at this job. At ten years old she'd been good at this job.

She beamed. "Who's next?"

Two whitefish salad sandwiches, a turkey and a sad-looking BLT later, the store was cleared out.

Ephie's coos turned into cries.

"You do this every day?" Lindy asked over her niece's wails.

"What?"

Lindy didn't know if Dee was playing dumb or she truly didn't get how crazy this was.

"Run this place with Ephie strapped to your chest?"

"Well, she doesn't like the high chair anymore. I keep forgetting to bring in the bouncy swing—"

"Delia…"

"Lindy. Your outrage seems to suggest that you think this is a choice."

"Delia," Mom said, screwing the cap back on her water. Her tone said, *Don't even bother, she doesn't understand.* This tone was familiar to Lindy from friends in the city who had kids.

"Oh my god, I may not have kids, but I can see this is nuts."

"It's almost summer," Delia said with a more patient voice. "Dan's fishing. Brin is finishing school, working and now she has community service. It's either have Ephie here or close down the store."

"We're not closing down the store," Mom piped up. Not exactly helpful.

"Okay, I get it. But…can we hire someone?"

"We?" Delia asked. Ephie was starting to cry in earnest, her little face a red knot of despair. "There's no we."

"Give me that baby," Mom said, walking between Lindy and Delia. "It's bad enough I have to listen to you two arguing. This sweet baby shouldn't have to, too."

They followed Meredith to the back room. Outside of the pack-n-play, mermaid mobile, a changing table and a rocking chair, it looked entirely the same. Dad's chair at his desk. The lighthouse calendar that Dee and Lindy got him for Christmas in 1990 was still pinned to the bulletin board.

They bought him a calendar every year for Christmas. That was his last calendar.

"There's no money to pay help," Dee said as Mom changed Ephie's diaper. Dee's face was tight and she was watching Mom like a hawk, as if she might run off with her baby. Lindy wanted to touch her face, turn her head so Delia had to look at her. See her. See that the solution was here, standing right in front of her.

"I can help," she said, almost forgetting she only had one week left in Port.

"Do you have money?"

"Some. But more importantly, I can help in the store."

"Lindy, cut the crap. Don't act like you're staying here indefinitely."

"It doesn't matter how long I'm staying. I'm here now. I can help. Now."

"Then who takes care of Mom?"

"We can figure it out, Delia. If Mom isn't feeling good we don't come down that day."

"Is that supposed to be helpful? Because it sounds like one more thing for *me* to worry about."

"Jesus, Delia, not everything is a fight. I want to help. I'm here. I'm willing to do more. I want to do more. This was supposed—" Lindy stopped.

*This was supposed to be my life.*

Now it was Lindy who couldn't meet her sister's eyes.

"I'm hanging out with Mom. We're going to doctor's appointments and we're doing crossword puzzles. We take naps, Dee. I can do more. We can hire Tiffany at night while Mom is sleeping and I can come down here and clean and paint—"

"You really want to do that?" Dee's face was incredulous. "Fix this place up?"

"Yes, Dee. It's all I've wanted to do."

It was the truth everyone knew about her. "Mom," Lindy said. "How would you feel about coming down here with me for a few hours every day? I can set you up in a chair out front."

"Great idea," she said.

"And I can talk to Garrett...Chief Singh, and maybe we can get some of the community service kids over to sand the front of the building and we can repaint it. We'll claim beautification."

"Don't," Delia breathed, like every word was burning her from the inside. "Don't come here and make everything seem easy when it has been so hard."

"Nothing's easy." Lindy used the tone she saved for women at the corner of the bar on their third vodka martini who weren't wearing waterproof mascara.

"No," Delia spat. "It's not."

"Which is why it's going to take all of us. It should never have been you all alone. It was never supposed to be either of us all alone," Lindy whispered, urging her sister to remember.

Dee bit her lip and finally nodded. It wasn't much, but it felt like a start.

"I think she's hungry," Mom said, lifting the baby.

Delia cupped her boobs like they were about to run off on her. "It's about that time." She took Ephie and settled down in the rocker.

"Do you need anything?" Lindy asked. This seemed too private a moment for her to witness. "Water or something?"

Dee blinked and Lindy realized how alone she must feel here day after day, Dan coming in off the lake after three, sometimes as late as five, Brin off living her own teenage life.

It had just been her and the lunch counter and a baby.

"Water would be nice," Delia said.

Lindy went out into the store to grab a bottle from the cooler.

As she walked across the wide-plank wood floors (original to the 1892 building!), she couldn't help but make mental changes:

First off it was time to get rid of the gross jarred tartar sauce and cocktail sauce. Lindy could make homemade, charge more for less. She could fill the shelves with proper picnic items. Water crackers, summer sausage and cheeses. Lindy knew the reps from local wineries and breweries, she could fill these shelves with local products. And produce. Tons of produce. Tomatoes and peaches, cherries, cucumbers. She could package cold salads; new potatoes with fresh corn and feta cheese, dressed in parsley pesto. Green apple coleslaw with ginger and sesame seeds. A better sandwich menu, for sure. That BLT she made earlier? Yikes.

*Stop*, she warned herself. *You're leaving.*

# NINETEEN
## *Delia*

*T*he high school was on the ridge opposite the ridge where Mom lived, the town of Port Lorraine sort of sandwiched between the two.

She'd dropped Brin off at the school earlier, so young and nervous in her black dress and carrying her violin case. Her hair curled just so. Dan and Ephie were inside holding seats while Delia waited in the parking lot for Mom and Lindy, who were, predictably, late, but somehow that didn't even bother her tonight.

Delia loved school assemblies.

When Brin was in kindergarten, Delia had been shocked when other parents joked about how awful those school holiday programs were, five-year-olds singing "Dreidel, Dreidel, Dreidel" and "Frosty the Snowman." Delia didn't understand how you could *not* love all those kids, hair brushed, faces shiny, trying so hard. How could you say all those sweet little voices were awful?

Tonight was going to be lovely. The air was just right, no humidity, a perfect breeze coming off the lake. Delia'd showered. She'd shaved her legs. Her hair was behaving. She'd managed to find a tube of mascara that hadn't dried out and a stretchy pre-pregnancy skirt that fit.

A beat-up Toyota pulled up next to the van. Delia was even happy that Lindy was here to see how amazing her niece was. In Lindy's eyes, Delia might have failed at the shop, but she hadn't failed with Brin.

The watch stealing was just a blip.

Lindy hopped out of the driver's side. "Are we late?"

"A little."

"Sorry. We just—"

Delia stopped her, not interested in the reasons or in making her sister feel worse. It was too nice of a night. "It's not a big deal. There's still plenty of time."

"Oh," Lindy said, then she put her hands up and cried, "Spring Assembly!"

Delia couldn't help but smile.

"Is it the same as when we were kids?"

"Almost exactly."

They'd done their share of Spring Assemblies. Delia had played flute in the orchestra and Lindy—off and on—had been in choir.

"Should be good," Delia said and opened the door for Mom. She had to admit, since Lindy had been back, Mom was looking a little more together than she had in the last few months.

"Are we late?" Mom asked under her breath so just Delia could hear. "I told her we needed to hurry but you know how that girl is in front of a bathroom mirror."

"You're right on time," she assured Mom.

It had taken Delia an hour of concentrated work to get ready. Lindy, however, looked like she just shook out her beautiful mane of hair, threw on a tank top and some lip gloss and called it a day.

Some things just weren't fair.

"Mom and I thought we could take everyone out for ice cream after," Lindy said. "I mean if it's cool and Brin's not in too much trouble."

"Yeah," Delia said. "That's a great idea."

Lindy's surprise hit Delia hard in her chest, like catching a glimpse of herself in the bathroom mirror after a 3:00 a.m. feeding, but worse.

*Why does everyone expect me to say no, all the time? To ruin everyone's good time? I can still be fun.*

"Dee?" Lindy asked, turning back at the steps to the high school. "You all right?"

"Fine," she said and took a few trotting steps to catch up.

The auditorium was packed, a small line of people shuffling their way into the side doors. She smiled and waved at a few old friends.

"Hey," she said to Janice Shultz, whose son had taken Brin's spot in the orchestra.

"Hi!" Janice said with a little bit too much enthusiasm. She'd been exceedingly friendly since Justin got first chair. "Big night, huh?"

"Yeah, should be good. Janice, I'm not sure if you know my mom, Meredith. Or my sister, Lindy—"

"Oh my goodness." Janice stared at Lindy, her hand pressed to the neck of her matching green sweater set. God, the woman had to be sweating buckets under all those layers. "I see where Brin gets her looks."

*Man,* Delia thought, *and I just resolved to be nicer.*

"Right? My sister cleans up pretty nice, doesn't she?" Lindy said with a tight smile.

There was some shifting behind them and a man in a suit made his way up through the line to Janice's side. "Hi, babe," said Janice's husband, whose name Delia could honestly never remember. "Sorry I'm late."

*Bill? Blake? I think it's a B sound.*

Janice kissed her husband on the cheek and he rested a hand against her shoulder. Delia glanced away only to catch Lindy looking like she'd like to hide.

"Holy cow, Lindy McAvoy?" Janice's husband said with a big wide laugh. "Is that you?"

*Barney? No. No one is named Barney anymore.*

"Hi, Brad," Lindy said with a half smile. "How are you doing?"

*Brad!*

"Oh my god, I can't believe it's you." His enthusiasm was a bit much for the small echoey hallway. Janice glanced around, embarrassed.

"Brad," she whispered. "Lower your—"

"Remember, babe?" Brad said. "The girl I went to high school with. I told you about how she stole that teacher's car. That's her!"

Poor Lindy looked like she wanted the floor to open up and swallow her whole.

"Actually," Delia said, because the story that had circulated wasn't accurate. It had been more of a misunderstanding. "The car was the same kind of car as the one Lindy and I shared in high school. And the teacher happened to leave the keys in the ignition."

Brad blinked at her.

"It was an accident," Delia clarified.

"It was legend," Brad laughed, apparently not interested in the truth.

"Excuse me!" Mom cried. She grabbed both Lindy and Delia by the hands and started pushing her way through the crowd. "Old lady, coming through."

And wouldn't you know it, everyone made room for her.

"Thanks," Lindy said.

"For what?"

"Trying to explain."

"Half the stuff people said about you wasn't true," Delia said. "And the other half was exaggerated. We should have set them all straight years ago."

Inside the gym Delia looked up at the stands and found Dan in their usual spot, half down and just left of the center aisle. He waved his hand, and the familiarity of the moment made her heart swell.

She led Lindy and Mom up the stairs.

"Hey," he said. "You found me."

"I will always find you," she said, and then she leaned forward and kissed him. He smiled against her mouth and she smiled back. Ephie got a hold of her hair and pulled.

"Wow," he said, blushing because it had been so long since she'd kissed him in public. Or private for that matter. "Good to see you, too."

"Garrett!" Lindy said, and Delia turned to find the police chief sitting just above them. "What are you doing here?"

"Spring Assembly," he said with a shrug and a smile. "Best show in town." He was wearing his uniform and Delia had to admit the man wore it well. "Actually the English teacher asked me to be here so I could give out a special award."

"That's great!" Lindy said with a little too much enthusiasm. Delia leaned forward and waggled her eyebrows at her sister. Lindy went bright pink.

*Oh, she has it bad for Garrett Singh.*

"Come on now," Mom said, tugging everyone down to sit. "Show's starting."

Mrs. Grath, the principal, was at the microphone, and the

students in the orchestra filed into their seats. Delia's heart leapt at the sight of Brin, looking so serious as she walked in. She glanced up at the audience to find Delia and Dan in their seats and gave them a tiny wave.

Delia exhaled, long and slow, and smiled with relief at Dan.

The orchestra took on an exceedingly lovely version of Lin Manuel-Miranda and Ben Platt's mash-up "Found/Tonight." Delia was a fountain of tears and even Mom, the crusty old bird, had damp eyes.

"That was beautiful," Chief Singh bent down to whisper.

"It was, wasn't it?" she whispered back, her heart just bursting.

The awards came last and Delia held out hope that Brin would win something. Last year she took home three different awards for honor roll, excellence in orchestra and peer leaders. But this year her name wasn't called once.

"You know—" Dan said into her ear.

"She's had such a tough year," Delia rushed to fill in.

She could sense in Dan's silence a kind of shock. Earlier this year, when she had lost first chair violin, Brin had been so angry and upset she'd barely left her room for a week and wouldn't let Delia in. Each night, after Dan went to sleep, Delia had leaned her head against Brin's bedroom door, hoping her daughter could sense her there, that she felt for her. Delia knew it wasn't much.

But Ephie had just been born and it was all she'd had to give.

Garrett Singh stood next to the English teacher, Mr. Rose, as he talked about a student who had made tremendous strides in his writing, so much so that he had won a state-wide contest.

"Troy Daniels," Mr. Rose announced, and the students sitting in the front rows gasped, their heads swiveling around as they looked for this Troy Daniels. Delia did, too, and caught Lindy's gaze, eyes all wide.

"What?" Delia whispered.

"Do you know Troy?" she asked.

"No. Do you?"

Lindy shook her head.

"Troy?" Mr. Rose said into the mic. It was obvious the kid wasn't there. "That's too bad," he said. "We'll make sure Troy gets his prize."

After, Mrs. Graft thanked everyone for coming, urged them all to drive safe and it was over.

"Ice cream!" Mom cried.

"I'll get Brin," Delia said. "And meet you outside."

Lindy and Meredith took off at a hustle as parents made their way down to the basketball court floor to hug and take pictures of their kids. Dan and Delia were no different.

Nirosha was there, trying to straighten the tie of her eldest son, a sophomore who'd made honor roll and won a prize with the robotics team.

"Hey!" Delia said. "Lindy's here. We're all going to get ice cream after. You should come."

"We'd love to!" Nirosha said. "I've been meaning to call Lindy now that she's home but...you know how things are at the end of the school year."

Delia did know. She knew all too well how time was speeding up and all she could do was try to hold on with both hands.

"There's my girl!" Dan cried when Brin finally got to them through the throng of people. "What an incredible job you did, honey!"

He hugged her and kissed her forehead and Delia put down the baby carrier to do the same.

She squeezed her extra hard. "I'm so proud of you."

"I didn't get any awards," Brin whispered.

"It's been a hard year."

Brin pushed away, looking at Delia like she'd just attempted to eat her.

"We're going to go get ice cream with Lindy and Gran!" she blurted.

Like the girl she really still was, Brin lit right up.

*We're going to be all right*, Delia thought. And for the first time in a long time it didn't feel like a lie.

By the time they got out to the parking lot Delia expected it to have emptied out a little. But instead a giant crowd of people stood at the very edge, on the grassy stretch before the fence.

"What's going on?" Brin asked.

"Something with the harbor?" Dan said and took off at a trot. Brin and Delia followed at a slower pace.

"Justin did pretty good, didn't he?" Brin asked. Justin, the kid who took her spot.

"He was awful."

"Mom," she laughed.

"The worst."

"Stop."

"I'm not joking. I don't—"

Dan turned to them, his face pale. "Dee," he said.

She stepped onto the grass, closer to the clutch of people.

"I heard half a million," someone said.

"For that wreck?"

"Someone will tear it down. The property is worth that. Probably more."

"Dan?" she said, growing cold in the warm night.

He pulled her close and then turned her slowly so she was facing the lake.

The harbor. Her town. Everything as it should be.

And the Fulbright House—all aglow.

A giant for-sale sign plastered on the front.

She couldn't force her eyes away. All these years avoiding the Fulbright House and now she couldn't look away.

"It's for sale." She wasn't sure why she said that. Everyone could see the sign. Big as life, right there.

People were still talking about the property value and the extensive damage to the house.

"Kids still go out there and party."

*I used to go out there and party. Me and Dan and Lindy.*

She stepped away from Dan. She wanted to throw up.

"Are they back?" someone asked. "The Fulbrights? Are they in town?"

A hand grabbed hers in the night. She would know that hand anywhere. Lindy.

# TWENTY

## *Delia*

After Dad died, Lindy and Delia had nightmares. Delia dreamt of terrible monsters with teeth and dark places and not being able to breathe. Lindy dreamt of falling and being lost in a big house. It got so bad they couldn't sleep. They'd lie in bed and whisper and try as hard as they could to be silent so Mom wouldn't come in. But one of them would drift off and the nightmare would start and so would the screaming.

Mom would come running in and wipe their eyes, brush the hair off their foreheads and tell them there were no monsters. She'd check under the beds and in the closet, the dark corners, but it somehow was never enough. The dreams had become so real.

It was nights. Weeks. Months of this.

Finally Mom told them to lie as still as they could, side by side, in Delia's bed. Lie still and not let any part of their bodies touch the edge of the mattress. Not their long hair. Or their big toes. Not their hands when they rolled over. That as long as they were fully on the mattress, nothing could hurt them.

It worked—the nightmares came to an end, but the paranoia of a finger or a stray hair, the bottom edge of a night-gown slipping over the edge of that mattress, began.

The sleep was often shallow, but it was sleep.

Delia still found herself waking up some nights, her leg kicked out under the blanket, her foot over the bottom of the mattress, and her heart would pound hard against her ribs.

The whole day on Friday felt like those nights. Everyone who came into the shop was speculating about the Fulbright House. Delia found herself standing in the corner of the restaurant so she could see the house from the edge of the front windows. Like a bruise she couldn't stop pressing her thumb into.

Ephie was napping in the back, and Mom and Delia were getting the fish ready to be fried. Perch and walleye filets, firm and slippery, dipped in egg and a time-tested mix of flour, paprika and cornmeal. Then set aside in a plastic tub for Dan and Brin to grab for the big fryer.

Lindy manned the lunch counter, chirping at everyone who walked in the door.

"Hi!" she said. "Would you guys like to sample our home-made whitefish salad? Secret family recipe." Lindy scooped some of the whitefish spread onto probably stale Ritz crackers and handed them over to anyone who couldn't say no.

*Everyone's had the whitefish salad. This whole town has been eating it their whole lives.*

"Should we tell them the secret is mayo and pickle relish?" Mom whispered to Delia, her fingers covered in thick bubbly batter.

"I added black pepper."

"Well, aren't you fancy," she said with a sly smile. Delia hadn't seen this woman in a while. The twinkly conspirator. The no-nonsense practicality.

"You never wanted this," Mom whispered.

"What?"

"The shop. It's not a secret. You always hated this place. Lindy loved it. You tolerated it on your best days."

Delia had helped out at the shop since Brin was in kindergarten. Dan took over the charters right out of high school. He and Mom had two boats going out, and the money had been good. Then Mom took a nasty spill on the deck during a storm, hurt her leg badly enough that Dan and Delia had to step in and convince her to retire to the shop.

She had not gone peacefully.

When Brin entered kindergarten, Dan had encouraged Delia to go back to school to get that degree she'd been planning on, but it felt at the time like that ship had sailed. She wasn't sharp as she used to be. Her brain had been softened and rounded down by the daily grind of parenting a toddler.

So she worked the shop, taking over more and more as Mom got older. Until it was Dan and Delia running things. A new generation Mom and Dad.

Delia never expected to be this person. Lindy, sure. But Delia had had plans to get out of Port, at least for a while. To see the world.

"Want didn't really have anything to do with it," Delia said.

"It should have," Mom said.

Dan came in through the back, Brin trailing with a smile on her face.

*I need to get back to that feeling from last night. I need to shake this off. It's just a house. It was all so long ago. I'm fine. I'm better.*

"Ready for the first batch?" Dan clapped his hands with pure enthusiasm.

"No!" Delia said and turned her slimy hand to check her watch. "Did you start the oil? It's only four! We don't have the coleslaw—"

Brin put a hand on her arm. "He's joking. He thinks he's funny."

"It's not funny?" he asked.

"No!" Mom said.

Delia forced out a smile at her mom's honesty.

"What can I do?" Lindy asked, coming to the fresh fish counter. She had her hair up in a ponytail and was wearing a pair of cutoffs. She looked so much like a teenage version of herself Delia had to glance away.

"Hello, Lindy," Dan said with a careful smile.

"Help Brin with the coleslaw," Dee told Lindy.

"Great. Have we got cabbage—?"

Brin opened the big cooler beneath the fish counter and pulled out the industrial-size jug of coleslaw.

"Oh, honey." Mom laughed at Lindy, who looked like they'd killed her cat. "You should see your face."

Dan brought out the small paper containers for the coleslaw and the newspaper for packaging the fish. The mound of fish ready to be fried grew into a mountain. At four thirty, Dan started the oil and by five they'd dropped the first batch.

The smell of crispy hot fried fish drifted through the shop. Even Delia's stomach growled.

And it must have drifted across the whole town, too, because soon the line was out the door. With Lindy there, the roles got switched around, and Delia, delighted not to have to talk to anyone, stood battering more fish. Brin worked the cash, and Lindy ran the tubs of raw fish to the back and returned with golden hot filets that she wrapped in newspaper and sold as fast as customers arrived.

"I heard one of Cleveland Cavaliers was going to buy it," someone standing in line said. "Tear the whole thing down and build a fancy new house."

"Swear to god," someone else said. "I saw Eric Fulbright this morning. Driving down Queen in that old BMW he used to drive."

"Don't be ridiculous. That guy's not showing his face around here. Remember what Jessica Mayhew said about him. Told everyone who'd listen—"

"Come on," someone interrupted. "There are kids here."

Sweating and huffing, Lindy arrived from the back with a tub of hot fish. "You okay?" she asked, blowing her hair off her forehead.

"Why wouldn't I be?"

"'Cause you look like you're gonna pass out. If you need—"

"I'm fine."

The bell rang over the door and suddenly the solid hum of voices in the shop stopped. It went so quiet Delia looked up to see if everyone had left.

They hadn't, but a woman had arrived, dressed in a navy-blue skirt with a white silk blouse covered in anchors. She was tiny, but carried herself in such a way that she seemed bigger. She had silver hair, curled and set impeccably, not a strand out of place.

"Oh my god," Lindy said and grabbed Delia's wrist. Her palm was hot from the pans.

The woman turned and faced them, and though it took Delia a second, in a way she had been bracing for this all day.

Gloria Fulbright.

# TWENTY-ONE
## *Lindy*

*They were frozen.*

Lindy felt like she couldn't move. One step and everything would break into a million pieces. Beside her, Delia had gone as rigid as a tentpole.

Brin, thank god for small favors, got her act together and started ringing people up again. Selling fish so fast it was like they were having a fire sale. Gloria Fulbright stood in the middle of the restaurant like she didn't know how to get in line. She'd probably never waited in a line for anything her whole damn life.

Lindy wanted to ignore her. She wanted to force that woman to stand there and be whispered about and pointed at. She wanted to watch Gloria Fulbright pretend that nothing was happening, that everything was all right.

But at the same time Lindy wanted her out of there. Before Mom came out from the back and saw her. Before Delia cracked right down the middle.

"Hey! What's the holdup?" Dan asked, coming into the room in big rubber gloves, his safety goggles pushed up into his hair. "I got hot oil— Oh god." He started to remove his gloves and Lindy knew—because Dan was a good guy—that he was going to handle Gloria Fulbright.

That pushed Lindy into action more than anything else.

"Mrs. Fulbright," she said in a low voice, approaching the woman in the middle of the restaurant. Brin had done a good job and the place was emptying out, but everyone still there was staring and whispering.

Gloria Fulbright smiled at Lindy.

"Are you Lindy or Delia?" she asked. "I thought that was you." Gloria pointed over at Brin, and it was all Lindy could do not to smack her hand down and say, *Don't you look at her.* "But time isn't that kind to anyone."

Time had seemingly passed right over Gloria Fulbright. She looked the same as the night Dad died. Not young, not old. She would undoubtedly call it *timeless. Classic.* Lindy had a different word for it.

"What can I do for you, Mrs. Fulbright?"

"I'm looking for your mother. All of you, really."

"My mother's not here," Lindy said. "Why don't you leave me your number and I can have her call you."

Of course Mom took that moment to step out from the back room, Ephie in her arms, rubbing her eyes with little fists.

"We out of fish already?" Mom asked.

Lindy gave Delia a look that was supposed to tell her to get Mom out of there, but Delia still hadn't moved. Dan, however, caught on and turned to block Mom's view.

They'd been having good days, Lindy and Mom. Real good days. And Gloria Fulbright would be the end of them, of that Lindy was sure.

"Mrs. McAvoy," Gloria said, her voice carrying across the shop.

Mom nudged Dan aside. "Can I help you?" she asked, polite and careful.

Lindy could tell that her mom didn't recognize Gloria but was aware that she should.

Gloria stepped around Lindy and she felt herself trapped. She could taste her own shame on her tongue, like she had that night, when she'd had to be so polite to a woman so absolutely awful to them.

*You made us beg.*

Still Lindy couldn't call her out. Tell her to get lost and take her fake…whatever with her. She only stood there.

"Meredith," Gloria said. "It's Mrs. Fulbright. I know it's been a while—"

"What do you want?" Mom asked.

Gloria Fulbright looked so pained, and Lindy felt the old instinct to make this awful moment better, to deflect the attention, to crack a joke. But she was speechless.

"I suppose…well, I wanted to apologize."

"For what?" Mom said. Her fingers toyed with the neck of her shirt and her face lost its presence, like some indelible muscle had let go.

"What happened that night your husband died. I just feel terrible. We were just as scared and worried as you—"

Lindy gasped. The *gall* of that woman.

"You should go." It was Brin from behind the counter, doing what none of the McAvoys could. She had one finger pointed at the door. "We don't want your apology. We just want you to leave."

Gloria looked from Brin over to the adults on the other side of the room, as if to see if they were going to handle the impertinent teenager.

"Dear," Gloria said, "I don't think this is a matter you understand—"

"I understand you're here and you're freaking everyone out," Brin said. "You should go."

"She's right," Lindy finally managed. She turned, held her arm out toward the door. "I think it's best if you leave."

"I only wanted—"

"I know what you wanted," Lindy murmured. "And you can't have it."

Mrs. Fulbright sucked a big breath in through her nose. So hard, Lindy was surprised she didn't turn herself inside out with it.

"Where's your son?" Delia's voice cracked and Gloria stopped dead still in front of the door.

"Eric's in Canada," Gloria said, her chin pointed up. "He's doing very well up there."

"I find that hard to believe," Mom said.

Someone laughed and Gloria's eyes narrowed.

"I have always hated this town," she spat as she walked toward the door.

Lindy opened the door and glanced back over Gloria's head to her family, strung out along the back of the store, shellshocked. The past had brushed too close to the present for all of them.

# TWENTY-TWO

## Brin

Lindy and Gran had left in Dad's truck, and Mom had grabbed Ephie and stormed out without a word to anyone.

Dad looked over at Brin, his sweaty hair pushed up by the safety goggles. He was still wearing one glove, and the fish in the bin beside him steamed into the air.

"Are you mad?" she whispered.

"Because you told that witch to get lost?" he asked and then shook his head. "No way."

"Is Mom?"

"Nope. I think she's grateful. And proud." He crossed the room and pulled Brin into a hug. "I'm proud."

Brin felt like crying and she wasn't sure why.

"Someone told you about the night Grandpa died, huh?"

"Gran and Lindy. A few days ago."

He nodded and pulled off the other glove. "Sometimes being polite can be a curse. This whole town has always been too polite to the Fulbrights."

"Is Mom okay?"

"Sure. Rattled, probably, but she'll be fine."

"Dad. She hasn't been fine in a while and we all keep pretending she is."

Dad's smile was the saddest she'd ever seen and he cupped her face like he used to. "When did you grow up, Brindaven? When did you get so wise?"

She jerked her head back. "I'm sixteen. I'm only a few years away from the age you were when you had me. I'm not a baby."

He took off the goggles and the one glove and she watched him, expecting him to say something. *Anything.* The longer he was silent the less she expected and the more she *hoped*.

Hoped that he would break all this silence they were living in.

"You hungry?" he asked. "Because we have a ton of fish."

At home, Dad went right upstairs to find Mom and Ephie, leaving Brin alone in the silent shadowy kitchen. She walked along the rug from the kitchen into the dining room and didn't even think twice as she swiped her phone from jail.

Which was just the bottom drawer of the old hutch.

Mom always made a big show of locking it up, but Brin knew the dumb lock didn't work. She slipped the phone in her pocket and sneaked upstairs to her room, shutting the door and flopping down on her bed.

The opening notification beeps were so loud, she flinched, turned off the volume and put her pillow over the phone because she was feeling extra paranoid. She kept one eye on the door and an ear out for her parents in case they came rampaging down the hallway.

But her parents never came.

She was forgotten tonight, like she had been for most of the year. And she was going to take full advantage.

She screened through her texts. Mostly Jenny, who really couldn't remember when Brin's phone was in jail and just kept texting. Amanda, Jay. A stupid emoji from Jamal. Andrea Sapp with questions about French homework and then a random number with no name attached.

Hey. Mom took xtra shift. Going to house tonight. Wnt to come?

Brin nearly dropped her phone.

It was from yesterday night when she had been at Spring Assembly. When Troy had won the award but hadn't shown up.

Troy? she texted, then held the phone to her chest so she wouldn't just sit there and stare, waiting for the typing dots to appear. He wasn't going to text back. It was Friday night and he was probably out. Jenny and everyone were probably at a bonfire on Ferris, the remnants of which she would have to clean up on Sunday.

If she wanted to sneak out she could. One text to Jenny and she'd have some boy in a car waiting for her at the top of the street. She could drink enough shitty beer to forget this weird night.

Ephie squawked and she could hear the low murmur of her parents' voices, the creak of the floor as one of them went to check on her.

Brin didn't get out of bed. She didn't text Jenny. She lay on top of her green-and-white duvet, staring up at the ceiling, feeling like if she left, something might go wrong.

Something had happened tonight when she told Mrs. Fulbright to leave, and she didn't just feel older. She felt like her family needed her.

# Lindy

At 7:00 a.m. on Saturday Lindy was pulling the empty garbage cans from the curb back to their spot outside the old garage. One of the neighbors must have put them out last night. She was so worn thin that the kind gesture made her weepy. Made her want to bake everyone on the street muffins.

*God, last night.*

Brin… When she saw that girl next, she was going to give her a medal.

*I wish I'd been more like her when I was her age,* Lindy thought. The recycling can tipped on its wheels and she wrestled it back square. She wished she'd fought for her family the way Brin had, instead of just running away.

Despite the warm morning, the realization sent chills across her skin.

*We were always worth fighting for.* She just never knew how.

Her cell phone, tucked in the back pocket of her cutoff jeans, buzzed with an incoming text.

It was Dante.

Do you know John Blakley? he texted. He says he worked

with you at The Harvest. Lindy winced. She had no glowing recommendation for John.

I did, she texted back.

Can you work with him again?

Is this like a referral thing?

There was a long pause and the texting dots flashed on his side of the screen.

You realize I'm hiring you as manager of the bar, don't you? You'll be working with me and Jill in the kitchen. If you don't think John's a good hire, I don't hire him.

Management. She hadn't realized. She'd never been manager before. His faith made her proud and uncomfortable at the same time.

No, she texted. Don't hire John.

Okay. See you in a week!

She tucked the phone back into her pocket and pushed the recycling and garbage into the garage.

Never in her life had a week seemed so long and not nearly long enough.

From the porch, she could hear the landline ringing in the house. She caught it on the fourth ring.

"Hello?"

"Lindy?"

"Yeah. Dan? Is everything okay?"

"Yeah. I mean… I just… I'm calling because I need some help."

"Sure. Of course. What do you need?"

"Can you run the shop today?"

Of all the things she'd expected this wasn't it. "Yeah. But… what about Delia?"

"She's taking a day. Brin will be there around noon and I have charters. I'm already late—"

"Taking a day?" That sounded really un-Delia-like. "Is she okay?"

*I should have gone to her last night. I should have checked on her. I was so focused on Mom I forgot about Delia.*

"Of course she's okay," Dan said. "She's been working so hard. She just… She needs a break."

She could hear all the cracks in Dan's voice, and she rushed to make it better. To smooth over what she could. "Of course."

"Can you come soon? I have the baby and my charter is supposed to leave at eight."

If Mom remembered what happened last night she didn't say anything. Lindy didn't bring it up either. Maybe that was part of the problem of their house, but today it was pure survival instinct. Mom was delighted to go down to the shop again, and Lindy got them ready in record time. Just to be on the safe side, she called Tiffany and let her know that she might be needed later. Tiffany said she could rearrange a few things if she needed.

Mom wanted to walk, but Lindy wanted the car there in case Mom or the baby needed a quick getaway.

Mom, the baby and the shop—it seemed ridiculous.

*This is Dee's life every day.*

She drove Dan's truck around back to the harbor side of Queen Street and parked in his usual spot. She still had it from last night, when she'd had to get her mom home as quickly as possible after the visit from a certain patron.

Dan was waiting for them behind the shop, near the harbor. He had the baby in his arms, a diaper bag over his shoulder and the carrier at his feet.

Calm, unruffle-able Dan looked frayed.

The *Dreamer*, Dad's old boat, was in its usual slip. A group of four men sitting on the deck, a cooler between them. They kept checking their watches.

"You sure we won't miss out on the bass?" one of them asked.

"Trust me, boys," Dan said. "I've been fishing this lake for twenty years. I know where the bass are any time of day."

"Hey," Lindy said and Dan turned with an almost reverent look on his face.

"Thank god, Linds. Thank you for coming."

"It's not a problem," she said, though she couldn't be entirely sure of that.

Dan handed over Ephie and the bag. "I've written down her schedule. She has tons of stuff in there and Brin will be there at noon to help. I'll be off the water at three at the latest."

"Dan," she said. "If it gets bad, I'm closing the store and taking everyone back to the house. Just so you know."

"Of course." He seemed to suddenly realize that this was an option. That not opening the store and not trying to keep everything moving in exactly the same way as it always had was something he could do. "Do you want to just do that now?" he asked.

"Don't be ridiculous," Mom said. "We'll be fine."

It seemed unlikely but Lindy echoed her. "We'll be fine."

# *Meredith*

"*T*his…this doesn't seem like a good idea," Lindy said, but Meredith could sense she was starting to waver. The lunch rush was about to start and this idea was surefire. One hundred percent gold.

"It's a great idea," Meredith said. "Trust me."

Lindy shot her a dubious look. "Don't you think Delia will have something to say about using her daughter as advertising?"

"The baby's got to go somewhere and Delia threw away the damn fish sign. Put the swing up."

Lindy hooked the jumpy swing contraption on to the top of the doorway to the shop. Not the office doorway or the storage room doorway. The main door.

Lindy opened both doors today, letting in the fresh air, sunlight and hopefully a bunch of customers. Meredith wasn't sure the last time she'd seen the shop with the doors wide open; it was a good thing.

Lindy had also been cleaning like the devil. Throwing away all the old stuff on the shelves and scrubbing them hard.

And now the baby was happily jumping in one of the doorways, leaving the other side open.

Meredith sat herself down in her old camp chair to the left of the doorway and let Ephie work her magic. The girl was a born flirt. Reminded her of Lindy as a baby. All smiles and spit bubbles. Never met a stranger, that was Lindy.

"Come on in," Meredith said to people on the street, and most of them did, because Meredith was an old lady and lots of people had a hard time refusing old ladies. And if by chance they were able to resist her, they fell for Ephie.

So much better than that old fish sign.

"This some knew kind of tactic?" a man asked, standing in front of the sun so Meredith couldn't quite make out his face. But she recognized the uniform.

"Hello, Chief Singh."

"Mrs. McAvoy," he said so polite. "How are you today?"

"Can't complain. You?"

"I suppose I can't either."

"You here to see my daughter?"

Oh heavens, that boy could be made to blush with nothing.

"No, ma'am, I'm here for a whitefish sandwich."

"Sure you are."

"Holy cats. It's getting warm in there." Lindy came out, cobwebs strung in her hair and a smudge of dust across her face.

A cloud slipped over the sun, and the sidewalk and shop were cast in cool, cool shade, and Meredith could see Chief Singh real clear.

*Good*, Meredith thought as she watched the two lovebirds notice each other.

"Hello, Garrett," Lindy said. She put a hand through her hair, trying her dangedest to be flirty, and ran into the cobwebs. Meredith smothered a laugh.

"Hey, Lindy," he said. "Whole lot of activity going on around here."

"Fixing up the joint," she said. "Making a few changes."

"As long as they aren't changes to the whitefish salad sandwich."

"I think we'd lose our license if we did that. You just passing by—?"

"Nope. I get lunch here on Saturdays."

"Every Saturday?"

"Every one."

"What will all the other restaurants in town say, Chief? If you're showing us all the love."

"I spread my love around."

Meredith wondered if she needed to get the hose, spray them down like two cats howling in the backyard.

"What's your Monday spot?"

"Leftovers," he said. "From Mom's Sunday dinner."

"Tuesday?"

"Subway."

"By the beach?"

"That's the one."

"Wednesday?"

"My day off."

"Thursday?"

"Cora's."

"Friday?"

"Drunk Duck. Your fish fry took a chunk out of their business."

"Am I supposed to be sorry?"

"No. But I think I am. Your fish fry is better than theirs."

They grinned at each other like fools, but Meredith kept her mouth shut because that Singh boy was one of the good ones.

"Well, come on in. I'd hate to mess with the system." Lindy

vanished back into the shop and Chief Singh followed, like he always did.

The cloud passed, leaving the sun high up over the harbor. There was something in the breeze that made her miss the boats. The whistle of the wind in the rigging.

"Hey, Gran."

Meredith shaded her eyes. It was Lindy standing there. Young Lindy. With red hair down her back, freckles across her nose. A girl on the edge of something, that was Lindy.

"What are you doing here, girl?" Meredith asked.

"Dad said I had to come down and work. Mom's not feeling well."

"I'm feeling fine," Meredith said. "Let's go get you something to eat."

It took her a few tries to push up and out of the camp chair. Her knees felt unpredictable and her vision was swimming at the corner of her eyes, but she got herself up and into the store.

The shop looked different. Messier. Lindy changing things around again. Girl had a lot of great ideas but she had a tendency to get halfway through them and then become distracted. Like she was right now. There was a boy leaning against the counter while Lindy made a whitefish sandwich.

It wasn't a boy, really. It was a man standing there. That damn Eric Fulbright sniffing around Lindy again.

"You have to go," she said, but no one heard her. Or if they did they ignored her.

Honest-to-god it amazed Meredith that Lindy could look at that boy and not see the night William died. Not see the sullen, pimple-faced teenager who had stood at the top of the stairs and watched them on that roof. He didn't help. He didn't talk. He just watched them work their hearts out on a lost cause. Meredith didn't like the boy then and she sure as hell didn't like him now.

If Lindy didn't have shame, didn't she have sense? Or respect?

"Eric Fulbright," Meredith said a little bit louder, and that got everyone's attention.

"You have to go."

"Mom?" Lindy's eyebrows creased over her eyes. She was embarrassed, but this was long overdue. This was what William would have done. Gotten rid of this tomcat sniffing around the back door.

She never did like the Fulbrights, building that big house that blocked out the lake.

Meredith crossed her arms and put on a disapproving parent face, and Eric's smile was gone for good.

"I'm sorry." Lindy was out from around the counter.

"Lindy," the boy said quietly. "I remember this with my grandpa. It's okay. I need to head on out anyway."

"Your grandpa was a nasty old man," Meredith said. "And mean as a snake."

But who was she saying that to? She didn't know Eric Fulbright's grandfather from Adam. And it wasn't that Fulbright boy standing there. It was Chief Singh, whose grandpa could find fault in a sunrise and was not kind to Chief Singh and his mom. The whole town knew it, and they smiled at him anyway. Called out hello when they saw him down at Barker's Hardware.

It occurred to her now, in a way it didn't then, that they should have done something. Said something.

But the town had been silent.

The mean people, who are cruel out one side of their mouth and smile out the other side, it took a lot of courage to stand up to them. The smile made the cruelty seem imagined. The smile made it feel impolite to say anything. And they'd been taught being polite was the most important thing. It made the community work. The family.

*My family.*

"Mrs. McAvoy?" he asked, his face all folded up with concern.

Lindy handed him a sandwich and he reached for his wallet. But Lindy shook her head, not accepting payment.

When he was out the door, Meredith turned to face her daughter, expecting to find her angry.

But all her glitter and shine were gone.

"You feeling all right?" she asked carefully.

"Right as rain." It was a lie and Lindy could probably tell, but the truth wasn't something she wanted to say out loud.

*I'm scared.*

# TWENTY-THREE

## *Lindy*

Mom went willingly with Tiffany, sitting in the passenger seat with the St. Christopher medal between her fingers. Her face worried. She hadn't recovered after mistaking Garrett for Eric Fulbright. Time just kept shifting under her feet and she knew something was wrong. But she gathered up her pride and made herself stiff with it. Prickly. A defensive strategy for sure.

Lindy, Brin and the baby waved goodbye from the front of the store, but Mom looked resolutely ahead.

"She's mad," Brin said.

"Yeah. But she'll get over it." She hoped.

Lindy pulled Ephie into her arms and stared out at Main Street, at the pretty spring Saturday and all the people enjoying it.

*Mom just thought Garrett was Eric Fulbright.* There wasn't any resemblance, not in body or character, and she felt like she needed to apologize to Garrett all day to make up for the mistake, for those awful things her mom had said about his grandfather. She'd never seen her mother that way. Maybe it was the disease. Maybe it was Gloria Fulbright showing up last night, throwing every McAvoy into a tailspin.

"How's your mom?" Lindy asked Brin.

"I don't know really."

"I'm sorry."

"It's not your fault."

"You were amazing last night," Lindy said. "Kicking her out."

"I thought everyone would be mad."

"Not at all. I'm erecting a statue in your honor."

Brin laughed and Lindy felt the sting of tears behind her eyes.

"Want something to eat?" she asked, changing the subject because she could hardly be the cool aunt and burst into tears.

"Is there anything other than whitefish salad?"

"You don't like whitefish salad?" Lindy said like such a thing wasn't possible.

"It's disgusting."

"I'm pretty sure that makes you not a part of this family."

Brin rolled her eyes but followed her into the shop.

"What are you doing?" Brin asked, looking around at the mess Lindy had been making.

Lindy put Ephie in the high chair behind the counter, and she immediately started wailing like she was sitting on pins. It was amazing what the sound of a crying baby did to her heart rate. Worse than a Saturday night rush behind the bar when one of the backs called in sick. She was panicky, losing track of where she was in the sandwich-making process.

"Aunt Lindy?"

She fumbled around, putting Cheerios on the high chair tray, which calmed Ephie down for the moment.

"You okay?"

"Yep. I've been cleaning mostly."

226

"I don't think some of this stuff has been cleaned...like ever."

"Yeah. I can tell," Lindy laughed. "I'm glad you're here."

"Are you going to make me clean?"

"Well, you have some options. Clean or babysit Ephie."

"I'll clean."

That seemed terribly sad, but what did she know about teenage girls dealing with the sudden appearance of baby sisters? Her sister had been the most important relationship in her life.

The truth of that was a little shocking.

Lindy handed her the hastily made sandwich.

"What is it?" Brin asked skeptically.

"The very sophisticated and hard to like, much less enjoy, smooth peanut butter and grape jelly sandwich."

"I have a peanut allergy."

"Oh." Lindy's mouth dropped and her shoulders slumped. "Oh god, I didn't... I'm sorry. I didn't know."

"It's okay," Brin said, handing back the sandwich. "How would you?"

"I'll make you something else," Lindy said. "Turkey?"

"Sure," Brin said with a shrug.

Turkey sandwich made, Lindy left Brin in charge of the shop and took the baby into the back. She managed to get Ephie to sleep, which frankly made her feel like some kind of superhero.

The bell over the door started ringing around 1:00 p.m, and didn't let up. At first Lindy thought people were coming in to pick up dinner, but she caught on soon enough. They were all buying just enough fish that it didn't seem like they were coming in simply to gawk. She braced for the worst. Some version of Jeannette Bracker over and over again, but she was pleasantly surprised when old friends showed up.

It went on that way for half an hour. Whitefish filets, one or two at a time, until they sold out.

She was bagging up the last of them for her old high school science teacher when Ephie stirred in the back.

"Aunt Lindy," Brin said. "Ephie's crying."

"Go grab her, would you?"

"Me?"

Lindy looked up at her puzzled and then she realized—Brin didn't help with the baby.

"You," Lindy said.

# Brin

The baby stunk. And she was wet. Like wet all the way through. She was wet in weird places like the top of her head, and Brin wondered if she peed in everything and rolled in it.

Ugh.

Gross.

Brin leaned over the baby and Ephie grinned up at her.

"You're gross," Brin told her.

Ephie laughed and reached for Brin's hair, grabbing it in her fists.

"Ouch," Brin said, but the baby pulled harder, jerking her hands up and down like she was just having the best time. Brin picked her up and untangled her hair from Ephie's fists. She immediately leaned forward to gum at Brin's cheek.

"Oh my god," she breathed, so grossed out. "My face is not Mom's boob."

Brin put her down on the change table and pulled off her onesie, trying not to gag.

At the beginning, Mom tried to get Brin to be "an active

participant" with Ephie and had her change a diaper a few times, but Brin made it clear that she wasn't interested.

Brin's stomach flipped and squeezed as she thought about her mom in that blue bathrobe today well past the time she was usually up and changed.

"Well, will you look at this," Dad said, and Brin whirled around.

"Whoa, whoa." He rushed forward from the back door. "You can't take your eyes or your hands off her on the table."

"Why? Where's she gonna go?" Brin asked, putting her hand down on Ephie's bare tummy. The baby absolutely shrieked with laughter.

"She could roll off. She's gotten pretty good at flipping over onto her stomach. Hey, happy girl," he cooed down at Ephie, who literally went ballistic at the sight of him. Like… it was kind of hard not to smile she was so freaking happy.

"You were changing her diaper?"

"Yeah." Brin motioned as if to move away, but her dad stepped back.

"Don't let me stop you."

She finished the diaper, but every time Brin put Ephie's foot in her pajamas, she kicked it out.

"She doesn't want to get dressed," Brin said, so over this.

"Sure she does," Dad laughed.

"No, she's like making this so hard—"

"She's a baby, Brin," he said. "Be the grown-up."

*Be the grown-up.* What a stupid thing to say. Since he couldn't see her, Brin rolled her eyes. Not much bugged Dad but rolling her eyes at him would have *consequences.*

"How did everything go today?"

"Lindy's been working really hard, cleaning a bunch of stuff. And we sent Gran home a little while ago. Tiffany came and got her."

"She got tired?"

"Confused. She thought Garrett Singh was that Fulbright boy."

Dad was silent and she looked up to see him wiping his hand over his face. She wanted to ask him about Gloria Fulbright but he seemed so tired.

"Hey," Lindy said, coming to stand in the doorway. "I thought I heard another voice back here."

Ephie had curled up against Brin's chest, her hand tucked into the neck of her shirt, and Brin couldn't say it was bad. Whatever was wet on her head was dry now and it didn't smell like pee. It smelled...well, kind of nice actually. Powdery.

"Lindy," Dad said with his careful smile. "Brin tells me you're doing some work here."

"I'm just...helping. Cleaning mostly."

"Does Delia know?"

"We talked about it yesterday. She said I could make some changes."

"Well, this place could use some changes. Brin," he said and reached for the baby, "go grab your stuff. We'll close up and head on home."

"We're closing early?"

"Why not?"

If Dad broke down in tears that could not be weirder.

Brin handed him the baby, swallowing down the urge to apologize, though for what she wasn't sure. It was just that nothing seemed right. And lots of things that upset her parents these days were her fault.

Brin walked through the door to the booth in front where she'd stored her bookbag. On the way she flipped the sign to Closed and locked the door. In the back room, Lindy and Dad were talking in low tones.

"We're out of fish," Lindy said.

"What? The walleye?"

"All of it."

"How?"

"Well, two filets at a time for most of the day. Lots of people coming in to see the prodigal daughter returned."

"Maybe we should have sold tickets, too."

"Maybe tomorrow," Lindy said and the two of them chuckled. "If that's…you know. Cool."

"It is with me. The work you've done today. It's amazing."

"I don't mean to step on anyone's toes," Lindy said, all the laughter gone from her voice.

"It's not that. It's your shop. Your family. I've just… I've been trying to make some changes around here for years. Delia shuts me down every time."

"I'm as surprised as you are. I think maybe…she's just really tired. I caught her in a weak moment."

"Yeah," Dad said. "I think it might be more than that."

It was quiet for so long that Brin realized she was holding her breath.

"Mom said Dee had postpartum depression after Brin. That maybe she has it again?"

"Delia says she's fine."

"Well, isn't there a chance that's the depression talking? And Gloria Fulbright showing up here last night—"

"Yeah. That didn't help."

Dad dropped his voice but Brin was an excellent eavesdropper.

"You haven't been here. You don't know what it's like. We trapped her here."

"Who?"

"You and me!"

"Dan," Lindy gasped. "It's been seventeen years. You can't still feel guilty."

"Don't you?"

The bookbag dropped from Brin's hand, a hard heavy thunk, and both Dad and Lindy stepped out of the back office.

"You all right?" he asked.

"Fine," Brin said, grabbing the bookbag with shaking hands and struggling to get it over her shoulder. "I just want to go home."

# Lindy

*A* few hours after Brin and Dan left, Lindy locked up the shop.

The shelves were now cleared and cleaned. So were the fridges. The stuff in the back corners and forgotten, expired jars of coleslaw and herring, all met their appropriate end.

If it was up to her, she'd spend the next week making calls to wineries and breweries in the area. Local farms. Maybe a beekeeper and a woodworker. She'd offer them a commission if they wanted to give her product to sell. She'd change the order from the paper supplier so they would have salad packaging and look for a used, cheap cold case online.

In two weeks' time, the McAvoy Bait, Fish and Lunch Counter could be completely different.

*But I'll be gone in one.*

Funny, she just wasn't as excited about the job now as she'd been this morning.

It was a clear May night and she could smell a bonfire in the distance. Probably Ferris Beach. Fulbright House out in the harbor was still lit up with its for-sale sign. The moon was full. Or if not full, at least close enough.

There was a familiar feeling under her skin. A restless achy itch.

*It's been seventeen years. You can't still feel guilty.*

*Don't you?*

Across the street the Drunk Duck had its doors open, the sound of Bon Jovi slipping out into the early evening summer sunlight, accompanied by a woman's laugh.

She pulled out her cell phone and called Nirosha.

"Hey, girl!" Nirosha yelled, over the mayhem in the background. "What are you doing?"

"Any chance you can sneak away for a quick drink down at the Duck?"

"Ahh! I'd love to. Can we do it at eight?"

Lindy looked at her watch. That was two hours away and if she went back to her mom's the night would be over. "I can't," she said. "I've got a little window right now."

"Sorry, it's dinner here and Brian isn't home for another hour and a bit. You could come." There was a crash and a shout and she heard a long slow exhale, like Nirosha was counting to ten.

"Nirosha, you go. We'll try again another time."

"Right. Okay. Thanks for trying."

Lindy hung up. Going in alone felt risky. Word would get out pretty fast that Lindy McAvoy was over at the Duck.

But she was tired of Port Lorraine having something to say about her.

Without a second thought she crossed the street and stepped up the cracked cement ramp. The Drunk Duck was the same as ever. Old Christmas lights up along the back. The printed sign on the graying and spotty mirror behind the bar: NO TABS. NO DOGS. NO ASSHOLES.

Lindy sat at the bar and felt a small ripple of awareness run through the place. The guy behind the bar, a handsome man Lindy didn't recognize, tossed a coaster in front of her. "What can I get you?" he asked.

"Gin and tonic. Tall."

He nodded and stepped away to make her drink.

"Well, well, look what the cat dragged home."

Lindy braced herself and turned to see former football player Phil Kincaid. The son of a bitch didn't look like he'd aged at all; his blond hair was still thick and his jaw hadn't lost its edge.

Lindy smiled at the first blush of memories. Jumping the fence at the country club to go skinny-dipping. Phil was one of the few guys who liked to dance and he was a good time out on that dance floor. He'd been in her history class the year they went out to Put-in-Bay when they were studying the War of 1812. She and Nirosha had smoked their first cigarettes with him.

"Phil," she said with a sincere smile. "You have not changed a bit."

"Neither have you, girl. I mean, look at you."

His eyes walked all over her and she was reminded of other memories. Rushing Phil to the hospital after he got into a fight with Jerome and they fell into the bonfire. Phil always rested hard on his image as a good guy. The guy you could count on for a ride home when everyone else had already left. The guy you could bum smokes off. Or who always had a flask at the school dances.

But at the end of the night, after a few drinks, that act ended pretty fast.

"Put that gin and tonic on my tab," Phil said.

"It's all right—"

"I insist. A little welcome home drink for an old friend."

He sat down next to her. Phil Kincaid still smelled like a

teenage boy, and at this moment, raw and fraught from the day, exhausted by the demands and pressures of adulthood, she found that smell outrageously appealing.

Like how the errant whiff of a Marlboro Light at the right moment could remind her of all the ways she used to love smoking.

Sometimes it was easy to ignore the bad, if you needed the good enough.

"So what have you been up to, McAvoy? Breaking hearts?"

"Only the ones that need breaking."

"Heard you were like a big-shot chef or something in Cleveland."

"Bartender."

"You can be a big-shot bartender?"

"Apparently. So, what have you been up to, Phil?" Her question got a litany from him about his two kids, one with an ex-wife and one with an ex-girlfriend, and how they don't let him see the kids unless he pays.

"Child support," she said pointedly. "That's kind of the whole point."

"I guess," he said petulantly into his drink.

After a little more small talk about former classmates, none of whom she stayed in touch with and most she wasn't too interested in, she was sorry Phil had sat beside her. She should have just gone home.

"So," he said, leaning close after he'd had another drink. "We had some good times together, didn't we, McAvoy?"

"Yes, we did," she said and leaned away. Lindy remembered with a kind of full body gag the way she'd let Phil feel her up in high school. She'd kiss him with tongue and hope that would be enough for him to let her out of his car.

"You gonna be nicer this time around?"

"Probably not."

He came closer and she could feel his breath. "You fucking McAvoys, always acting like your shit don't stink. But I know what happened to your sister. How she begged that Fulbright—"

Lindy smacked him hard across the face. His head snapped back and when he got it on straight again, she jumped out of her chair in case she needed to make a run for it.

But then a big hand clapped down on Phil's shoulders.

"Phil. I think it's time you went on home," Garrett announced.

"Did you see what that bitch did? You gonna arrest her?"

"No, Phil. I'm going to give you to the count of three to get the hell out of here."

Garrett lifted his hand from Phil's shoulder. Phil pounded back what was left of his drink and set it back on the bar with a heavy thunk. "Later days, Linds," he said. He did one of those jerk moves, fake lunging for her, but before she could even jump Garrett had him pulled around by the neck and was walking him to the door.

She collapsed against the bar, adrenaline pulsing through her body.

"I'm sorry," the bartender said, his face creased in sincerity. "I should have booted him an hour ago."

"You all right?" Garrett asked when he came back. "A glass of water," he said to the bartender. "I never did like that guy."

Lindy nodded and took her time drinking her water, gathering up the frayed and fragmented parts of herself before finally turning to face Garrett.

The sight of that man out of uniform never got old. He wore a T-shirt and jeans that hung just right over his body. Whatever product he used to keep those curls in line had given up.

All the adrenaline in her bloodstream shifted direction and

she managed to flip back her hair and put her hand on her hip with sheer white-knuckled bravado.

"I've been a bartender for over ten years, Garrett. The day I can't handle a drunk is the day I have to turn in my cocktail shaker."

"Is that so?"

"Official bartender rules," she said with a small smile. She lifted her almost full gin and tonic. "Why don't you join me? Unless you're meeting someone."

It was hard to imagine Garrett just stopping at the Duck for a beer by himself.

"No, once a month I have a beer with the fire chief and we just finished up."

"The fire chief?"

"And the coast guard commander when she can make it."

"That sounds like the beginning of a joke."

"I've been working on the punch line for a few years, but really all we do is argue about whether or not we should try to get another stoplight put in on South Shore."

"Public safety is no laughing matter."

His grin, the way it curled up at the side, was a powerful force, and she was simply too weak to resist.

"Well, then how about you let me buy you a drink?" she offered.

"I'd love a drink," Garrett finally said, his knee brushing her thigh, his elbow touching hers and then shifting away as he sat down.

"Chief?" the bartender said.

"Bud Light. Draft."

"Have you tried the Great Lakes Brewery?" she asked, recognizing one of the microbrews on tap. "It's a lager. Light. Way better than the Bud Light."

"That's your professional opinion?"

"Well, it's not that pinot grigio you brought over the other night, but it's very good." Garrett changed his order and she tried not to feel a little thrill.

"I'm sorry about what my mom said today," Lindy said.

"It's okay. It's not like I was unaware that my grandpa was a mean old man."

"She thought you were a Fulbright." The insult of that was shocking; never were there two more different men.

Garrett sighed. "It's the disease, Linds," he said, and her heart warmed at the old nickname. So different out of his mouth. "That's all. It's not personal. It's hard to remember that some days, but it's the truth. It's not personal."

"Your granddad must have made it pretty hard as he got sick."

"You know, it's strange actually. Some days he was so sweet, sweeter than he'd ever been. Like whatever was keeping him from showing his feelings would be taken out by the disease. I remember him just holding my hand and telling me how proud he was of me. It was a shock. But then, you know the next day he'd throw his bedpan at my mom's head and say something racist about my dad. So, it wasn't like he was a totally different man."

"God forbid," Lindy said.

"Exactly."

They both took a sip of their drinks and Garrett made a happy sound. "That is good."

"Always trust a professional." Lindy smiled. "So, how did you decide on police chief?"

"I wanted to get into the academy since I was a kid."

"I didn't know that."

"You were too busy kissing me to ask about my career path."

Unbelievably she felt herself blush and Garrett bumped her shoulder with his.

"For the record," she said. "You kissed me."

"That's...not how I remember it," he said, a fake furrow in his brow. For a second their eyes caught and the bar fell away, and it was just the two of them like no time had passed. The memories of that summer like tiny fires between them.

It would take nothing to stoke those fires. She could press her knee just slightly into the side of his thigh. When she set her glass down it could be just that much closer to his, so when she let go the backs of her fingers might touch the backs of his.

But he shifted out absentmindedly, opening up the cocoon of their bodies, letting in the rest of the bar and the cold air from the open door.

"So," she scrambled. "Tell me now, why a police officer?"

"My dad was a cop in Cleveland. Killed by a tweaker robbing a corner store with a semiautomatic rifle."

"Oh my god, Garrett. I never knew..." Lindy whispered.

Garret nodded, his mouth pulled taut. "Mom buried Dad and packed us up and we moved back here. With her dad. But I always planned on following in Dad's footsteps."

"But you stayed here, in Port."

"It's home. Good, bad or otherwise, it's home. I like the idea of a small community. Being a part of that. Working with kids. Helping to keep it safe."

She realized she liked that, too. The idea of feeding her neighbors. Watching the town grow up through the windows of the store...

"I always thought you'd stay in Port, too," he said, turning his pint glass on the cardboard coaster in front of him. "Take over the shop. Ed's, too, while you were at it. Make a monopoly of things on Queen Street."

"How is your mom?" Lindy said. She remembered Garrett's mom as a sweet woman until it came time to cheer Garrett on at his lacrosse tournaments, when she became bloodthirsty.

"Changing the subject, Lindy?"

"Trying to," she said, looking down at the bar, pretending with all her might to be casual.

"In Florida most of the year," he said after a moment. "She comes back for the summer to sit on the beach and harass me over not giving her grandbabies."

"Why aren't you giving her grandbabies?"

"Not you, too!" He smiled and took another sip and then set the glass down carefully in the center of his coaster. "I was married a few years ago."

That made her freeze. That he'd met someone, been married and divorced in the years that had passed. And yes, she was aware that it had been seventeen of them.

It's just that she'd done so little with that time. A couple of shitty jobs that led to better jobs, that led occasionally to a great one she loved, until somehow she screwed it up and started the cycle all over again. A series of boyfriends she knew she was never going to love, and who were never going to love her either.

"What happened?"

"We just weren't...right. She kept thinking I had bigger goals than Port Lorraine and I kept thinking she'd stop pushing me to have bigger goals. Luckily we figured it out before there were grandbabies."

"Another?" the bartender said and Lindy realized she'd finished her drink.

She nodded but Garrett declined.

"What about you?" Garrett asked. "You giving your mom any grandbabies?"

"No babies. No exes of significance."

"Just a string of broken hearts?"

"Not even that."

"I find that hard to believe."

242

She laughed. "Why?"

"Because you broke my heart." He said it lightly, but the words fell like granite.

When she was silent, he laughed and said, "Don't pretend you didn't know."

"There's nothing to pretend. I didn't know."

"Why do you think I showed up at the ice cream shop all the time?"

"Your sister liked ice cream?"

"She's lactose intolerant," he said. "She ate cotton candy all those nights."

"You're joking."

"Cross my heart."

"I thought…" Her drink arrived just in time and she put her lips around the little red straw to stop herself from revealing too much.

"What?" he asked. "What did you think?"

"That you were trying to get a piece of the *wild* McAvoy sister," she said dramatically to lighten the mood.

"A piece—?" He put down his beer. His eyes on hers were serious and sure. "No."

"Come on," she cajoled. His seriousness made her uncomfortable. "I knew my own reputation."

"Lindy. That wasn't why I came to the ice cream shop. I liked you. I liked everything about you and I could not have cared less about your reputation."

She opened her mouth to make a joke, but none came.

"I wish I'd been able to talk to you. Any girl, really. But especially you. There wasn't a whole lot of time in my house for me to talk to my mom about girls. Not between my grand-dad and my sister and her job. I turned fifteen, Mom gave me a box of condoms and told me that I could never have sex without one. I hadn't even kissed a girl at that point."

"Oh my gosh." Lindy laughed and couldn't wait to tell her sister. "At least you got the condoms. Would you like to hear the sex ed conversation my mother gave me and Delia?"

"Lay it on me," he said with a sweep of his arm.

She swiveled on her stool to face him and projected her best Meredith McAvoy with one finger up in the air, sort of declarative but also a little accusing.

"You play. You pay."

He blinked, clearly expecting more. There was no more.

"That's it?"

"That. Is. It."

Garrett shook his head. "What...what does that even mean?"

She returned to her drink. "Excellent question, Chief Singh. Excellent question."

"I'm sorry I never got myself together to ask you out," he said, leaning toward her. "For real. Not just making out behind the ice cream shop."

"I don't know, that making out was better than a lot of dates I've been on. I'm sorry I broke your heart."

She was electrically aware of him. Of the precise distance between their knees. The inches between their fingers on the edge of the bar. If she were braver or as bold as everyone in this town believed, she would touch him. Put her fingers against his and see what would happen.

"So you're fixing up the shop," he said, his hands on his knees.

"Just cleaning it for now."

"That place deserves to be something special."

It was breathtaking how clearly—how casually—he said what was in her heart.

"No offense to your sister. She's worked so hard. But if anyone can make it special, it's you."

She tilted her head and studied him sideways for a second. Where did all this faith in her come from? Was it just smoke? But to what end? Lord knew if he wanted a piece of the wild McAvoy girl now, he would not have to work so hard.

"That's nice of you to say. Delia's got her hands full. Mom, the baby, the shop. Brin."

"I work with a lot of kids," Garrett said softly, quietly, and Lindy leaned in so she could hear him. "The after-school program and community service. And this stuff with Brin—it's not serious—"

"I know."

"But it could be. She's angry and she's smart. And that can be a pretty lethal combination."

Lindy realized that everyone had been banking on the smart part of that equation leveling out the angry. "That's very true, Chief Singh."

Garret finished his beer and stood up. "How are you getting home?"

"Taking the shortcut."

"Walking?"

Lindy nodded.

"I'll give you a ride."

"Can I turn on the lights?"

"No."

"Can I try the siren?"

"You can sit in the passenger seat and wear your seat belt."

"I'll take it," she said and placed a tip on the bar. There was a time in her life when she wouldn't have left a half-finished drink behind. But finishing every drink was a young woman's game.

"You're paying Cleveland prices." Garrett tried to hand her back one of the fives.

"Overtipping is my religion," she said and put the five back down.

245

They walked from the bar down Second Avenue toward the station. The night had the warm kiss of summer in it. A hint of July's breeze. The promise of August's heat. The stars were bright overhead. The moon skewered by the masts in the harbor. For the moment, hopeful and pure, Lindy was happy to be home.

Even with the Phil Kincaids. Because for every Phil there was a Nirosha.

A Garrett.

She was in fact so deliriously happy that she reached out and grabbed Garrett's hand.

On the side street where his cruiser was parked, it was dark and quiet, the businesses of Queen Street behind them, on the other side of the shadows. It felt like they were in a pocket. Hidden. Secret.

Garrett's hand was warm and solid in hers. She touched the calluses at the base of his fingers and grew reckless at the sensation of his rough skin against hers.

"I'd like to kiss you," she whispered.

He shifted to face her and she could feel the light bump of his body against hers. His fingers brushed her cheek, her jaw-line, slid into the hair at the nape of her neck.

"I would like to kiss you, too."

His lips, when they touched hers, were careful—two teenagers all grown up. She stepped closer; he pulled her in.

Things became less careful. Their hands found their way under shirts and onto skin.

"Take me home," she said into his mouth. "To your house."

She thought about Tiffany up at Mom's, probably wanting to get home. About Delia and what she would say when she found out she went home with Garrett.

And then, with the old skill, she just stopped thinking about them. It's how she'd survived her long exile.

But he pulled away, leaned back when she tried to kiss him again. His fingers let go of her hair and gripped, instead, her shoulders. Air brushed between their chests and then their stomachs.

"Are you going to pretend you don't want to?" she asked.

He shook his head. "No."

"Then what's the problem?"

"No problem. I just… How about a date before we go back to my place?"

"A date?"

"Dinner. Drinks. Maybe a movie? A *date*."

"Oh god, Garrett. If you don't want—"

He stepped forward, grabbed her waist. "Of course I want you. You know I do. But you've never understood that I want more."

"More what?" she said, stunned.

"More of you. More than sex. More than a piece of the wild McAvoy sister."

Lindy rolled her eyes and stepped back. This had been a weird day followed by a terrible rejection. She just wanted to go home.

"I'll walk," she said.

"You know," he said, grabbing her hand, gathering up her fingers in his. "In high school, I didn't know how to tell you how much I liked you. I thought you'd figure it out, some-how. But I know that by not telling you, you thought I was like every other guy who was just interested in seeing how wild the wild McAvoy sister could be. And now you're back. And maybe it's nothing. Maybe it's a second chance. But I'm not making that mistake again."

She was aware, standing in that pocket of Port Lorraine evening, with this boy that she'd liked but dismissed, that she was still the girl she'd been. Because the last seventeen years, despite moving away and living a new life, lovers and jobs and success and failure, she'd been stuck. Waiting.

To come home.

But, as she knew now, she'd only turn right around and leave it—this man, this town, her family, all of it. All over again.

It made her sad, the years she'd wasted, building a life that meant so little. She'd kept her life small, filling her pockets with things she didn't really want so it wouldn't hurt if she lost them.

"I'm not staying," she said. "I'm going back to Cleveland in a week."

She could sense his shock, but he recovered quickly. "That's too bad," he said and took a step back.

"I have a life to get back to," she said, forcing her hands not to reach for him. Hold on to him.

"I'm sure you do."

"And it's not like Delia's made it easy—"

"Lindy?"

"What?"

"Who are you trying to convince?"

# TWENTY-FOUR
## *Delia*

*T*hey were home. All of them. The kids and Dan. She could hear them downstairs in the kitchen. The smell of a frozen pizza in the oven wafted upstairs and she wanted to go down and smile and eat and tell them she was okay. She wanted to laugh with her daughter and her husband.

She got as far as the stairs and sat down on the top step.

Dan's voice in the kitchen was a low murmur, but then his footsteps grew louder as he walked down the hallway, turned up the staircase and stopped in front of her.

"Hey," he said and she could tell he was surprised to see her.

"Hey."

"You okay?"

"Better." That wasn't quite a lie. Or maybe it was.

"Good."

"How was the day?"

"Action packed apparently," he said. "We sold out of fish because everyone wanted to come see Lindy. Lindy cleaned the place pretty much top to bottom. She's making a lot of changes."

"Good."

"You think so?"

"Yeah. Don't you?"

"I think it's really good." He took another step and then another and then sat down beside her. She leaned toward him, putting her shoulder on his, just to see if she could feel anything.

He leaned back against her, turned his head so he could kiss her temple.

"I'm scared," he whispered. "I don't know how to help you when you're like this."

"I know." She didn't know how to help herself.

They sat in silence for a few more seconds and it wasn't comfortable. If she went downstairs she'd bring the silence with her. Brin would stop laughing. Take her pizza and go to her room. Exhausted, Dan would yawn and she would tell him to go to sleep. That happiness downstairs, she'd ruin it. She was already ruining it now from the top step.

"I want to go see my mom and Lindy," she said.

"Really?"

She imagined Mom and Lindy back up at the house. Playing gin rummy on the back deck, pushing the cats off the table when they insisted on sitting on the discard pile. Iced tea and chips. Maybe Lindy would make tomato sandwiches and she could pretend for just a few hours that the years had not passed. That life could be simple.

"Yes." She said it again. "Yes." And then again until it was true.

"Then go."

"The girls—"

"I got it, babe," he said.

"I pumped," she said. "It's in the fridge."

"Then we're good. Go see your sister and then come back to us. We'll be here."

# Brin

$M$om left. She just left without saying anything. Dad got weird and sad, and Brin ate her pizza alone at the kitchen counter. It was so quiet in the house that the buzz of her phone deep in her bookbag made her jump. But no one was there to hear it.

Or care.

She dug out her contraband phone. It was a text from Troy.

Going 2nite. Want 2 come.

Her heart leapt a little. The Fulbright House.

What time?

After 12. Waiting for full dark.

There were a million reasons it was a bad idea. A million.

Where do I meet U?

# Delia

Delia took the van, not noticing until she was parked out front that she was wearing old yoga pants and a fleece that had seen better days.

Tiffany's car was in the driveway, and Lindy's Toyota was nowhere to be found.

"Mom?" she said, opening the door and poking her head in. "Tiffany?"

There was the squeal of the ancient couch and then Tiffany walked into the kitchen.

"Hey there, Delia."

"Tiffany? What are you doing here?"

"Lindy called me from the store when your mom had a little trouble."

*A little trouble?* "Where is Lindy?" Delia asked, setting down her purse on the kitchen counter.

"On her way. She called a few minutes ago."

"Why don't you go on home?" Delia said. "I can wait here with Mom."

Tiffany took the opportunity and headed out the back door.

Delia found Mom in her chair watching TV. *Modern Family*, her favorite.

"Hey, Mom." Delia leaned down and kissed her forehead.

Mom smiled up at her. "Dee," she said. "You hungry?"

"I'm good. How about you?"

"Tiffany made sandwiches. Not half bad. What are you doing here?"

That was a big question with a lot of answers.

"Mom, do you have any wine?" she asked.

"Under the sink."

There was an ancient bottle of Asti, probably a holiday gift from a neighbor years ago, and Delia found two wineglasses from the cupboard above the fridge where household goods went to die. She put ice in both glasses. Asti in one. Sprite in the other.

"You want to sit outside?" Delia held the wineglasses in her hand. "Bugs aren't bad."

Mom got up and made her way to the back door. Her left foot was moving slower than usual and Delia had to wonder if going to the shop was a bad idea.

"Are we celebrating?" Mom said, pushing open the screen door and holding it for Delia to follow.

"You bet," Delia said.

"Where's Lindy?"

"I'm sure she'll be here soon."

Mom took a sip from her wineglass and immediately scowled at Dee. "You drinking Sprite or do you have the real stuff in there?"

"The real stuff."

"That's not fair."

"You're right. But it's just kinda the way it is."

Car lights illuminated the lilac bushes at the top of the driveway. There was a door slam and then the car drove away.

"William?" Mom said, turning toward the walkway.

"No, Mom," she said just as Lindy came around the corner, looking tired. But once she caught sight of the two of them, she smiled so big it was contagious.

"Hey," she said. "Is this a party?"

"What have you been doing?" Mom asked, sipping her Sprite and then scowling again.

Lindy put her bag on the table and collapsed into her old spot.

*Look at us*, Delia thought. *Almost like it used to be.*

"I finished up at the shop and then ran into Garrett Singh."

"You get arrested after all?" Delia said over the edge of her wineglass.

"No. We just had a drink at the Drunk Duck. Is there any more of that?" Lindy pointed to the Asti.

"On the counter," Delia said. "Needs ice."

Lindy came back out with the bottle and a coffee mug filled with ice, a couple of which she used to refresh Delia's glass before adding in the Asti.

"How are you?" Lindy asked Delia.

"Better," Delia answered, though she wasn't sure anyone believed her, because she sure as hell didn't believe herself. "How was the shop?"

"Well, Dee," Lindy said, stretching her long legs out under the table to rest them on the empty seat across from her. "What you do every day is not easy. Running the shop with a baby in the back room is no joke."

Delia laughed, because it did kind of seem like a joke. "Tell me about it."

"But Brin was a huge help. We did a big cleanup."

Mom picked up her glass and drained it.

"Was that Asti?" Lindy asked, wide-eyed.

"No, the sneak gave me Sprite," Mom said.

"What a mean sneak," Lindy said.

Mom lifted hopeful eyebrows and held out her glass but Lindy shook her head. "No way. Sorry, Mom."

"I don't remember the doctor saying I couldn't have a sip of wine," Mom protested.

"Mom." Delia laughed. "The doctor didn't say anything about wine. We're not giving you any because you get rowdy."

Mom scowled. "Stop that nonsense."

Lindy's mouth fell open. "You don't remember?" She looked to Delia for backup and Delia nodded emphatically. "Was it my high school graduation?"

"And mine," Delia added. At the very beginning of that summer.

"You kept challenging our friends to arm wrestling matches."

Mom looked real ornery and then she winced. "That does ring a bell. Did I win?"

Delia and Lindy howled with laughter. Because Mom did win a few and at the time it had been so embarrassing.

Now Delia would pay a fortune to have that summer back. That moment.

Mom pushed herself to her feet. "On that note, time for bed, girls. Stay out of the tequila under the sink."

She opened the screen door, humming the theme song to *Modern Family*, and Delia slowly turned to face Lindy, who was grinning like a kid on Christmas morning.

"I've got limes in the fridge," Lindy said.

"I'll get Mom to bed. You get the tequila."

# TWENTY-FIVE

## *Brin*

*A*round 11:00 p.m. the stairs creaked and Brin could hear Dad softly shushing Ephie. The door to the baby's room opened and closed and then, predictably, there was a knock on Brin's door just before it slid open.

That knock thing was such crap. Her parents always came barging right in anyway, so the knock was barely enough warning to slip her phone under the blankets.

"Hey," he said from the doorway. "I'm heading to bed."

"Yeah." She faked a yawn. "Me, too. Is…Mom back?"

"No. I haven't heard from her. I think her phone died."

"She's still up at Gran's?"

Dad nodded and she wanted to say something to comfort him but didn't know how. Or what. Or if it even mattered anymore.

"Good night." Quietly he shut the door, and the moment passed.

Mom not being home at night felt wrong, but it for sure made sneaking out of the house easier to pull off. Brin headed downstairs, making it sound as if she was getting a glass of water and a snack, all the while really packing her schoolbag with breaking-and-entering supplies. Or what she thought would be breaking-and-entering supplies.

Gloves. An old ski mask of Dad's. Granola bars.

She went back upstairs for one final "good night, Dad" and then waited in her bedroom.

At 11:45 p.m., she crept down the stairs, skipping the creaky ones and avoiding the squeaky banister. At the front door she paused, her ear tuned to any sound coming from upstairs. There was only the white noise machine in Ephie's room, projecting its usual whooshing through the house.

Easy as pie.

*Oh my god, Brin, do not use those words in front of Troy.*

She slipped out the front door and ran the four blocks, over the bridge to the end of the spit. She didn't run down Queen Street but instead picked the side roads, Seventh Avenue with the big stone homes that were mostly cheap rooming houses now.

The road to the spit was blocked by a gate, so cars couldn't get down there. It was deserted, and the bright moonlight made the shadows under the trees seem super dark and the pale sand and stone of the road seem super light.

A glowing path right out to the old ruin of a house.

At 12:05 a.m., Brin glanced at her watch and started to feel like an idiot, like maybe she'd been duped. Troy and his friends were probably someplace laughing at how eager she'd been. How lame.

There was a scuff of a boot over gravel and all the hair on her arms prickled and she stepped back farther into the shadows of the trees. A guy, tall and thin, stepped from the road to the edge of the gate. He stood in the moonlight like he wasn't worried at all about being caught.

"Troy?" she whisper-yelled. If it wasn't him, she'd make

a run for it. She was only four blocks from her house. She could slip inside the back door and no one would ever know what happened.

In fact, that didn't sound like a bad idea right about now. She'd chalk this night away as a stupid mistake. Whenever she saw Troy she'd pull one of Mom's tricks and smile real big and pretend like nothing happened.

The guy turned to face her and she nearly crumpled with relief.

"Wow." Troy's smile glowed white in the moonlight. "You came."

"I said I would."

"Still. Big move."

She shrugged like it was no big deal. But she held on to her backpack straps with shaking hands.

"You ready?" he asked.

"Yeah." She pulled her backpack off her shoulder and started to open it. "I brought some flashlights."

"No flashlights." He put his hand over hers and the touch of his fingers on her skin made her breath stop. "People see the lights and call the police."

"We're going to walk out there in the dark?"

"That's the plan."

At least there were the floodlights that lit up the house for boats on the water. But then what? She imagined there might be lock-picking involved. "Didn't the real estate people put a lock on the door or anything?"

"There are a hundred ways into that house."

"Right. Yeah. Of course."

"Don't worry, Brin," he said, and the sound of her name in his mouth made her giddy. "There's a whole lot of moon tonight." He held his arm out. "Ready?"

The spit was endless from this perspective. A longer walk than she thought.

If she got caught, she was going to get into so much trouble…

"Let's do it," she said.

They ducked under the chain that was supposed to keep them out and started walking. Wheels, from when cars were let out here, had worn ruts into the gravel and sand, and there were two dirt stripes all the way down to the house. But on the sides were all types of dandelions and nettles. Milkweed. The leaves brushed against her knuckles as they walked.

"My second-grade teacher had us come out here and plant plants that would attract butterflies. She thought she could turn this whole thing into a butterfly garden," she said.

"I did a report in the eighth grade about how we should just put solar panels all along this road. Use the power to get Port Lorraine off the grid."

"Would it have worked?"

He shrugged.

"That's…really cool."

"You don't have to act so surprised," he said.

"I'm not." She was. "I don't know you very well… Sorry."

"Whatever. I know my reputation. What else is in that bookbag?"

"Ummmm…" God, it seemed so dumb now. She'd brought snacks to a crime scene. "Just some stuff if we get hungry and a couple of drinks."

"What kind of drinks?"

She wanted to die. Just die. Because they were juice boxes. Because her mom shopped for her like she was still eight years old.

"Apple juice. You want one?" she asked, sure that he didn't. But to her surprise he accepted. He seemed so much older, but she was reminded now that he was the same age as she was as he jabbed the little straw through the top of the juice box. It was kind of adorable.

"I heard about you and the watch," he said. The spit was narrowing and they stepped closer together. His knuckles grazed hers ever so slightly and she jumped in surprise. "You okay?" he asked.

"Yeah." Her laugh sounded fake to her own ears.

"So, what are you doing stealing a Rolex from Baumgartner's?" He took a sip of the juice and arched an eyebrow at her over the box.

Her whole body flushed and she looked down at the glowing toe of her beat-up Converse.

"I wasn't actually stealing it," she said. "I was just being an asshole so my parents would pay attention to me."

"Did it work?"

"Not really."

"So now you're sneaking out to the Fulbright House with Troy Daniels so if you get caught they'll *really* have to pay attention."

"It's not like that."

"It's okay if it is."

"It's not. I actually have a whole other reason for coming out here." She told him the story of her grandfather's death and how awful the Fulbrights were to her family.

"Jesus. That's shitty. So, what? You want to trash the place in revenge?"

"No." Maybe. "I just want to see it."

"I would want to trash it," he said. "I'd want to burn that place down."

"You know what else?" she said.

"Tell me."

"I just found out about that night. No one ever told me that story before. About my own grandfather."

"Adults don't tell kids shitty things," Troy said with a shrug. "My mom didn't tell me my dad got remarried for three years."

"I think my dad cheated on my mom with my aunt." The words exploded out of her mouth and she wanted to clap her hand over her lips. She wanted to gather them up and swallow them back down. But they were out. They were out and they were attached to a truth she couldn't quite believe.

"Whoa," he said. "Because of the picture? Like…your aunt is your mom?"

"No. That's ridiculous." She looked up at him, only to find him watching her. No judgment on his face. "Isn't it?"

"I don't know, I've heard crazier. I got an uncle who is actually my cousin. No one said shit for a long time. Now it's just the way it is."

"Something for sure happened the summer before I was born and no one *ever* talks about it."

"So what are you going to do?"

"What can I do?"

He shrugged. "Don't let them off the hook. It's your life, too."

*It's my life, too.* The words were comforting and inspiring at the same time. She walked a little taller beside him.

"Why weren't you at Spring Assembly?" she asked.

"I've never gone to any assembly. Why would I go to that one?" He looked at her like she was crazy. Not just for asking him, but for going herself.

"Didn't anyone tell you to go? You won a big award," she said and he shrugged. "Chief Singh was there to present it and everything."

"I heard."

"I didn't know you were a writer?"

"I'm not a writer," he muttered. "I just wrote something. Mr. Rose submitted it. I didn't know about any of it."

"Are you mad?"

"No. I just don't care."

They walked in prickly, uncomfortable silence the rest of the way until they were standing right in front of the Ful-bright House. The big for-sale sign to the left. The lake endless and black to the right.

"It's bigger than I thought," she said, her neck craned all the way back. She still couldn't see the widow's walk on top. From here it looked even darker and scarier.

Realer.

She looked back over her shoulder at Port. Queen Street and the harbor. She could see the big houses on the ridge and imagined Gran's house, all slumpy and out of place. This view of the town was one she hadn't seen since the days she would go out on the boat with Dad. They'd go cruising and fish with rods and worms. Dad would let her drink brown pop and they'd ignore the egg salad sandwiches Mom made and instead eat themselves sick on gummy candy from the bulk section of the grocery store.

"I think I should go back."

"What?" Troy asked. "Are you joking?"

She imagined walking back by herself. She imagined climbing into her bed. Waking up in the morning and telling her dad she wanted to go fishing. It would make him so happy.

"You came all this way. You're gonna bail now?"

She had wanted to come out here. To see the house. She'd wanted to be wild.

*This is what it's like, being wild.*

"No," she said and shook her head, turning away from the harbor. "No. Of course not."

# TWENTY-SIX

## Delia

As she tucked Mom into bed, Delia listened to the sounds coming from the kitchen. The high-pitched whine of the ancient KitchenAid blender. Lindy's faint humming. Drawers—lots of them—opening and closing.

*It's just shots of tequila. What is she doing?*

The truth was Delia was nervous.

*What do Lindy and I actually have to talk about? That won't start a fight? Or make us cry? Dogs? Does Lindy still like dogs?*

"Don't be a chicken," Mom said.

"What?"

"Go sit and talk with your sister."

"What if…?" Delia looked up at the one picture Mom had on her bedroom wall. The two of them, Delia and Lindy, asleep in Delia's old twin bed. They were ten, curled up together like kittens. "What if we don't know how?"

"To talk? She's not a stranger. Hiding out with your mother isn't going to get you anywhere," Mom muttered and rolled over onto her side, her body a lump under the blankets. "Go, honey. You'll remember how."

Delia found Lindy in her old spot around the patio table. She'd lit candles and put out chips and salsa. The blender was in the middle of the table, white slush dripping down its sides. She'd poured margaritas into Mom's old champagne glasses. The glasses had been Meredith's mom's, heirlooms that rarely saw the light of day.

"Oh my gosh," Delia said, lifting up the beautiful old glass at her spot. "I haven't seen these in ages."

"Christmas and birthdays," Lindy said.

"Remember the year you broke one—"

"That wasn't me!" Lindy shook her head "It was you."

"Lindy—"

"No," she insisted. "It was you. It was Christmas and I was seventeen, you were fifteen and Mom let us have Asti— the real stuff instead of that fizzy grape juice she usually let us have."

That rang a bell.

"We got so drunk," Lindy said.

"Mom, too." Delia remembered falling off her chair and taking the glass down with her.

Delia took a huge sip of her margarita. "Wow." She looked down at the drink. "This is amazing… What did you do?"

"Didn't use a gross bar mix. And added a little beer I found in the back of the fridge, cuts the sweetness. You hungry?" Lindy asked. "I have some soup I made yesterday. Minestrone. Mom really liked it."

Delia took another sip. Then another. "When did you become such a good cook?"

"The first job I got in Cleveland was waiting tables at a reasonably nice restaurant. A local place with a menu that never changed. The chef was a good guy and when I expressed interest, he let me work in the kitchen."

"You didn't have to go to school or anything?"

Lindy shook her head. "From there I got a job in a nicer kitchen. And then a nicer one. And then I worked behind the bar and…" Lindy shrugged "…I don't know. The years passed."

"Do you like it?"

"I'm good at it. Really good at it if I'm being honest. And if I cared about the place…I think I would be amazing." She sat up a little straighter and Delia realized how rare it was to see her sister proud of herself.

Delia leaned forward. "I'm sorry. I'm sorry I haven't taken better care of the shop."

"It's okay, Dee."

"Don't do that. You always…do that. I stayed and I took it on and I never loved it like you would have. The first time you saw it the other day I was so embarrassed."

"You've been busy raising a family."

"I have. But I have help. I just don't take it…so everything flounders. The shop most of all."

"I'm here," Lindy said. She put her hand over Delia's and Delia forced herself to feel it. To not flinch away. "I can help."

"You're here, but you haven't said for how long."

"I'm supposed to go back for a job in a week."

Delia tried to pull her hand back, but Lindy would not let go.

"I'd stay if you let me," Lindy said.

"Let you? You don't need my permission."

"Don't I? Look, I'd stay if you made room for me. If you'd really let me help."

Delia looked down at their hands. Lindy had chipped nail polish. Sparkly black. Sparkly black was always her color. In their bedroom, in the middle drawer of the desk, there would probably be three dried-up bottles of the stuff.

"You've brought back all these memories, you know."

"I'm sorry," Lindy whispered and this time it was Delia who held on.

"No. No. Good memories. Camping and Spring Assemblies and sleeping in the same bed until we couldn't fit. Things I'd forgotten. Good things I'd put away with all the bad."

"I haven't been able to go into our room," Lindy admitted. "I'm scared."

Dee stood up. "Let's go."

"Where?"

"Our room. I haven't been in there in years."

Immediately Lindy was on her feet, the margarita pitcher in one hand, her glass in the other.

The drink had gone to Delia's head and as they crept down the hallway past Mom's room, she actually giggled. Lindy shushed her and then giggled, too.

At the door to their old bedroom they stood side by side, close enough that Delia could feel her sister's hair against her shoulder. Could see, from the corner of her eye, Lindy's chest rise and fall. Delia reached out and touched the sparkly sticker on the doorframe. A rainbow or a ladybug, too worn to tell anymore. The knob turned in Dee's hand and the door swung open with a squeak.

Inside the old room it was dark and stuffy. The window closed for who knows how long.

Their single beds, one on each side of the room, were made up like they'd just left for school or work. Lindy's quilt was yellow. Dee's a blue-and-white check.

Lindy walked in, disturbing the still air and the memories that had settled like dust. She set her glass and the pitcher of margarita on the table between the two beds and wrestled the window open. A cool breeze swept in and Lindy sat down on her bed with a sigh.

Delia did the same on hers, their knees only a few inches apart.

"It hasn't changed," Lindy whispered, looking around at the shadows in the corners where the bookshelf stood, filled with paperback romances and old textbooks.

"Nothing really does around here, does it?"

Lindy laughed and lay down, staring up at the ceiling, her arms crossed over her chest. Delia scooched back until she could sit cross-legged on her own bed.

"Oh!" Lindy said and rolled onto her side so she could open the little drawer of the table. It was sticky and came out lopsided but she was able to get her fingers in there and pull out some hair ties and pens. A pack of Marlboro Lights.

"These yours?" Lindy asked.

Delia shrugged. It had been a terrible habit that they'd shared for a year or two, trying to look cool in the school parking lot.

Lindy went in one more time and pulled out the notebook.

"I'd forgotten," Delia whispered with a giddy laugh.

"Me, too," Lindy said.

In big letters on the front cover it read NOTHING TO SEE HERE. Lindy had written that. Fooling no one, but they'd thought they were clever.

The walls in the house were thin and Mom had to wake up so early that if they got caught talking after lights out, there was usually some kind of punishment the next day involving cleaning and fish. So, they'd started writing notes to each other.

Their book of secrets.

"Scooch," Delia said, getting off her bed and climbing into Lindy's. Like they used to. It was awkward at first. They were bigger, taller, took up more space. The intimacy felt foreign. But all intimacy did these days for Delia.

She forced herself to relax into the place she always occupied next to her sister, and her body began to remember.

Her soul did, too.

They lay on the lumpy mattress and opened the notebook.

Mostly it was nonsense.

*Did you empty the dishwasher? Mom's gonna be pissed.*

*Stop borrowing my shoes!*

*Can you tell Mom I'm at Nirosha's tomorrow night?*

*You need to stop making out with that Garrett kid. You're leading him on.*

Delia nudged her sister with her elbow.

"Give me a pencil," Lindy whispered and Delia contorted herself sideways to grab one off the bedside table.

*Garrett won't have sex with me,* Lindy wrote.

Delia gasped and grabbed the pencil and notebook.

*What? Why?*

*He wants to go on a date.*

*And you don't want to?*

"I do," Lindy whispered. "I would. If I was staying."

"Lindy McAvoy and the police chief. Gotta say, I like that very much," Delia said.

As Lindy flipped through the notebook, Delia spotted Dan's name often. Plans for Europe. Excitement about college.

On the bottom of one page Delia had written:

*Will you go with me to Yorkville to get a prescription for BC?*

Birth control.

Lindy had responded, *Yes.*

Delia remembered that day so well. How nervous she'd been walking into the Planned Parenthood. How cool Lindy had been. And in the end the antibiotics she'd been taking for a sinus infection made the pill moot.

"Tonight Garrett told me his mom gave him a box of condoms for his fifteenth birthday," Lindy whispered.

"That's…progressive. Remember what Mom told us?"

"You play. You pay," they whispered at the same time.

"What have you told Brin? Hopefully something better." Lindy rolled onto her side, but Delia stayed on her back, staring up at the ceiling.

*What have I told her?*

There'd been an awkward conversation full of euphemisms that was probably far more confusing than enlightening. She remembered being so relieved that she'd done it—that it was over—she'd had the talk. She ran into Nirosha that night at the grocery store and Nirosha had said, "Congrats. The first one is the hardest. Now you only have a hundred more to go."

And Delia had thought, *No way. No way am I doing that again.*

"You've talked to her, right?" Lindy asked.

"Of course," she said, flipping a page in the notebook. "But she's not having sex."

"She's a teenager, Dee. And she's pushing back against you. You can bet sex will be a part of that—"

"She's not that kind of kid."

Delia knew how she sounded and she hated it. She wanted to have an open line of communication with her daughter about all this stuff, she just didn't know how.

She knew when it came to sex there weren't good kids and bad kids. She knew as a measuring stick of worth or value it was total garbage.

*But how do you talk about it? Talk about any of it?*

Theirs was a generation of women who had believed that *no means no* would protect them. It hadn't. How could she grow *You play. You pay* into something meaningful for her daughter? Something that said sex was a beautiful miracle but it could also hurt her. Endlessly.

How did she turn *You play. You pay* into a conversation about consent and trusting her instincts? About following that slithery worm of dread in her stomach out of a situation and not trusting a partner to have her best interests at heart—until she met one who did.

About owning her desire so someone else couldn't take it and use it against her.

She barely knew those words herself. She'd grafted herself right onto Dan and left it at that.

But Lindy…somehow Lindy had been born knowing those words. Or at least more words than Delia had. And she hadn't been embarrassed to go out in search of the ones she didn't have.

Delia leafed through the notebook and caught the name Eric Fulbright in the corner of one of the pages. She immediately shut the notebook, tossing it to the floor.

"Dan read a book," Delia said.

"What?"

"Junior year of high school. He read some kind of Kama Sutra book with pictures."

"Oh my god, that's the best thing I've ever heard."

"I was so…" Delia shuddered, remembering "…uncomfortable with it. I didn't even want to know that my body could do that."

"But he wore you down?"

"He totally wore me down." On the bench seat of his old pickup, on the turnoff past Ferris Beach, he wore her down *plenty*.

"After that summer…" She didn't actually know how she was going to finish that sentence.

"Yeah?" Lindy asked, just as carefully.

There were a thousand things she could say about Dan after that summer. He'd been patient and kind. His fear and his anger he'd tried to keep to himself, but she'd felt it like a whole other person in their lives.

After that summer it had taken her a while, but they'd found a way to bring back that part of her.

That part of *them*.

Her sister's chuckle floated through the room, and Delia realized she was smiling, which must have told Lindy all she needed to know about her sex life. At least until Ephie had been born. She had hope—she really did—that they'd get back to each other that way.

"I'm glad," Lindy said and left it at that.

The sounds of the night swelled into the room, insects and an owl in the trees behind the house. The lake and its endless waves lapping against the shoreline.

"I have champagne glasses at home," Delia said, thinking about the ones they'd left on the table outside. "Dan and I got them for our wedding and for years I brought them out for birthdays and holidays. I'd get Brin that fizzy juice like Mom got us and we'd all toast each other. I thought, when I had Brin, that I would do all those awesome things Mom did. Champagne glasses and bedtime stories and responsibility and the chore jar and... God, there were so many good things, weren't there?"

"Weekend breakfasts outside. Picnics at the beach."

"Midnight swims," they said at the same time.

"And I did those things with Brin," Delia said. "But I do the other things, too."

"What do you mean?"

"If something's bad or scary, I shove it aside and don't let anyone talk about it. Like we're children with our heads under the covers. If we can't see the monsters, they're not there."

"She's a good kid. You raised her right."

"Did you miss the part about how my daughter is doing community service for attempting to steal a watch?"

"Your daughter came to the store and worked all afternoon with me today." Lindy filled their glasses back up. "And I know it's hard for you to imagine being so angry and frustrated that it seriously makes sense to try to steal a watch, or pretend to or whatever it is she did. But I do. I get that anger. I was an angry sixteen-year-old just like Brin. But when you were sixteen you were already an adult. You already had Dan and you put your grief over Dad away and you understood that sometimes Mom couldn't show up to stuff."

"I didn't just put my grief away!" Delia cried, then lowered her voice again. "I was hurt when Mom didn't show up. But I just didn't make it a big thing. And Brin right now, she's just so mad—"

"Maybe she's mad because you're mad," Lindy said.

"I'm not mad!" she said at full volume. Such a terrible lie that she actually burst out laughing like a mad woman. "How amazing was she last night?" Delia sighed.

"Telling Mrs. Fulbright to leave? Amazing. Really amazing."

"You know she was always like that. This little warrior. She'd be the first to tell kids—adults even—if they weren't being fair. Or kind. It used to embarrass me."

"What? Why?"

"Because it wasn't quiet. Or polite. And I think, at least a little, I was scared. Of how righteous she already was at that age. The same way Mom was scared of you." She cleared her throat. "The way I was scared of you, too. Especially that summer. You wanted everything to be talked about and dealt with. You wanted justice and I...and Mom and Dan, too...we just all wanted it to go away. So I made you go away. I made you leave that summer because it was easier to pretend nothing happened without you there."

"I know. And I left because I didn't know how to be what you wanted me to be."

Delia had spent so many years knowing deep in her gut that she had hurt her sister, too.

"I know I messed up, Dee. Me and Dan."

Delia shook her head, because it didn't matter. They'd made a mistake. But in the way of small mistakes it had snowballed into something out of everyone's control.

"I was just trying to survive," Dee said. "But I should never have made you leave."

And that's all she could say. More words didn't come.

Delia took the pencil and wrote:

*Stay. Please.*

And Lindy wrote back: *Okay.*

# TWENTY-SEVEN

## Brin

She was going to stay. She wasn't going to back down and run home.

Troy put his hand at her waist as they stepped over the broken front door, holding her hand to help her around what looked like a campfire setup in the middle of the old foyer but was really a big round table, half ash, half gray and black from being burnt.

The light from outside illuminated the room, but it made the walls bright and everything else shadowed. It was dark and murky at her feet, and when she stumbled, he grabbed her hand again and this time didn't let go. Immediately she freaked. Was he just being nice? Was he coming on to her? Did she want him to come on to her? What did this mean?

Finally, she couldn't take it.

"Just a second," she whispered and pulled her hand free so she could make a big show of rearranging her backpack on her shoulders. And then she left her hands on the straps.

Off the main hallway were two side rooms and there were mattresses in the corners of each, broken glass everywhere.

Paintings had been cut up and the fireplace had half a table sticking out of it. There were holes in the walls.

But as much as the old house was ruined, there was something still fancy about it, too. The walls were made of intricate carved wood and the ceilings in some of the rooms were domed with painted scenes. Cherubs and angels. Fluffy clouds.

"So, like, what happened?"

"To the house?" Troy shrugged. "Bad locks."

"No. The Fulbrights. Why…why did they leave it like this?"

"No clue. Someone said the kid, that guy in the picture you showed me, he killed a man and left the country."

"Eric? He's in Canada. That's what his mom said."

"You just randomly talked to his mom?"

"She showed up at the shop the other night. My mom asked about Eric."

"So, maybe he killed a guy and went to Canada?" he said and started walking up the dark stairway.

"Where are you going?"

"Upstairs?"

"Why?"

He glanced over at her, and he was just far enough away that all she could see was his face, the pale glow of his skin. The rest of him was smudged shadow. His hair and body. His eyes.

That trickle of dread came back. That itchy worm of worry. Awareness that they were so totally alone. And she barely knew him.

"Because I haven't looked through the upstairs yet. And that's where the painting is."

Right. The painting of Eric Fulbright.

When she flicked the flashlight on its lowest setting and cast it down to the floor, she expected him to complain, but he just let her lead the way. Her flashlight caught the tail of a mouse running across the top step and she screamed and jumped a mile high.

"You okay?" he asked, his hand again on her back, sending shivers up her spine.

"Oh! Just great!"

He laughed behind her, his breath ruffling her hair.

His hand still at her back, they climbed the wide staircase to the second floor. There was another flight, but Troy turned left into a small room that held a desk and another fireplace. The walls were lined with empty bookshelves, and she tried to imagine what the shelves might have looked like full.

"Look," Troy said and pointed to the wall behind her. She turned and saw in the ghostly glow of the flashlight the portrait of the kid in the picture. There was a sailboat in the background and he was looking off to the side like a teenage Ahab.

"He still doesn't look like a killer," she said, holding the flashlight over his face.

"You know what killers look like?"

She tilted her head and stepped closer, staring into his blue eyes. "No. But…do they have sailboats?"

"Assholes come with everything."

"So, what do we do now?" She turned and faced Troy, who had taken off his own backpack and pulled out a sledgehammer.

"Whoa. What's with the hammer?"

"You scared?"

"It's…it's a little weird."

"There's copper wire in the wall and if I strip all the shit off it, the scrapyard will pay me for it."

"Do they pay you…a lot?"

"Enough. Don't be scared."

"I'm not scared."

He turned and found the light switch and smashed the hammer into the wall about five inches above the panel.

She knew it was coming but she jumped all the same.

The summer Brin turned nine, it took her three months to jump off the high dive at the Lorraine pool. Every day she climbed up the twenty-four steps to the board, telling herself today was the day. Reminding herself that Jenny had already done the high dive the year before. Listening to her mom yell, *You can do it!* from the edge of the deep end.

Every day for three months she took baby steps out to the end of the board, curling her toes over the edge just like the lifeguard instructed, and she looked down at that drain in the bottom of the pool. The thick black square under all that water. So. Far. Away.

And every day for three months, she looked over at her mom, and shook her head no.

*Okay*, Mom would yell. *Don't move.*

The pool had strict rules about two people on the board at one time, but Mom didn't care so much about that, maybe. Brin wasn't sure. All she knew was that when she got the courage to turn around and walk back to the ladder, Mom would be there. And they'd climb down together, agreeing with every step that she'd do it the next day.

When she finally did jump on the very last day of the pool season, Mom clapped and bought her a frozen Snickers bar from the concession stand. At a picnic table in the shade she'd said, *That wasn't so bad, was it?*

Brin had never known how to say just because she didn't die or belly flop and get hurt or get stuck in the drain, didn't mean the fear hadn't been real. The fear was one thing and the jump was another entirely.

She could be exhilarated and happy, but that did not erase the shadow of the fear she'd felt seconds before.

Walking home from the Fulbright House Brin felt the same she had that day.

They were sticking to the shadows of her street as Troy walked her home. She was glad she'd done this wild and crazy thing, but she never wanted to do it again.

"Hey." Troy put his hand against her arm and they stopped under the branches of the Svensons' elm tree. "I'm really sorry."

"For what?" she asked, pulling her backpack tighter around her shoulders.

"I think you...were scared, and I was kind of a jerk."

She had this urge to tell him that it was okay. To minimize. But instead she said, "You were."

"I've only gone out there with my cousin and he's kind of a jerk and I didn't know what to do when you were scared. So, I did what my cousin did the first time we went out there."

"Thanks," she finally managed.

"You made me nervous."

"Me?"

"Girls like you aren't into guys like me."

"Guys like you aren't into girls like me." Saying *that* felt more wild than breaking into an abandoned house.

"I'm into girls like you. You're pretty and you're smart and you're tough when you're not screaming about mice."

His hand was still on her arm.

"Anyway, I'm really sorry, Brin. I was not cool out there. I knew you wanted to go home and I should have just walked you back. If you ever want to go out there again, let me know. You were really a lot of help."

And there under the elm tree, the dust of the Fulbright House in their hair, she felt the potential in the air. The potential of them. Of what was next.

She stepped back and broke the moment. "I better go."

"For sure," he said. "See you around, Brin."

She turned and walked the rest of the way down the block. *Don't look back*, she told herself. *Don't. Don't be that girl. Don't—*

She looked back, a quick glance over her shoulder. Troy was still standing there, under the elm, watching her. He lifted his hand in a wave.

Their family never locked the doors to their house. Or their car doors for that matter. Only the boat got locked up. So Brin eased open the front door and stepped into the dark and quiet living room.

"I thought you might not come home."

Brin screamed and Dad, sitting in the dark at the kitchen table, turned on the light.

"Brin?"

"Dad?"

"What are you doing?" they said at the same time.

"You want to go first?" she tried for a joke but Dad clearly didn't find it funny.

"What are you doing sneaking into the house at 3:00 a.m.?"

"I didn't want to wake you up."

"Brin!"

"I snuck out. I snuck out after you went to bed," she said so fast the words flew across the room.

"Where did you go?"

For a second the lies came fast and furious to her lips. The beach with Jenny. She could say that and he would believe it and she'd get grounded and nothing would really be any different.

"I went to the Fulbright House."

Dad's eyes practically popped out of his head. "Why?"

"Because I wanted to see it."

"Brin. You know it's dangerous there."

"It's not that bad."

Twice he opened his mouth and shut it again. "Were you by yourself?" he finally asked.

"No."

Brin could tell him about Troy. But Troy was a secret she'd be keeping safe for now.

"Why, Brin, why did you go there?"

She opened up the small outer pocket of her bookbag and pulled out the pictures for her dad.

"Jesus," he breathed. "Where did these come from?"

"I was helping Aunt Lindy clean some stuff out of the closet at Gran's. I found them."

He was holding the picture of Eric Fulbright.

"Is it true?" she asked.

Dad closed his eyes. "Is what true?" he whispered.

"Did he murder someone and leave the country? Is that why the house looks the way it does?"

"He didn't murder anyone," Dad said and crumpled the photo into a ball.

He wiped his face with his hand.

She looked at the holes in his shirt, an old McAvoy Bait, Fish and Lunch Counter, and remembered for some reason falling asleep in his winter coat in the back seat of the car when she was a kid out of her booster. How comforting that had been. How she'd believed her father would keep her safe from anything…

*Don't let them off the hook. It's your life, too.*

"Is Aunt Lindy my mom?"

"What?" he yelled and she jumped, wishing she could suck the words back. "What are you asking me?"

"Is Aunt Lindy…? It's just… We look so much alike and…"

She took the rest of the pictures from him. "Mom and I are nothing alike and I overheard you and Lindy talking at the shop."

"What? What did you hear?"

"That what was going on with Mom was all your fault. That you and Aunt Lindy did something that summer. Something you weren't able to forget."

"Something?" His voice was getting louder, the white lines around his eyes even whiter. "You mean I could have gotten Aunt Lindy pregnant?"

"Yeah," she murmured.

"I can't hear you, Brin."

"Yes."

"And then what? After getting her pregnant I forced Lindy to give me the baby and chased her out of town?"

"Or Mom did."

His mouth dropped open. "Is that what you think of us? Is that the kind of person you think I am? The kind who would cheat and lie and run a person out of town?"

"No. Dad." She'd thought about this. About a thousand different scenarios. "But what if she wanted an abortion and you convinced her not to by telling her you would keep the baby and raise it—?"

He shook his head. "Do you hear what you're saying?"

"Dad. No. I'm sorry. I'm just—"

"What? You're just what? Mad at your mom so you con-cocted something so hurtful so you could stay angry?"

Her heart squeezed so hard she saw stars in the corner of her vision. "We just… We're nothing alike," she whispered lamely.

"Oh my god, honey. You're exactly alike. You're so the same, when I look at you it's like I'm looking at her when she was seventeen."

"Lindy?"

"No! Your mother. You have the same look in your eye and the same set to your shoulders. You lift your chin when you're angry like you're ready to take a swing. You're yellers, not criers. You're grumpy in the morning but silly at night. You're stubborn. The two of you. So damn stubborn you'd go down with a ship that wasn't even yours."

"Dad—"

"No, you need to listen to me. It kills me to hear you say that you're nothing like your mother when I see in you all the things I love most about her. Your intelligence. The way you walk into rooms like you already know everyone there and love them. And they love you."

She blinked to hold back the hot tears pooling in the corners of her eyes.

"You are your mother's daughter, Brin," he said. "And you may not love that right now. But trust me, in a few years, when life gets real and the challenges get harder, you'll be so glad to have the mother you have."

"I'm sorry." It was all she could say.

"Yeah. You should be. And frankly, you will be. Sneaking out? Brin?"

"I know." She ducked her head because the shame she felt was real. It all seemed so stupid now, all those things she thought. All the suspicions.

He wrapped her in his arms. She turned her face to the side so she could hear the beat of his heart in her ear.

"But something happened, right? Between you and Aunt Lindy?" she said to his chest. "Tell me, please."

He stroked back her hair like he used to when she was a kid and had a nightmare.

"I was nervous about going to Europe and even more nervous about your mom going off to college. I was sure she'd get a taste of the world and never want to come back to Port.

Lindy was working on the apartment above the shop and she was planning on taking over the shop and she was nervous about Dee leaving, too. I know it's hard to imagine but they were inseparable, Brin. Anyway one afternoon I was helping Lindy move stuff into her apartment and she kissed me. And for a second I kissed her back."

"Mom found out?"

"She walked in."

"Dad," she breathed.

"It was one of the worst moments of my life and one of my biggest regrets."

"Was she mad?"

"Furious."

"And she forgave you and not Lindy."

"We never talked about it again. Go to bed, kiddo. We'll talk about your punishment in the morning."

She nodded and wiped her face. When she reached the doorway she stopped. "Hey," she said. "Why are you up if you weren't waiting for me?"

"I'm waiting for your mom. She's up at Gran's."

Mom never spent the night out of the house. Even when Ephie was born she was already back home that same night.

"Is everything okay? Did something happen to Gran?"

"No. She's fine. Lindy's fine. Mom will be home soon." He put a smile on at the end, but Brin was not convinced. She was a million miles from convinced.

# TWENTY-EIGHT
## *Delia*

*S*plinters of light were trying to drill through her eyeballs and right into her brain.

She sat up from the couch only to find Mom in her chair, watching her with a smile.

"You smell, girl," she said, eating a piece of toast way too loudly.

"Oh my god, my head." Delia lifted her arm to try to keep the light away, but she accidentally brushed her breast and it was so rock hard it hurt. She cupped her breast through the grimy, sweaty shirt and immediately started to leak.

"You okay?"

Lindy's feet appeared on the floor near the edge of the couch. Delia couldn't even raise her head.

"No."

"Margaritas and Asti on an empty stomach are a pretty bad combo." Lindy's palm held two aspirin, and Delia contemplated just sticking her tongue out and licking them out of her sister's hand.

"Here." Lindy put a glass of water under Delia's nose.

"Thank you."

"Coffee?"

"No. I…I have to get home." She tried to get to her feet but couldn't quite make it and collapsed back against the old couch.

"Dee," Lindy laughed. "Why don't you rest—?"

"I can't. My boobs. I have to get home."

"Don't you go feeding my grandbaby that milk," Mom said, pointing at Delia's seven-hundred-pound boobs. "You'll get her drunk."

"I'll pump and dump," Delia said. "What time is it?"

"About eight."

"Oh my god, the baby. Dan has charters today and the shop." She felt homesick and nauseous.

"Hey, it's okay."

"It's not okay, Lindy," Delia said, looking for her purse. Did she bring a purse? Keys? How did she get here?

"Girl," Mom said and jingled Delia's keys. "Here."

"Thanks, Mom. I'll see you later." Delia kissed her cheek and headed for the back door.

"Dee." Lindy followed her onto the back deck. "Do you need me to drive you?"

"I'm fine."

"I really don't see what the big deal is, Dee."

"I didn't call. I didn't call him. I didn't let him know. He asked me to come home, to come back to him and instead I got hammered and stayed out all night. And now I don't know where my baby is. I don't know where my teenager is but I'm pretty sure wherever my husband is, he is not happy with me…" She stopped, shaking her aching head. "And after yesterday?" She couldn't put yesterday into words. "I don't do this kind of thing."

Lindy shrugged. "Maybe it's time you did. Just so you can see that the world goes on without you there to control it."

"Are you trying to start a fight?" Delia asked. "Because last night was good. It was fun."

Lindy lifted her hands. "Go," she said. "Go and martyr yourself on your breast pump. Mom and I will open the shop."

Dee broke every speed limit. Rolled through every stop sign until she was in her own driveway.

"Hello, Mrs. Higgins!" she said to the neighbor waving over at her, roses in her hand.

"Delia," she said. "Did you see the Fulbright—?"

"Sorry, Mrs. Higgins," she cried, her arms crossed over her chest. "I'm running late."

Mrs. Higgins waved again and Delia burst through the front door of her house. The living room was empty. So was the kitchen. She was half hopeful and half full of dread as she charged upstairs, tossing her shirt off as she went.

The baby's room was empty. So was Brin's.

Maybe Dan took everyone fishing.

Delia pushed open the door to her bedroom and there on the bed napped baby Ephie, her bum up in the air, her thumb in her mouth.

And lying beside her was Dan.

He was in his pajamas at 8:00 a.m. on a Sunday and it was so out of place, like a cat walking on hind legs. She hadn't seen him not in work clothes during the day...ever. Even when he got the flu, he got himself dressed.

Slowly he stood up from the bed and they faced each other, the three feet of the flowered blue rug they never agreed on as wide and as deep as the lake outside the window.

When they'd bought this house it was just a bungalow. A seventies thing covered in wood paneling. Delia wanted something new, something easy, but Dan convinced her that they could make this their dream home. It took so many years. Little renovations and huge ones. Dan did most of the work, calling in help from friends when he needed it. She washed dishes in the bathtub for what felt like a year. Brin called the sawdust in the air wood glitter.

Now the view out the window was her dream view. The harbor and the flags over the bridge. A tiny green corner of the park with the gazebo and then just lake. Just the wide wild lake. There was no Fulbright House.

"You didn't go out?" she asked, a stupid question. She caught sight of herself, standing there in just her bra, in the mirror over the dresser. She hadn't shown Dan this much skin in months. She shifted sideways so she couldn't see herself.

"Rescheduled. I said my wife was sick. They understood." Delia nodded.

"You spent the night at your mom's?" he asked. "You're okay?"

"Yeah," she said through gummy lips. Nervous. "We... Lindy and I had some drinks. A lot of drinks. She made margaritas."

"Sounds fun."

"It was. She hit on Garrett Singh at the Drunk Duck. Classic Lindy, you know." She laughed awkwardly but his face didn't change. "She's staying. Here. In Port. We'll have to figure that out, I guess. Maybe I should have talked to you first?"

"Dee," he whispered, and she broke.

"I'm sorry. So sorry that I didn't call. That I didn't ask—"

"You don't—" he snapped, then composed himself again. "You don't have to ask permission. Dee. You deserve a night out. You deserve to have fun. Have too much to drink. That's not what I'm angry about."

"The not calling," she said.

"You know?" He laughed, but nothing was funny. "I'm not even mad about that."

"Then why are you mad?"

"Yesterday was one of the worst days of my life. I didn't know what was going on with you. I didn't know how to help you. I didn't know what you were going to do or what I was going to come home to. I did that charter job like everything was fine all the time thinking you might have just left us. Driven away in the van. Or…hurt yourself—"

"Dan," she sighed. "It wasn't that bad."

"It was!" he cried, and the baby on the bed whimpered. He dropped his head in his hands and whispered. "It was, Dee. It is. We're broken, Dee. Somehow, someway, we broke. And last night as the hours ticked by and you didn't come home I started to get mad. I got so mad. That you wouldn't let me in. That you didn't call. That you left me yesterday to deal with our entire life. And then I got scared again. I feel like that's how I live my life now. I'm mad or I'm scared. I don't want to be this guy. I don't want to be this husband. This father."

"I know," she exhaled and the truth just came out of her. "I don't want to be this woman."

He rubbed his face, pushed his hands up into the thick brush of his hair. She wanted to say, *Let me cut your hair*, like she used to.

"I swore I'd never leave you," Dan said. "Seventeen years ago. Remember?"

She nodded, her throat thick.

"I love our life. I love you. I still do. I will love you forever. But…we need to figure this out. Constantly disappointing you is hard. But constantly worrying about you is killing me."

This was all true. And yet she didn't know what to say. How to make any it better.

"Brin snuck out last night." His voice broke through the fog, and the change of subject caught her by surprise.

"What?"

"She went down to the Fulbright House sometime after I went to bed. I caught her sneaking back in after three."

Delia's entire body broke out in a cold sweat.

"There's more," he said and something in his face made Delia brace herself.

"She asked if Lindy was her mother."

Delia gasped but there was no air. No air anywhere at all.

"It's okay, Dee," Dan whispered.

"What did you tell her?" Part of her, held in breathless anticipation, wanted him to say that he told her everything. That while Delia was off getting drunk, Dan did what she'd never been able to do.

"That she is your daughter." She waited, but that's all he said. "I've gone with your wishes all these years. Because I loved you."

*My wishes?*

*Loved?*

"And maybe your silence, Dee, has been easy for me, too. I don't know how to talk about the past. I don't know how to talk us. About what's gone wrong. But it's not working anymore. Pretending. Or shoving everything under the rug."

"We have to talk," she said with a nod. "We do. I know I'm bad about that. I know I can make it hard—"

He grabbed her shoulders and she lifted her eyes to his, his beautiful blue eyes so different from his daughter's. Blue eyes had a thousand variations.

"We have to tell her," he said.

She had thought about telling Brin. Of course she had. She thought about it until she was sick. Until she'd imagined every single horrible outcome. Until she couldn't bear to think of it anymore.

"How?" she whispered.

"I don't know. But we need to figure it out."

They stood there, in the center of the blue rug. Somehow they'd met at the middle and the notion was comforting. He slid his palm, flat and wide, from her neck down over her bare back, and he was close enough that if she bent her head and took one tiny step forward, she could put her head on his shoulder.

And then she could wrap her arms around his back and they would be hugging. She could turn her face into his neck, breathe in that familiar warm smell that smelled, even after all these years, like home.

But then he stepped back, over to his side of the rug. "Since I canceled the charter I'd like to go get caught up with some paperwork at the shop," he said. "Is that okay?"

"Of course," she whispered. "Lindy was going to be there with Mom later."

"Brin's at community service."

"How did she get there?"

"I had Chief Singh pick her up. He's going to drop her off, too."

Oh. That was just perfect. She glanced, delighted and horrified, up at her husband who was nodding.

"I know, right?" he asked.

They grinned at each other, a breath away from laughter.

*See*, she thought. *See? We're still us? I'm still me!*

Dan turned to get dressed, to put on his sunglasses and his white-soled shoes and go on with his day as if she wasn't standing there in shambles. She grabbed his arm, didn't actually realize she was going to do it until it was done. Until the rough hair of his forearm was rubbing against her palm.

He turned and they looked at each other, really looked at each other, and a spark drifted upward from the dead center of her body. *What would he do if I kissed him?* she thought. She stepped closer, knowing she was a little wild-eyed and gross.

*Too wild-eyed and gross?*

She hesitated but Dan did not. He pulled her in the rest of the way and the kiss, when it came, was perfect. Familiar and beautiful. Her body, the last few months, had not felt her own, but right now, pressed up against her husband, she was reminded of who she was. That she was more than the trauma that had happened to her body. More than a source of food for a child. More than the hormonal thunderstorm mother of a teenager.

She was Delia McAvoy and she'd loved Dan Collins from the moment she saw him. And they'd survived a lot.

And they could survive this.

# TWENTY-NINE

## *Lindy*

The shop was open but quiet and dark.

*If Delia's here I'll be amazed*, she thought. Her poor sister was hung *way* over.

"Hello?" she called out.

"Hi! Just a second." Dan came bounding out of the back room with a smile that faded slightly when he saw them.

"It's you guys."

"It's us guys," Lindy said.

"Were you expecting someone better?" Mom asked.

"Well, I was hoping Delia."

"How is she doing this morning?"

"I haven't seen her that hungover since her one and only effort at joining a book club."

Lindy laughed as she started flipping on the overhead lights. They buzzed and hummed and then illuminated.

"I'm just in the back working on some paperwork. I kept the lights off hoping people wouldn't come in," Dan admitted sheepishly.

"Quite a businessman," Lindy teased. "Go on and finish your paperwork, Mom and I can handle things up here."

"Brin will be here after lunch," he said. "She got in some trouble last night."

"Again?" Mom asked.

"She's going through some stuff," Dan said. "But I think last night might have cleared the air."

"Well, we got work for her, too," Mom said.

Lindy surveyed the McAvoy family kingdom. It was still in rough shape, but it was slowly improving.

"Hey, Mom," she said. "You feel like washing windows?"

"No. But I'll do it."

"That's the spirit."

Brin arrived at noon, her face hidden by the long veil of her auburn hair.

"Hey." Lindy treaded carefully. She wasn't sure what the girl had done, but the weight on her shoulders looked heavy.

"Hey," Brin said, lifting her head in a tight nod.

"How was community service?"

"Gross."

"You hungry?"

"No. Where's my dad?"

Lindy jerked her head to the back. "He's working."

Brin glanced at the office door like it was too far away. Or she didn't have the energy.

"What about my mom?"

"At home with the baby."

For a moment all that teenage posturing cracked right down the middle and she saw the confused little girl who just wanted her mom. Lindy hauled her niece into her arms.

"I know things are weird right now," she said. "But your

dad is smiling and cracking jokes. And last night your mom seemed really good. Things are going to be okay."

"What if they're not?" Brin whispered into her shoulder.

"Then you just keep going until they are."

"I thought you were my mom," Brin breathed, and Lindy recoiled, leaning back to see into her niece's face. She was not joking. "I thought that was the big secret my family was hiding."

"How...?" Lindy started to ask, but then realized that wasn't the point. The point was Brin felt so foreign to her mother that she went looking in the wrong place for a connection.

"I'm not your mom, honey. You are Delia McAvoy's spitting image."

"Dad told me you guys kissed a long time ago."

Lindy shook her head, disoriented by hearing the words spoken out loud. "A momentary lapse," she whispered. "One I really regret."

"I get it," Brin said. "I mean it's so gross. But I get it. Sometimes you just really want something to be yours. Even when it's only what it is because other people have it."

"Sometimes," Lindy said. "That's exactly it."

Lindy put Brin to work washing the windows while Mom sat in that old camp chair next to the open door.

"What'd you do, girl?" Mom asked Brin.

"I broke into the Fulbright House," she said.

"What?" Mom asked, like she didn't hear her.

"Nothing, Mom," Lindy said and then lowered her voice to talk to Brin. "No wonder you're in trouble. Isn't it all closed up with it being for sale and everything?"

"Every window in the place is broken. There's like a thousand ways in."

"Sounds like a real blast."

Brin shrugged, spraying Windex at the glass and then wiping it off. The towel she used was immediately dark and grimy.

"There's a portrait there," Brin said. "That Eric guy and a boat."

"I remember that portrait." It had been in the den with all those bottles of booze and bookshelves. That summer, that's where the McAvoy sisters hung out. Lindy, because she liked really expensive rum, and Delia, because she liked books. Dan, when he went with them, would stare out the windows at the lake and ask if they were ready to go yet every fifteen minutes.

"Guy looks like a jerk," Brin said.

"Hey," Lindy whispered. "Let's try not to talk about the Fulbrights today. Gran's having a good day and it always really upsets her."

One day. Just one day without the memories of that family making themselves at home here. But maybe that was just the way it had to be in Port. There was no pretending that family didn't exist. That the trauma they'd inflicted hadn't happened.

*How does Dee stand it?*

"Yeah, sure," Brin said and continued spraying down the windows.

Lindy went back inside to get more towels, because the girl was going to need them to get all that grime off.

"Mom?" Lindy asked as she walked by. "You okay?"

"Right as rain," she said and shooed away curious seagulls.

# THIRTY

## Meredith

She remembered when William got the trap net license. It was a big deal, a chance for better money. It'd been rare then, to get one of them. They weren't a big outfit.

*This is gonna change our life,* William had said. *This is gonna make it so the girls have something they can hold on to. Something real.*

She'd celebrated, making a big pot of stew with hunks of beef and carrots. William's favorite. That night he started designing his trap so that the big nets, tied with the big rope, would scare the fish and they'd swim right where William wanted them, down a funnel of smaller and smaller nets until finally they reached nets so fine, the fish couldn't even see them.

Those fish thought they were doing the right thing, escaping danger, and then they were trapped by a danger they couldn't even see.

The wind blew right up Queen Street, a thick hard push, like it wanted to keep Meredith in her seat. She waited until Brin went inside with Lindy and then pushed right back and out of her camp chair.

The seagulls made a fuss.

For years after William died, she kept the McAvoy family on the path of least resistance. *Keep the girls safe, make the girls happy.*

Safe. Happy.

It was the net she got trapped in. They all got trapped in.

And now Brin was going to get trapped there, too. Going out to the Fulbright House.

Someone had to stop this nonsense.

The police station was right down the street, the red brick building next to the harbor. She remembered when they built it. She and William donated money. They had a brick in there somewhere with the girls' names on it.

It was a five-minute walk, even for an old bird like her.

Janet Evans waved at her from the CutNRun and Meredith waved back as she walked by.

Jonah Bishop, a boy she remembered from the shop, was heading out the police station doors just as she got there. Jonah and his dad used to come in for bait every other weekend and fished off the pier.

"Ma'am," he said and held the door open for her.

She nodded as she walked past, managed a smile, but didn't say anything because the next words out of her mouth were not meant for him. She wouldn't get distracted by casual chit-chat.

Inside, the air-conditioning was turned up too high and she got goose bumps all up and down her arms.

"Can I help you, Mrs. McAvoy?" a woman police officer asked.

Meredith opened her mouth wide enough to say, "Chief."

The lady glanced around her. "Are your girls with you, ma'am?"

*Oh brother.* She opened her mouth again, tipped her chin up a little. "Chief," she said louder.

"Chief Singh," the woman said. "I'll take you."

She attempted to guide Meredith by the elbow, but Meredith shook her off.

"Follow me then." The woman walked ahead, glancing over her shoulder every time she skirted a desk as if making sure Meredith was still in her wake.

*Calm down. You ain't so fast.*

The door with Garrett Singh's name on it was open and she could see him eating lunch from a Styrofoam container. The lady police officer went in first.

"Meredith McAvoy is out here asking for you," Meredith heard her say. "She seems real confused."

Meredith was clear as the May sky. She hadn't been so clear in years.

A roller chair squeaked against the floor and then Garrett Singh appeared at the doorway, smiling.

"Well, hello, Mrs. McAvoy. You want to come in?"

"Sit down," she said to Garrett Singh. "We don't have much time."

# Lindy

"Excuse me?" someone said from the doorway, and Lindy poked her head up from behind the counter. A cop was standing next to Mom's empty camp chair.

*Uh-oh.*

"Are you Lindy?" the woman asked. Brin, who had still not finished cleaning those windows, came over so the three of them stood in the doorway. "Your mom is down at the police station."

"I thought you were watching her," Brin said, a horrified look on her face.

"And I thought you were…"

"Well, someone needs to," the police officer said and walked back toward the station.

"You want me to go?" Brin asked.

"No. Stay here. I'll go get her."

"Do you think… Like she's not telling Chief Singh that I was out at the Fulbright House, is she?"

"I don't know," Lindy answered truthfully, and Brin to her credit only nodded and headed back into the shop.

As Lindy walked to the police station, she gave herself a stern talking-to. This wasn't working, having Mom at the shop. Lindy was too distracted.

A block away she stopped at the sight of her mom leaving the station.

With Garrett.

With a hand at Mom's back, he started walking her in Lindy's direction.

"Lindy," he said, when they were face-to-face.

"Hi, Garrett," she said, but her eyes were on Mom, the way she was worrying the hem of her sweater, pulling a pink thread loose.

Lindy grabbed her mother's hand. "Hey," she said quietly.

"Hey yourself." She put her nose up like it was Lindy who had done something odd.

Lindy could tell she was trying hard to be brave. As Lindy pulled her into a hug, she felt Mom grab the back of her T-shirt and hold on for dear life.

"Your mom just walked down to talk to me in my office," Garrett said.

"Yeah?" Lindy smiled at her mom, who did not smile back. "You reporting a crime?"

Neither Garrett nor Mom laughed.

*Uh-oh. Maybe Mom did tell him about Brin. Breaking into the Fulbright House was serious.*

"I'll walk you back to the shop."

Once in the store, Lindy fetched a bottle of water and sat her mom down at the booth.

"Everything all right?" Dan came out from the office.

"Is there a place we can talk alone?" Garrett asked.

"Sure," Dan said and shifted sideways, putting an arm out

like he was formally inviting them into the dingy office. Brin, white-faced, stayed back to watch Mom.

Lindy closed the office door behind her and then leaned against it for support.

"She did come into my office to report a crime," Garrett said.

Lindy and Dan shared a look. *Not Brin. Don't be Brin.*

"She said Eric Fulbright raped Delia."

# THIRTY-ONE

## *Brin*

$D$ad put a sign on the door: "Closed for the day. Be back tomorrow. Sorry for the inconvenience."

She read it like five times.

Dad never closed the store. Not for the flu. Or crazy storms. When Ephie was born he shut the store down for a day. That was it.

Brin couldn't stop staring at the sign.

Because it might as well have read: "Collins family falling apart—get your fish someplace else."

She and Dad drove home in total silence.

She thought about demanding to know what was going on, but for the first time in a long time, she wasn't sure she really wanted to know. Maybe things were a secret for a good reason.

The house was cleaned up for once. The laundry baskets that sat on the floor next to the steps were gone, and the table between the couch and the TV, usually sticky and covered in crusty baby clothes and half-drunk cups of coffee, had been cleared off.

Ephie swung in a contraption hanging from the top of the

kitchen doorframe, all spit and smiles. At the sound of the front door opening, Mom appeared in the doorway. Her hair was washed and her clothes were clean and she looked...nice.

Like yesterday didn't happen.

"Hey," Mom said quietly, and the baby screamed and did twenty jumping jacks, launching herself toward Brin. "Everything okay?"

Brin shrugged. Honestly? She had no freaking clue.

"Brin?" Dad said. "Can you take Ephie upstairs?"

The way he looked at Brin made the strength run out of her bones. "How do I...?" she asked, staring down at the baby all buckled into the swing.

"Well," Mom said. "It's very complicated—"

She was making a joke.

It hurt Brin to hear it, because the world was falling apart and Mom didn't know it yet. She was making jokes like everything was fine.

Mom pulled the baby out of the jumper and handed her over. Ephie smiled and laughed like the best thing in the world was being held by Brin. And Brin found herself smiling back at Ephie even when she grabbed on to Brin's hair with two fists.

Brin walked up the stairs, whispering against her sister's head.

"It's going to be all right. Don't worry, baby. It's going to be all right, and if it's not, we will just keep going until it is."

# Lindy

She scooped cottage cheese into the divots of canned pears, one of her mom's favorites. Years ago Mom would eat the pears and Dad would stand over the sink, drinking the juice right out of the can. Risking botulism and cut lips.

"Mom." Lindy crouched down beside her chair. "Look what I made."

But Mom's eyes were on the dark clouds outside the window. "The storm is coming."

"Mom, please eat something."

"You better close the windows in your room. You girls better run down to the store, too. See if there's any milk or bread left. Radio said this was going to be a bad one."

Lindy's head rested against the wooden arm of her mother's chair. "Please come back to me."

"Where's William? Is he back? He was only going to check the nets. He said he'd be back before noon."

Lindy closed her eyes and when she felt her mother's hand on her hair she squeezed them shut. *Don't cry*, she told herself. *Just don't cry.*

"Honey," Mom whispered, and her fingers stroked Lindy's hair, down to her scalp. Her thumb touched the edge of Lindy's ear and it was more comfort than she'd had in years. She forced herself to soak it up, carefully, bit by bit, when all she wanted was just to gulp it down.

"Lindy," Mom said.

*Mom. Please be here. Be now. You kicked a hornet's nest and now it has to be dealt with. And we need you, Mom.*

"They're calling it a November Witch," Mom said. "We need to get ready."

There was a knock at the door and Lindy got to her feet, knees creaking as she stood.

"Hello?"

She recognized Garrett's voice and felt relief and dread in equal parts.

"Hey," she said. "Come on in."

Mom was still fixated on the window and Lindy didn't know how to pull her back from the night of the storm. It caused her so much pain, and to relive her dad's death again and again seemed unnecessarily cruel.

"I'm sorry to intrude," Garrett said.

"You're not intruding."

"I went back to the office after I left the shop and did some digging." Lindy braced herself. "Eric Fulbright got kicked out of Carnegie Mellon, at the beginning of November 2001."

Lindy had left Port Lorraine in October.

"Okay," she said.

"There was a warrant out for his arrest, fifteen girls had filed cases against him."

"Cases?"

"Sexual assault. Rape. Forcible confinement."

She flinched at the sound of those horrible words. "What happened?"

"He left campus and was never seen again."

"So? What does that mean? He ran away?" Lindy asked. The other night Mrs. Fulbright had said he was *doing well in Canada*. "His parents put him in some rich kid rapist protection program in Canada?"

"Maybe." He said it with zero faith. "But I called a friend in the RCMP. There's no record of Eric Fulbright in Canada."

"Maybe he changed his name. Or moved on from there."

Garrett licked his lips. Wind rattled the screens in their windows.

"Did Dan know what Eric Fulbright did to Delia?"

# Brin

*E*phie slept with her butt in the air and sucked her thumb.

Brin used to suck her thumb. She did it until she was ten. Mom put that gross stuff on her thumb but even that didn't stop her. She sucked it right off. Mom tried hot sauce, too. That was harder to stomach, but Brin kept at it. Finally, at ten, a girl in her cabin at summer camp took a picture of her sleeping with her thumb in her mouth and showed it around to everyone.

She never sucked her thumb again.

Brin hooked her finger inside her baby sister's palm and pulled her thumb out of her little baby mouth.

"Trust me," she whispered. "It's for the best."

Ephie made a whimpering sound but settled back down without replacing her thumb. Brin couldn't hear her parents fighting downstairs, and she wasn't sure what that meant.

They'd gotten really good over the last year at whisper-fighting, but even that she could usually hear. It was dead silent downstairs.

She tapped the text box on her phone and pulled up her messages with Troy.

Hey.

When she saw the typing bubbles appear on his end, she smiled and scooched down in her pillows.

What up?

A lot. Shit hitting the fan here.

U OK?

Sort of.

Want to sneak out? Meet at spit?

R U crazy? It's about to storm.

I sold the wire and got a shit ton of money. I'm going to spend the night see how many rooms I can clear out.

What about UR mom?

Told her I had an end of year party. That I might stay over. She was so happy I was going to a party she didn't ask any more questions.

LOL

Text if U want to come.

OK

There was a thump and what sounded like one of her parents coming up the first step. She shoved the phone under her pillow. They were going to come in and sit at the foot of her bed like they used to. Maybe Mom would even lie down with her, head on the pillow. And they would talk to her, really talk to her, tell her everything. They'd answer her questions and they wouldn't treat her like she was a baby.

But no one came up.

Ephie sighed and collapsed over onto her side.

Still no one came up.

And Brin didn't go down.

Not until she heard the bowl break.

# *Lindy*

The laugh burst out of her. "You're asking if Dan, Dan Collins, made Eric Fulbright disappear? Have you met Dan?"

Garrett shook his head. "People do unbelievable things when they're upset. Mad. Grieving."

"Dan doesn't even swear when he's upset, mad or grieving."

"Lindy—"

"Wherever Eric Fulbright is, Dan had nothing to do with it."

Mom stood up from her chair and walked down the hallway to her room. It had gotten dark, but the rain had held off.

*Dinner,* Lindy thought. *I need to get dinner.*

"Your sister—"

"Is there an investigation?" she asked. "Is that what you're doing? Investigating?"

Garrett looked at her for a long time with those sweet steady eyes. But these weren't her secrets to tell, and her job had been, had always been, to protect Dee, so she kept everything she could give him locked behind bars.

"I'm not the bad guy here, Lindy."

"Is there an investigation?"

"No investigation," he said.

"Okay then. I need to get Mom settled for the night."

"Sure," he said, backing his way out of the kitchen. Away from her. "Of course. I'll see you later."

That date seemed miles away now. As impossible as ever.

"See you later."

When he was gone and she could no longer hear his footsteps on the back porch, she walked down the hallway to find Mom back in the closet, pulling out all the things Lindy had put away just a week ago.

"Mom, what are you looking for?"

"Where are all our flare guns?"

# Delia

"But what do *you* want?" Dan repeated like a chant that would raise the dead.

They'd been talking for…hours? It felt like hours. It was quiet upstairs and she strained to hear Ephie or Brin. Anything that would pull her away from this conversation.

Her eyes burned from the tears.

"What do you want?" she asked like a child, because she didn't have an answer. "It's your marriage, too. Your life."

Dan turned to the window and she followed his gaze. Outside the trees were being tossed in the wind. Leaves slapped against the glass. It sounded like a woman moaning out there. Or maybe the sound was coming from her.

"We were happy, right? Those years? I didn't make that up? You weren't…pretending? I wasn't seeing something just because I wanted it to be true?"

She nodded so fast. "We were. We were happy. I don't know what happened."

"Dee," he said. "You know that's not true. We never dealt

with that summer. With what happened and all the plans that changed. I don't even know if you grieved for all those things."

"We had a baby," she said. "I wasn't going to *grieve* a trip to Europe."

"It wasn't just the trip," he said. "It was college and being a teacher. It was leaving this town, even if just for a little while. You can grieve that and still be glad for what you have. It's not black and white."

It felt that way in her brain sometimes. The line of judgment was clear.

"And I think when you got pregnant with both the girls that brought it all back. Everything that happened."

It didn't really work like that, but she didn't know how to tell him how the depression changed her from the inside. Her brain with all its chemicals liked to make a flip book of the past and play it for her on repeat. Until all the wounds were fresh.

Her stomach was cramping and she couldn't sit there any longer. She pulled out the frozen chicken breasts so she could make that pasta Dan and Brin loved with the cream sauce.

"Dee."

"I need to make dinner."

"We're talking."

"I can make dinner while we talk." She grabbed the big bowl for the pasta. They'd sit at the table, all of them. It had been a while since they'd done that.

"Dee, you're doing what you always do—"

"Making dinner? Trust me, I know."

"Pretend nothing happened."

"I'm not pretending—"

"He raped you, Dee."

She dropped the bowl and it shattered spectacularly—thunderously—in the quiet house.

It was just a bowl. Just a bowl. Nothing at all to cry over. Sweep up the mess and it was like it never happened.

*Clean it up*, she told herself, but her hands were shaking too hard to do anything.

She felt him next to her, not touching, but there. Solid.

"No one has said that out loud," she whispered. "Not to me. Not for so long."

Once a long time ago, seventeen years ago, actually, Lindy had. Lindy had said it out loud and tried to get her to the hospital. To the police. To the counselor at the high school. Once even the priest.

When that didn't work, Lindy had told Dan.

And Delia had made her leave.

"I know."

Dan loved her and he didn't push. Not once. He held her when she cried. Understood when she couldn't be touched. Promised her he'd never leave.

*I have spent seventeen years pretending it didn't happen. I made them all promise never to tell. A terrible wrong happened to me and so they let me be right for all these years.*

This big secret had rotted them from the inside. Rotted her from the inside.

"You've never even said the words, Dee."

She nodded, still unable to say them.

"You asked me what I want," he said. "And I want you to get better. To feel better. Medication if you need it and counseling. For all of us. You, me and Brin."

She nodded, because she wanted it, too. To feel better. To feel like herself again. To dig out this rot and see who she could be without it.

"We have to tell Brin who her father is."

"You are, Dan. You are her father."

"You know she's spent the last week thinking your sister was her mother. She knows—"

"She doesn't know *that*."

The house creaked and settled in the shadows all around them. The windows rattled. Thunder boomed like a slamming door.

Upstairs the baby started crying, and when Dan went to get her, Dee turned and crumpled against the kitchen counter. It barely held her up. The weight of her grief and her rage was pulling the whole damn house right into the lake.

Dan's feet thundered down the steps, or maybe that was real thunder. She glanced out the window and saw the wild slash of lightning.

The first fat splatters of rain fell on the glass.

"Dee?" Dan said from the doorway, holding their beautiful baby. "Brin's gone."

# THIRTY-TWO
## *Meredith*

$T$he pill they gave her was blue on one side. White on the other. And when she took it her thoughts turned to mist. Her body got real heavy. She still had the same worries—about the stove being turned off or wondering where her keys were. But the pill made it so she couldn't do anything about it.

"It's been a crazy day, huh?" her sweet Lindy said. Meredith reached out and touched her hand. Held it in hers.

"I'm so glad you're here," Meredith said.

Thunder started. But still no rain.

But it would come.

"I remember when you were a girl," Meredith said. "You'd stand on your bed so you could see out the window and watch the storms roll across the lake."

"You let us go stand on the ridge when we were older."

Of course that all stopped after the night William died. They no longer went out to see the thunderclouds, those big cumulonimbus castles with the black bottoms and white spires.

"I had a condo, once," Lindy said. "In Cleveland. Way up on the tenth floor, right on the water."

"Fancy." Meredith imagined her beautiful daughter in a world she'd never seen.

"Sublet studio with an incontinent cat. It wasn't that fancy. But I liked watching the storms roll in from there."

"I imagine that was something."

Lindy nodded, tucked the blanket with the silk blue trim up higher under Meredith's chin. "You got your pill?"

Meredith opened her hand and showed Lindy the pill with its blue half and its white half. Sky and cloud.

"Here." Lindy handed Meredith the glass of water on the bedside table, next to her lotion and the book she pretended to read.

When Meredith handed it back, Lindy yawned, big and loud. "I'll see you in the morning," she said through her fingers.

Meredith nodded and shifted down into the bed, making a real show of getting all comfy.

When Lindy was gone, she spat out the pill, dropped it in the water and watched it dissolve.

# Lindy

Storm watching was in her head now and she couldn't shake it. With Mom asleep Lindy stepped out onto the back deck and tried to get a view of the clouds and the lake, but the neighbors' trees had grown too big. She followed the deck around to the front, smelling the storm, feeling it in the hair on her arms. The back of her neck.

From the road she caught a better glimpse of what was building over the lake. Lightning turned the big black clouds pink and orange. The wind was wet and it blew back her hair and cooled down her skin. She closed her eyes as she walked, letting the force push away some of the day, too.

Down the street, the view was even better. She stepped around the trees so there was nothing between her, the sheer drop-off and the storm on the lake.

The front of the Fulbright House facing the town was dark in the oncoming storm and occasionally, briefly, was illuminated. She thought it was lightning again but then realized there were flashlights glowing inside the house.

*Crazy kids.*

She turned around and went back home.

# Delia

"She's not answering her cell," Delia said and hung up her phone. The cell phone jail drawer, they'd discovered, was open and empty. Neither of them knew when she'd gotten it.

"How did she even sneak out?"

"I don't know?" Dan said. "The storm... We were talking. It might not have been that hard."

She whispered her worst fear. "Do you think she heard us?"

"I don't know," he said, and she could see that it was his worst fear, too.

Tree limbs brushed against the window, the sound deeply unsettling. "It's really storming, Dan."

"Maybe she's gone up to your mom's?" Dan rocked the baby while he fed her a bottle from the fridge.

"Good thinking," Delia said and called Lindy's cell. It rang three times and went straight to voice mail. "Great. Lindy's not answering either."

Mom's landline must have been out from the wind—all they got when they called was a busy signal.

"Okay," Dan said. "Here's what we're going to do. You go

up to your mom's. I'll take Ephie and run by Jenny's and then I'll go talk to Chief Singh."

"The police?" Did that seem extreme? Surely they weren't at the call the police stage, were they?

"Yeah, Dee. The police."

She had the urge to downplay the situation. To be more reasonable. That's what she'd been trained to do all her life.

And Dan, because he knew that was her first instinct, didn't even stick around to listen.

"Is your cell phone charged?" he yelled from the other room.

"I'll charge it at Mom's."

"Okay. You take my truck. I'll take the van."

"I can take the baby," she said.

"So can I," he said and was out the door, Ephie against his chest.

# Lindy

Lindy made herself a cup of tea and went through 1970s Jell-O-a-thon cookbooks. Mom never made anything from one of these books. Lindy would have remembered a dish called Jellied Ham Salad.

Thunder boomed and she jumped, spilling hot tea on her hand.

"Shit." She put her mug down on the counter and rinsed off her hand. Rain splattered against the window with such force that it sounded like ice pellets hitting the glass. She grabbed her phone from the counter and her notebook of recipe ideas and went to sit on the couch, the shell lamp sending its half-hearted illumination over the old pillows.

She saw the three missed calls from Delia just as the back door was thrown open to the wind and rain, and her sister was standing there in the flesh.

"Dee?" She got to her feet.

"Brin's missing. She here?"

"Here?" Lindy said. "No."

Dee took off for the back hallway, tracking in rain and leaves.

"Mom's sleeping." Lindy raced after her. "Can you just—"

Dee pushed open their old bedroom door, but it was empty as expected. Dee's bed perfectly made. Lindy's a mess with twisted sheets and pillows sliding off the mattress from where she'd slept when Dee spent the night.

Just like the old days.

Dee opened Mom's door and Lindy stumbled to a halt against her sister in the doorway, staring down at her mother's empty bed.

"Mom?" She threw back the blankets like Mom might be hiding under them. She checked the closet, got on her knees and looked under the bed. She put her elbows on the mattress like a little girl doing her nightly prayers.

Then she remembered going out on the ridge to see the storm. And the lights.

*Oh god, she asked for the flare guns.*

"I think," Lindy said, "I think I know where she might be."

Lindy ran out the back and around to the front. The screen of the front door was hanging open, caught on the giant hydrangea bush she and Dee planted for one of Mom's birthdays. The tightly furled green buds, which wouldn't bloom until the heat of the summer, hung drunkenly off broken stems.

She ran right on to the end of the ridge, stepping in front of the trees so it was nothing but cliff and storm before her. Cliff, storm and the Fulbright House.

One window held a ghostly light. Yellow and pale.

And she saw now, on the spit, a light bobbing through the night, making its way toward the house.

"There," Lindy said and pointed to the light on the spit. "She's going out to the Fulbright House."

"And Brin's already there," Dee said.

# *Brin*

Brin was breathing hard like she'd been running one of her cross-country meets. She hated it, but she kept going, the sledgehammer falling forward against the wall.

*You have to tell Brin who her father is.*

"What did you tell your parents?" Troy asked.

"About what?" She swung the sledgehammer again and her arms shook at the contact with the wall.

"About where you're spending the night."

"I'll go home at some point." Sneak in probably before they even realized she was gone.

"Brin. The road is going to be washed out soon. You're here. You're not going anywhere."

"I get why you like this," she said.

"Stealing copper wire?"

"Smashing walls."

"Brin," he said. "Is this another one of those things you don't want to talk about?"

"What do you mean?"

"Like how you didn't want to talk about your aunt being your mom."

"She's not my mom." Brin lifted the hammer and used its weight, just like Troy taught her, to smash it into the wall. It barely made a dent so she did it again and then again until the wall cracked and then broke out into a spider web of cracks. "My mom is my mom."

She was not in the mood for talking.

*You have to tell Brin who her dad is.*

*You are her dad, Dan.*

She was in the mood for smashing.

The storm outside was growing strong, thunder rolling through the house like a train.

"Hey," Troy said.

"What?" Brin put the head of the hammer through the wall. This time she broke through the wood on the second swing.

*I'm getting better at this.*

"Stop."

"What?"

"Brin! Stop!" he yelled.

She stopped.

"Someone's here," he whispered.

She heard it again, the squeal of the front door. The creak of the rotten wood floor.

A vagrant hiding out from the storm? Other kids looking to party?

The creak of the steps echoed in the study.

Whoever it was was coming upstairs.

"Brin," he whispered and waved her over. She ran across the room to stand behind him.

"I'm scared," she said right into his ear.

"It's probably just someone looking for a place to wait out

the storm," he said. He had just pulled the flashlight from the mantle when a voice—a painfully familiar voice—said:

"I know what you did."

Troy turned, pointing the light at the doorway.

And there she was with her white hair and old foul-weather gear.

"Gran?"

# THIRTY-THREE

## *Delia*

*Everything is okay. Everything will be fine. Everything is okay. Everything will be fine.*

She'd repeated those same damn words to herself seventeen years ago, walking away from this house in the milky cold light of a shitty dawn.

It had been the beginning of the armor she'd built over herself. The shell she lived in.

She hadn't been back since the night of that last party. Had looked at this house only when she had to. Ignoring it out in the lake had become a part of a survival mechanism.

And walking back out here was dismantling her. Piece by piece.

She fixed her daughter in her mind, a north star to follow when she wanted, so badly, to turn away.

"Do you have reception?" Lindy yelled over the wind.

Delia held up her phone but the screen was black and unresponsive. "It's dead," she shouted back.

The lake was rising, the cold water seeping through the net

of her tennis shoes. A confluence of terrible memories pooling in one awful spot.

"Garrett?" Lindy yelled into her cell phone. "Mom is missing. Yes…my mom is missing," she enunciated every word. "We think she's out at the Fulbright House and we…" She looked down at the phone. "Shit. The connection keeps dropping."

"Reception might be better once we get to the house."

"Once we get to the house we might be stuck there," Lindy said. The spit was getting treacherous. The water and waves up over their ankles at this point. "Jesus, I hope it's Mom out here and not some teenagers throwing a shitty party."

"Unless the teenager throwing a shitty party is my daughter."

"Right. Worst family reunion ever." It wasn't funny but points to Lindy for trying.

There was a sharp pop and a red flash in the window.

"Did the lightning strike the house?" Delia yelled. One of the second-floor rooms was glowing yellow. "Is that a fire?"

They both took off running. By the time they got across the spit, they were splashing through knee-high waves. Soaked and cold from the rain.

The front door hung open and cockeyed and once they were inside, they could smell the smoke. The sulphur chemical smell of a burnt flare. Lindy tripped in the middle of the hallway, and Delia got her back to her feet.

"You okay?" she asked.

"Fine," she said, though she was limping.

"Mom!" Delia shouted as they stumble-walked, arms over each other's shoulders, to the stairs.

"Mom?" Another voice. Younger.

Delia's heart stopped. "Brin?"

"Go," Lindy said.

Delia took the steps by two, her lungs burning with exertion and the acrid taste of the smoke. "Brin! I'm coming!" she yelled, tearing down the dark hallway in the direction of the fire. She staggered to a stop in the doorway, stunned for just a moment. Breathless.

The window curtain was engulfed and the edge of the old rug was smoking. Brin stared at her with a soot-and-tearstained face as she knelt beside the body of a boy.

Mom beside her.

# Brin

*T*he fire was hot at her back. Troy lay still and unmoving in front of her, and she was trying to protect him from the sparks flying around the room. The curtains were on fire and it was spreading.

Was he dead? Could you die from getting hit by a flare gun?

When Gran shot him, Troy got knocked off his feet, and he hadn't gotten up. Or said anything. Or opened his eyes since. She burned her hands putting out the fire in his hair and now they pulsed and itched. The shoulder of his T-shirt was gone.

Did he hit his head when he fell?

"He's breathing," Brin said to her mom, who showed up in the doorway as if she'd heard Brin's prayers.

"That's good, honey." Mom slid onto her knees next to Brin. "That's really good." She wrapped Brin in a hard quick hug.

Over and over again Brin lifted her hands up as if to touch Troy and then put them back in her lap, unsure what to do with them.

"We just need to move him, okay, honey? Everything's okay, we just need to move him."

Aunt Lindy appeared from the smoky shadows around the door.

"We need to move him away from the fire," Mom said. "And...maybe disarm Meredith."

Gran looked down at her hand as if surprised to see the still-smoking flare gun. She placed it on the wooden floor and pushed it away.

Behind Brin there was a creak and the curtain rod fell.

"We gotta get the hell out of here. Grab his feet," Mom yelled to Lindy and then grabbed Troy's arm, lifting it so she could pick him up. He groaned, his head rolling.

"Mom!" Brin cried. "You're hurting him."

"Drag him," Gran said. "You gotta drag him by the feet."

Mom and Aunt Lindy took Troy's feet and began to pull him across the floor. His phone fell out of his pocket. "Grab that!" Mom yelled.

Brin snatched the phone and scuttled out of the room after everyone.

"Where do we take him?" Lindy asked. "The road's going to be washed out. No one can come get us that way."

"Call Dad," Mom said. "Maybe he can come with the boat."

Brin used Troy's phone while Mom and Lindy carried Troy, arms around his waist, down the stairs.

"Who is this?" Dad said before the first ring finished.

"Dad?" Brin said and her voice broke on a sob. "Daddy?"

"Oh my god, Brin. Brin, baby, where are you? Are you okay?"

"We're okay. We...well, there's a fire and we need help."

"A fire?"

"We're out at the Fulbright House."

"We?"

"Me and Mom. And Aunt Lindy. And Gran."

Dad swore under his breath. "Yeah," she heard him say to someone in the background. "The Fulbright House. Yeah. All of them. Every damn McAvoy is out there."

"Dad?" Brin cried. "Can you come and get us? I'm scared. I'm really scared—"

"Shhh, Brin. Brin, I'm coming. I promise. I'll be there as fast as I can. Get to the docks at the back of the house. Tell your mom, I'm coming to get you."

Brin hung up and raced down the steps, but the house was dark and she didn't know which way everyone went. "Mom!" she yelled, fear spiking into her heart again. "Mom? Where'd you go?"

"Here I am," Mom said, stepping out of a dark, murky doorway. "Here I am."

Without thought Brin launched herself into her mother's arms. Which, as they always had, even when she forgot, even when she pushed away and put them all in danger, swept her right up and held her tight.

# Meredith

*T*he best days on the lake were never the ones you'd think. The beautiful hot August days without any wind, they were fine. The fish practically jumped into the boat, making life so easy.

Those were fine days, for sure. But not the best.

The best days were when things went wrong. When the wind shifted and the lake had something to say. Those were the days Meredith earned her money. And her title: Lake Erie fishing boat captain. She came home proud those days. She'd see the other captains around the harbor, Jimmie with his new nets and Gary, nice guy who always wanted to go for a drink, and they'd nod their heads at each other.

"Some kinda day out there," they'd say.

And they all meant the best.

Meredith smelled the smoke and the wet and she felt the fear of all the women around her. Her daughters. The wild one and the brave one.

"Don't be scared," she said.

"What?" Lindy asked, ducking her head down.

"Don't be scared."

This was some kinda day. Hard things got done.

The sky was black and so was the lake, far as the eye could see. An endless darkness.

*William's out there*, she thought.

And smiled.

# *Lindy*

*I*t seemed like hours, but really it was only about twenty minutes before they saw a boat with a giant klieg light leave the harbor, make a sharp left turn and head out toward the house.

"That's not Dan's boat," Delia yelled. She and Brin were huddled around the boy, trying to keep him warm and dry in the lashing rain. He'd woken up on the trip down the stairs but was still and quiet, probably knocked out again from the pain in his shoulder and head.

Lindy had one arm around her mom's thin shoulders. She'd thrown her own cheap raincoat over Mom's foul-weather gear because she'd been shaking so hard.

But the shaking had stopped a few minutes ago. She'd told Lindy not to be scared and then went still and soft against her. She was breathing, shallow and faint. Lindy could feel it against her cheek. But she wasn't sure if she was conscious.

Lindy held her mother as tight as she could and willed her to hold on just a little bit longer as the shallow-bottom boat approached the broken-down dock. The light swept the water, searching for debris, floating wood or broken supports under the surface.

Because that would be the McAvoy luck—the rescue boat sunk before anyone managed to get saved.

Delia walked out from under the eaves and waved her arms. The light caught her, throwing her in black relief against the bright glow.

"Mom," Lindy whispered into her mother's ear, her own ankle throbbing. "Mom. We're going home. If you can hear me, just…stay with me. We're almost home."

The boat idled up next to the most complete part of the dock, and Dan jumped off. He wrapped an arm around Delia's shoulder and she grabbed on to him like the wind might tear them apart. Brin sobbed hard and raced out there to join them.

"Lindy?"

She turned and saw Garrett.

"You okay?" he asked.

Lindy knew she was crying. "Mom," she said and wiped her nose.

He looked down at Mom, huddled against Lindy's shoulder. "We need to go, Lindy. I can take her."

"The boy—"

"I got him," Dan said, coming to stand under the eaves.

Garrett picked Mom up and out of Lindy's arms like she was a child. Her arms splayed out to the side, and Lindy took her hands and crossed them in her lap.

"It's okay," Garrett said. "I swear, Lindy—"

"Don't," she said. "Don't make promises you can't keep."

# THIRTY-FOUR
## *Delia*

*I*t wasn't another stroke.

When Dr. Alvarez said the brain scans were clear, Delia stopped listening. She bowed her head and grabbed her mother's hand. She'd climb right into bed with her but there were so many wires and her body under the sheets and blankets was so small.

*Thank you, God. Thank you.*

"Why isn't she waking up?" Lindy asked.

"She will," Dr. Alvarez said. "In her own time."

Dee looked across Mom's body and met her sister's eyes.

"I'll give you two a minute," the doctor said and slipped out the door.

"I have to go talk to Brin," Delia said. If she waited, if she gathered herself first, she wouldn't follow through with it. She wouldn't do it the way it needed to be done. She hadn't slept, moving between one hospital room and then the other, stress and grief and relief moving right along with her.

"Go," Lindy said. "I'll stay here with Mom."

Delia nodded and walked down the hallway, past Troy Daniels's room—that was the boy's name, Troy Daniels. The boy's mother was in there, Delia could see her sitting in one of the uncomfortable chairs, could hear the low rumble of her voice.

Delia had been in there earlier to apologize, and his mother had been gracious but confused as to why Meredith McAvoy, a seventy-year-old woman, would shoot her son with a flare gun.

Brin's room was four down from Troy's. The palms of her hands had second-degree burns and the doctor had wrapped them in thick gauze from the elbows down. The sight made Delia's breath catch in her throat. It made her think that it all could have been so much worse. That they were lucky.

She knocked on the door and slowly pushed it open, only to find Brin sitting up in bed, Dan beside her, a sleeping Ephie in his arms.

"Hi," Delia said hesitantly.

"How's Gran?" Brin asked.

"Her brain scans are clear."

"Is she gonna get better?"

"She'll be her own ornery self in no time."

Brin nodded, tears starting fresh in her eyes. Dan put his arm around her, and Delia, weak and terrified, sat down on the other side of the bed.

"It's not your fault," she told her daughter.

"But I ran away. And Troy—"

"Oh, we will be talking about Troy. You can bet on that. But none of that has anything to do with what happened to Gran. You need to know that."

"Before she shot him, she said, 'I know what you did.'"

Delia stared at the linoleum under their feet. Squares of white with a black and gray swirl. There were ten squares between the bed and the door. Another twenty to the chair in the corner. Two from the chair to the window.

"Mom? What was Gran talking about?"

She didn't have the words she required. She'd never had them. She looked over at Dan but he couldn't say them for her.

Brin put her bandaged mitt in Delia's lap. "I can't…" Brin said "…hold your hand."

And it was funny and awful, so the laughter and the tears spewed out together.

"I'll hold yours," Delia said and carefully, applying no pressure, rested Brin's bandaged hand in her palm.

"I've been angry for a really long time," Delia finally said. "It probably seems like I'm angry at you and at Dad. It's not fair that I've treated you that way because I'm angry about something else entirely."

She talked about that summer. About Europe.

"Dad drinking wine in the middle of the afternoon in Paris?" Brin said.

Dan smiled. "I was ready to give it a try. I was excited. But I was also out of my comfort zone. I was worried about the food and the language and the train stations and I was… I was just scared that I would lose your mom to something bigger than what I could offer."

"We fought," Delia said, catching Dan's eye over their daughter's messy red hair.

They would not talk about the kiss in the apartment upstairs. That desperate moment between Dan and Lindy that really—in the grand scheme of all that had happened, of the life they had lived—meant nothing.

"And I went out to this party. At the Fulbright House… alone."

Here was where the words got tricky. Where she felt like closing her eyes against the memory. Or at least putting her hand over her ears so she couldn't hear the soundtrack.

She told her daughter—beautiful and kind and smart— about the drinks she had. Lots of them on an empty stomach.

"The drinks don't matter," Dan said and she knew that. But somehow in her head it still did. All these years later, she still felt the urge to adopt guilt where there should only be outrage.

"I was mad at you," she whispered to Dan. "I was so mad at you."

"I know."

So she had kissed Eric Fulbright and she went up to that bedroom with him.

And there the words stopped.

"Mom?" Brin looked between Dan and Delia, panic forcing her eyes wide.

*Stop. Take it back. You're scaring her. Tell her another time. Any other time. It's too much.*

"Dad?" Brin asked, when Delia didn't continue. "What happened?"

Delia met Dan's eyes over their daughter's head.

"I can't," he said. "You have to."

"Mom." Brin's eyes were now full of tears, her poor bandaged hands like birds with no place to land. "What happened? Did he hurt you? Is that...?"

"No, it's okay," Delia said, struggling somehow to salvage this moment, to turn this story around. To save her daughter from having to carry this burden, too. This fear. "I mean... I went to his room. I had those drinks."

"Mom."

"It's complicated—"

"Dee," Dan whispered. "Don't."

"I didn't scream," she whispered. "I didn't fight. I let him—"

Delia was holding her breath. Because she was terrified the next one would ruin something. End something.

"Breathe," Dan said and she sucked in air.

"I got up there and I immediately changed my mind. I told

him to stop," Delia said, remembering something she'd tried so hard to forget. "I said no. I pushed at him. And he was mad." She gagged and shook her head. The memory there now, on the loose, and she couldn't look at her family. She couldn't bear to have them see her.

Eric Fulbright had pinned her on the bed and told her she could leave if she wanted. The door wasn't locked. But he didn't get off her. And she thought, with adrenaline-fueled clarity, that he *wanted* her to fight. To struggle. He wanted it to escalate so he could really hurt her.

His face above her had been the cruelest and ugliest she'd ever seen.

She couldn't finish. Those memories, those awful dark bruises, had been hers and hers alone for so long.

"Mom," Brin said. "It wasn't your fault."

"Thank you, honey. And…I know." Which wasn't a lie. She did know. She just needed to be reminded.

Brin turned to Dan, and Delia could sense her daughter connecting the dots.

"I heard your conversation last night. I came down when you dropped the bowl," she whispered, then looked up and straight at Dan. "This person, this terrible person is not… *You* are my dad."

Dan took a deep shuddery breath that came out in a sob. He leaned over and kissed Brin on the forehead. Ephie in his arms made a happy sleeping-baby sound.

Delia had told Dan she was pregnant in his truck the day they were supposed to leave for Europe. When he'd asked if she wanted to keep the baby, she didn't have an answer. In the vacuum she'd become, she'd lost the ability to move purposefully. She'd drifted through days. Bouncing off Mom, retreating back to her room.

When Dan said *we'll get married*, she'd said *yes*. Because that direction felt good. Because she could put her hand in Dan's and he could lead her out of the nightmare.

And he did. In so many ways.

He helped her back to sex. And love. The years they'd had together had been so sweet. Even for all the bitter. It wasn't perfect. Nothing ever was. But it had been good.

"Brin," she whispered and looked at her daughter. "You are an amazing girl and you have brought such wonder into my life. Into our lives. I thank the universe every day for you."

Delia's baby, her bright and sharp and fierce girl child, her mysterious and mercurial teenager, collapsed against her, and Delia at long last collapsed, too, right into her family's arms.

# Lindy

Lindy curled her body against her mother's. It took some work to arrange the wires so she wouldn't accidentally pull anything loose. She put her mouth to her mother's ear and told a story about every summer she could remember.

She'd gotten to her tenth when there was a knock at the door.

"Hello?" Garrett Singh poked his head in the room.

Lindy met his eyes. "Thanks for saving us," she said.

With a wry smile, he tipped his imaginary hat, and she let herself be charmed.

"How's your mom?"

"Okay. A little banged up but the brain scans are good."

"Oh, Lindy." He sagged with relief. "I'm so glad."

"Me, too." She wiped her nose. "She went out there to get revenge. To hurt Eric Fulbright for what he did."

"I hope wherever he is, he's being punished."

They both knew how unlikely that was. How he probably escaped justice on a cloud of wealthy white privilege.

"I'm telling Mom about my favorite summer memories."

"Should I leave?"

She considered. Maybe it was the adrenaline or the grief or the tired lines around his eyes, but his presence was a comfort she didn't want to take for granted. "No, stay. I'm glad you're here."

He smiled and took a seat in a chair on the other side of the bed. "I'm glad to be here, too, Lindy."

Another time she'd tell him she was staying, too. That they'd go on that date and see what happened with second chances. But right now they were there for her mom.

Lindy stroked back Mom's puffy white hair and reminded her of Lindy's tenth summer. The year they went camping out on South Bass Island and Delia chipped a tooth and the tent leaked and the sleeping bag Lindy had packed still smelled like vomit from a sleepover party gone horribly wrong.

"We ate s'mores for breakfast," she said. "And we played Scrabble on the beach and the second night it was so clear we saw all the stars. Every single one..."

# EPILOGUE

*August, one year later*

## Brin

*T*he McAvoy Bait, Fish and Lunch Counter was open for business. Newly remodeled, with a fancy new menu—thanks to Aunt Lindy. The old fish sign was back, too. With the flag, which Ephie was currently trying to eat.

"Ephie," Brin said. "Leave it." Ephie squawked at Brin and fought when she tried to pull her away from the flag.

"Ephie." Troy came out of the store and Ephie squealed because Troy was her favorite person. Mostly because he let her climb all over him like a jungle gym.

Troy was also Brin's favorite person because he treated Brin like…he loved her.

"Are you being a pest?" Troy asked Ephie, all serious.

"Pest!" Ephie yelled and smacked her hands against Troy's ears before trying to climb his shoulders.

Troy's mom walked toward them.

"Hey, Ms. Daniels," Brin said. "Thanks for coming!"

"My blood, sweat and tears are all over this place," Troy

said. He held Baby Pest with one arm and Brin's hand with the other, smiling at his mom as if he'd been doing it his whole life.

The doors opened and Aunt Lindy stepped out in a red dress and white apron and polka dot shoes. Her hair was long and smooth down her back.

She looked freaking awesome.

"You guys here to help or what?"

# *Lindy*

*I*t was just about perfect. The shelves looked amazing. Dan was in the back, manning the fryer. Brin was cutting tomatoes. Troy was watching her cut tomatoes like a puppy dog in love.

"Lindy?" Garrett said, breathing heavily as he stepped in the front door, rolling a keg of Great Lakes Brewery lager. "Where do you want this?"

He was off duty today, wearing one of Lindy's new McAvoy Bait, Fish and Lunch Counter T-shirts. And a pair of jeans that fit him just right.

They'd finally gone on that date. And then about a hundred more.

"Right over here," she said. She had the old barrel packed with ice and set up in the corner behind the bar. There was some local wine, too. Garrett would be bartending thanks to the new liquor license.

"Whoa." Garrett dusted off his hands. "Look at this place."

"Not too bad, huh?" She'd put flowers just about everywhere. Tied a few balloons to the front door.

"You are some kind of magic, Lindy," he said, and when

he put his arms around her and kissed the top of her head, she felt it.

The magic.

It was all of them. The McAvoys. And this town. This old building.

It was everything she ever wanted.

# Delia

"And then we're going to go to Paris," Delia said, readjusting her grip on the handles as she started the incline up Queen Street. She had been planning to drive but the day was just too perfect, so she decided to walk. "We're going to drink wine in the middle of the day. Not a lot. Just a little. Just to say we did it."

They rounded the harbor and there, freshly painted and festooned with balloons, was the shop, a group of people milling around on the sidewalk outside, waiting for the party to start.

Mom made a short, sharp grunt. A laugh maybe, and Delia put the brake on the wheelchair and crouched down beside her.

Mom was buried down in a body that didn't work well anymore. She'd had another stroke about six months ago. She couldn't walk. One hand curled stiff and unusable against her stomach. Her face was impassive, the left side of her mouth drawn down. There were days when Delia and Lindy went to visit and they couldn't see their mom in her eyes. But some days she was present and her eyes flashed with joy and humor.

Either way, Lindy and Delia sat themselves down in the chairs in Mom's room and they propped their feet up and sometimes they brought dinner. Sometimes they brought Ephie. But every time they talked. They talked and they talked. Geysers of conversation.

Mom's hand, the one she was still able to use, jerked forward, pointing at the store.

"All right," Dee said. "Let's get there."

They'd had six good months before the stroke. They went camping—all together. Built a giant bonfire on the beach and ate s'mores for breakfast. They played gin rummy on the back deck and went fishing. Lindy crammed it all in like she'd been on a mission to make up for lost time.

Dee huffed and puffed her way up Queen Street, until finally they made their way through the knot of people waiting. Most turned and said hello to Mom, touched her hand and smiled real wide in her face. She could feel Mom wanting to roll her eyes.

"Excuse me," Delia said, pushing the wheelchair slowly through the crowd. "We just… Yes… Thanks. We just need to get inside."

"Mom!" Lindy cried, seeing them in the doorway.

"Mom!" Brin put down the knife she was using to cut tomatoes. "Look what came in the mail today?"

She held up a big brown postage box that could only be one thing.

"The guidebook?" Delia asked.

Brin made an exceedingly happy teenage-girl squeal. One month in Europe, just the two of them. Delia could not imagine a better traveling companion. They were going in two weeks, before Delia started classes at a University of Ohio satellite campus in Yorkville. Growing up she'd wanted to be a teacher. A high school English teacher. Seventeen years later she was going to see if she could make that happen.

Lindy was wheeling Mom around the store, pointing out the changes she made. There had been a lot of discussion about whether to bring her today. Mom tired easily. Became distressed. But right now, in that moment, she was vivid with pleasure. Joy beamed out of her like sunlight.

"Hey," Garrett said. "Quite a place, huh?"

Delia laughed at the understatement. "You could say that."

"Your mom seems good."

"She is." She turned toward him. "Dan?"

"Out back."

Right. The fryer.

She walked through the office. Gone were Ephie's baby things. The old fishing charter pictures. The ancient bank boxes. It had all been replaced by clean shelves and a new computer system. It was painted white and blue and red, just like *Dreamer*.

But Dad's calendar remained, and Delia pressed a hand against the Maine lighthouse and all those surrounding waves as she passed by.

*Dad*, she thought. *I wish you could see us. See what we've done. You'd be so proud.*

Dan was out back, sitting in a lawn chair a few feet from the big silver fryer. Beside him was a big plastic tub of fish ready to go into the oil. Troy was there, too. He was still nervous around Dan, which Dan was in no hurry to change.

"Hey," she said, and Dan turned to her with a bright smile.

"Hey yourself. Everything go all right with your mom?"

"Yeah, it was such a nice day we decided to walk."

"Good call."

There was an awkwardness in their silences these days, but there wasn't any anger. Or at least not any that lasted more than a moment. Counseling had helped. Dan moved out, spent a few months in the apartment above the shop, while Delia spent most of the year trying to figure out if the pain she felt was missing him or missing what they'd been. Fear of losing him or fear of losing the life she'd grown used to.

They'd found their answer and he'd moved back home.

"I love you, Dan," she said.

He got to his feet and stood in front of her, his body a tantalizing inch away. There was a teasing glorious newness to him, and to her, too, maybe.

That was the awkwardness.

"I love you, too, Delia," he said.

And when they kissed, she felt her family safe and secure around her. She would carry the past with her forever, but it was a dim light now. Especially when, ahead of her, lay the beautiful uncontrollable future.

# AFTERWORD

## November 2001

## Meredith

*A*fter that party, the one Delia came home from so different, the Fulbright House sat dark. That boy gone. The parties over.

Night after night, Meredith found herself out at the ridge. On the other side of the trees so no one could see her. She'd stand there and stare out at that dark house floating on the lake.

And then, one night in November, thirty-four days after Lindy left, a light appeared in the house. The second-floor window glowed.

A Fulbright was home.

For the first time since Lindy told her what had happened to Delia, a week after it happened, she felt like there was something she could do. Something she could make right.

She took the boat, because no one could see her dock at the back of the house. She brought the flare gun, tucked in the back of her pants like some kind of bandit.

"Hello?" she called as she knocked on the back door. It

opened under her knock, pushing into a brick kitchen with shiny appliances. "Hello?"

There was a thump on the ceiling above her, the sound of fast moving feet on the stairs.

"Hey!" a voice yelled, getting closer. "Coming."

She tried to prepare herself, but it didn't do much good. It was Eric Fulbright in the doorway. Duffel bag in his hands. Coat on.

"What the—?" he asked. "You do this kind of thing?"

"You betcha," she said, not sure what he was talking about.

"We gotta get going. Someone's going to meet us at a campground in Point Pelee." He glanced at his watch and then opened a drawer and pulled out an envelope.

"Canada," she said.

He handed her the envelope. "Five grand. Cash. They said that was your fee."

She stared at the envelope for a second while it all came together.

"You got Canadian papers?" she asked.

He tapped his chest pocket and smirked.

She lifted the envelope. "This doesn't include gas money."

He sighed and pulled out his wallet. "How much?"

She had never prepared her girls for someone like this. The wolves in handsome boys' clothing. And they'd paid. They'd paid so dearly.

"All of it."

"Fuck no."

"Well, you can pay me. Or I'll turn right back around without you."

"Fine," he spat and gave her the cash. "Can we go now?"

She bowed slightly and held her arm out to her boat and the lake beyond.

It took some time to get out into the middle of the lake,

where it was the deepest and coldest. She kept her running lights off, so they were just a shadow passing in the night.

"How much longer?" he asked, shouting over the wind. She glanced back at him, shivering in his coat, small and vulnerable in the back of her boat.

"Not long. It's warmer up here," she yelled, and he got up and sat in the chair next to her. "What are you gonna do in Canada?"

"Be Canadian."

"Must have been bad."

"What?"

"Whatever you're running from."

"Did I pay extra for the conversation?"

He stared off at the edge where the water met the sky. He probably thought he was looking at Canada, but it was just Port back there. Port and her daughter. Her other daughter was someplace else in the darkness and that was his fault, too.

"You know who my daughter is?" she asked.

"Nope." He didn't even look at her.

"Delia."

"Doesn't ring a bell."

She swerved the boat, cutting it hard to the left, and he was knocked sideways. Barely caught himself from going over.

"Careful!" he yelled.

"Sorry. Waves."

They were quiet, the engine purring along.

"Delia was the girl you raped at the end of summer," she said real casual. She never said those words before. "You raped my daughter."

"I've never raped anyone," he lied, faking outrage.

She didn't even need the flare gun.

"Hold this, would you?" She handed him one of the nets,

and he was surprised enough to take it with both hands, hold the heavy, unwieldy material in his lap.

"What? Why?"

She swerved the boat again and Eric Fulbright went right over the side. He floated for a second before the weight of the net began to pull him under. It happened quickly, and before she knew it, the lake had swallowed him whole.

★ ★ ★ ★ ★

# ACKNOWLEDGMENTS

*A*bout twenty years ago, when I sold my very first books to Harlequin and the editor who bought those books left the company, I was handed off to a brand-new editor from whom I received a ten-page revision letter. In this letter she explained the basics of writing: POV, conflict, stakes and dialogue and basically how I'd managed to write a book without any of those things.

In this letter she was also patient, enthusiastic, kind and funny. And never once in those pages did I feel defeated. I felt instead like I had someone invested not just in my book but future books, and we were in it together.

That editor was Susan Swinwood.

We worked on three books together before she went one way and I went the other.

Flash forward nearly twenty years later and The McAvoy Sisters end up in her care at Graydon House. My first thanks are for Susan. Thank you for that revision letter all those years ago and for your championing now. The world is small and it is my honor to keep running into you.

The first thing Susan did was hand the McAvoys off to my fantastic and endlessly patient editor, Melanie Fried. Melanie turned a messy convoluted manuscript into this shiny, lean and lovely book that I am just so proud of. Thank you for all your incredible hard work, Melanie. The McAvoys and I were so lucky to have had your guiding hand.

For this beautiful cover I need to thank designer Mary Luna and art director Alexandra Niit. Thank you so much.

My steady partner in all the chaos—Pam Hopkins. Without you this wouldn't have happened.

All the author friends who kept me calm and read versions of the McAvoys and still returned my emails: Stephanie Doyle, Simone St. James, Annika Martin, Skye Warren, Shari Slade and Maureen McGowan.

My amazing readers, old and new. Thank you for continuing this journey with me. I'm not me without you.

And finally for Adam, Mick and Lucy—for everything.

# THE McAVOY SISTERS BOOK OF SECRETS

MOLLY FADER

Reader's Guide

GRAYDON
HOUSE

1. Of the McAvoy women—Meredith, Delia, Lindy and Brin—whom did you like best? Separately, which McAvoy woman did you most relate to?

2. Discuss the character of Brin. Did you understand her rebellious behavior? What kind of teenager were you?

3. Talking about sex—or in the case of the McAvoy sisters, not talking about sex—is an important part of the novel. How did you learn about sex when you were growing up? How would you discuss sex with a teenager today?

4. Silence is a key theme of the story. How did staying silent about certain parts of their lives affect each of the McAvoy women? Do you think the McAvoys will be able to keep up their new approach to life in the long term or will they revert back to their old habit?

5. Was it right for Brin's parents to withhold the truth of her biological father? What would you have done if you were her guardian?

6. At one point in the story Delia thinks that no matter how much we grow and change, we're never really far from the kids we'd once been. Discuss how this idea is reflected in the larger novel. As it applies to your own life, do you agree or disagree with Delia? How do you think our perceptions of who we were color who we become?

7. Discuss Lindy's relationship with Port Lorraine. What does it represent to her? Do you understand why she ultimately stayed? What would you have done in Lindy's place? And how do you feel about your own hometown?

8. How did living in a small fishing community shape the McAvoy family's lives? How do you think their lives might have been different had they lived elsewhere?

9. How did you feel about Meredith's actions toward Eric Fulbright at the end of the novel? What was your initial reaction to this scene, and did it change after some reflection? What would you have done if you were in her position?

10. What would you like to see happen to the Fulbright House? Should it be sold to another family? Should it stay as is in its decaying form? Be torn down?